Bruce Beckham

Murder in the Round

Detective Inspector Skelgill Investigates

LUCiUS

EVIL AFOOT

LAKELAND'S most famous 24-hour fell running feat was accomplished by local man Bob Graham, who in June 1932 scaled 42 peaks over a distance of 66 miles, with an attendant height gain just a little shy of Mount Everest – arriving back at Keswick Moot Hall with 21 minutes to spare. 'The Bob Graham Round', as this route came to be known, is etched into Cumbrian folklore, not least because the 42-year-old Keswick B&B owner ran in tennis shoes, long shorts and a pyjama jacket. His record stood for 28 years. Fell running gear has evolved beyond recognition in the near-century since, but the *Bob Graham's* arduous nature, the fickle mountain weather, and competitive spirit mean this challenge is fraught with risk. Throw in a malevolent actor, and jeopardy spikes. And when something goes wrong in the fells, help is not always at hand.

BRUCE BECKHAM brings a lifelong love of the outdoors to the contemporary crime novel. He is an award-winning author and copywriter. A resident of Great Britain, he has travelled and worked in over 60 countries. He is published in both fiction and non-fiction, and is a member of the UK Society of Authors.

His series 'Inspector Skelgill Investigates' features the recalcitrant Cumbrian detective Daniel Skelgill, and his loyal lieutenants, long-suffering Londoner DS Leyton and local high-flyer DS Emma Jones. Set amidst the ancient landscapes of England's Lake District, this expanding series of standalone murder mysteries has won acclaim across five continents, with over 1 million copies downloaded, from Australia to Japan and India, and from Brazil to Canada and the United States of America.

"Great characters. Great atmospheric locale. Great plots. What's not to like?"

Amazon reviewer, 5 stars

TEXT COPYRIGHT 2024 BRUCE BECKHAM

All rights reserved. Bruce Beckham asserts his right always to be identified as the author of this work. No part may be copied or transmitted without written permission from the publisher.

This is a work of fiction. Names, characters, places and incidents either are the product of the author's imagination or are used fictitiously. Any resemblance to actual persons, living or dead, events and locales is entirely coincidental.

Kindle edition first published by Lucius 2024
Paperback edition first published by Lucius 2024
Hardcover edition first published by Lucius 2024

For more details and rights enquiries contact:
Lucius-ebooks@live.com

Cover design by Moira Kay Nicol
Beta reader Kathy Dahm
United States editor Janet Colter

EDITOR'S NOTE

Murder in the Round is a stand-alone mystery, the twenty-third in the series 'Detective Inspector Skelgill Investigates'. It is set in the English Lake District, in particular the area surrounding Keswick, which is both start and endpoint for the 66-mile circuit of the Bob Graham Round. All but the 'tip of the toe' of this route can be found on Ordnance Survey Landranger Map 90.

Absolutely no AI (Artificial Intelligence) is used in the writing of the DI Skelgill novels.

THE DI SKELGILL SERIES

Murder in Adland
Murder in School
Murder on the Edge
Murder on the Lake
Murder by Magic
Murder in the Mind
Murder at the Wake
Murder in the Woods
Murder at the Flood
Murder at Dead Crags
Murder Mystery Weekend
Murder on the Run
Murder at Shake Holes
Murder at the Meet
Murder on the Moor
Murder Unseen
Murder in our Midst
Murder Unsolved
Murder in the Fells
Murder at the Bridge
Murder on the Farm
Murder at Home
Murder in the Round
Murder Mere Murder

Glossary

SOME OF THE Cumbrian dialect words, abbreviations, British slang and local usage appearing in *Murder in the Round* are as follows:

Abeun – above
Alan Whickers – knickers (Cockney)
Alreet/areet – alright (often a greeting)
ANPR – automatic number plate recognition
Any road – anyway
Arl fella – father/old man/husband
Arl lass – mother/old lady/wife
Bait – packed lunch
Beck – mountain stream/brook
Blank – catch no fish
Bookie – bookmaker
Brownie – wild brown trout
Cadge – borrow/scrounge
Chippy – fish & chip takeaway outlet
China – mate (china plate, Cockney)
Chuffin' – in place of an expletive
Clemmed – hungry
Coomb – rounded glacial hollow on mountainside
Cur dog – fell sheepdog
DAA – Derwentdale Anglers' Association
Dabs – fingerprints
Deek – look/peep
Dwam – trance, reverie (Scots)
Fell – mountain
Fettle – health
Gan – go
Gather – rounding-up of sheep from the fells
Gimmer – ewe between 1-2 years old
Ginnel – narrow alley between buildings
Girt – great
Ghyll – ravine (also Gill), or its tumbling stream
Gollop – swallow greedily
Griff – information
Gurn – make a distorted face

Happen – maybe
Hotch – budge/fidget
Hause – small plateau at head of a pass
Hen – dear (Scots, as in greeting)
Howay – come on
In-bye – walled pasture close to the farmstead
Jessica Ennis-Hill – Olympic gold heptathlete
Ken – know
Knott – craggy hill
La'al – little
Lowp – leap
Lug mark – notch in ear to identify sheep
Marra – mate (friend)
Mash – tea/make tea
Meet – shepherds' gathering
Mind – remember
Mither – nag/bother
MOT – certificate of roadworthiness
Nark – annoy
Natural – a fishing fly that mimics an invertebrate
Nicht – night (Scots)
Nowt – nothing
Oor – our
Ower – over
Owt – anything
Parkin – oatmeal & treacle bake
Polis – police (Scots)
Rake – rocky path
Reet – right
Rise – mickey (take the)
Shieling – shepherd's hut (Scots)
Shooting brake – station wagon
Smit mark – paint to identify sheep
Spring-heeled Jack – folklore character who can leap over buildings
Summat – something
Swim – a pocket of water inhabited by fish
T' – the (often silent)
Tarn – small mountain lake in a coomb (corrie)
Theesen – yourself
Thour – your

Tup – ram (male sheep)
Us – often used for me/my/our
Wainwrights – 214 fells listed by Alfred Wainwright
Watter – water, lake
Wuk – work
Yat – gate
Yatter – chatter
YHA – Youth Hostels Association
Yon – that
Yowe – ewe

The Bob Graham Round

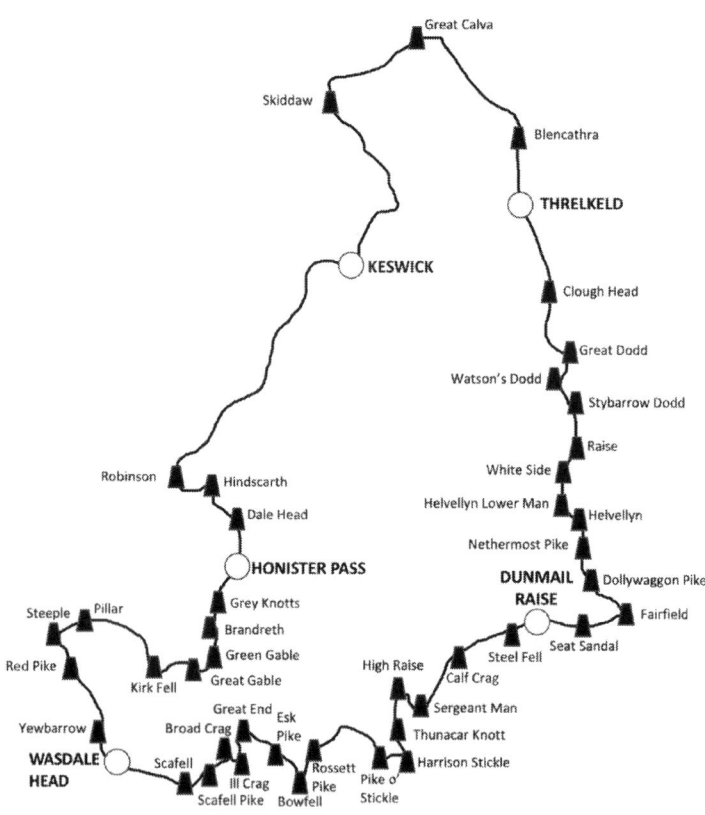

1. TORN

Bassenthwaite Lake – 6.25 a.m. Saturday 18thMay

SKELGILL, TO THE uninitiated, and subject to circumstances, might be regarded as taciturn and mildly hostile – or possibly even brash and arrogant. Certainly, caught on the hop, he is prone to unguarded moments of schoolboy bravado. And perhaps it is true that a boy has to learn – and learn twice – how to display his reaction to the likes of *first* an accolade, and *second* admiration. The former, amongst peers and rivals, is tempted to playground triumphalism – when dignity and humility in victory offer best stead in the long run. The latter – later, in teenage – is the primal urge to preen, to peacock beneath the gaze of the fairer sex. No easy judgement for a callow youth, when one girl's shining hero is another lass's vain bighead.

But he is not essentially one for self-aggrandisement – a view supported by those select long-suffering 'biographers' (such as sergeants Jones and Leyton) patient enough to peel away abstract nouns that would better have their place in a Dickensian novel – recalcitrance, capriciousness, belligerence. To know the man beneath is to understand that these traits were laid down in sedimentary genealogy and warped by tectonic life experience, only to be exposed by eruptions beyond his control.

He, too, would deny an excess of egotism. Albeit this particular day, while his own perspective is hardly a reliable barometer, he rests awkwardly upon the horns of a dilemma, in the matter of a long-brewing pet project.

His idea for a novel Lakeland challenge.

Thus, as he floats, becalmed by introspection, a vague sense of disquiet permeates his feelings, without actually deflecting the general direction of his thoughts; much like the mist on the surface disguises the imperceptible drift of his boat. Dawn sounds – the sharp *kirruk* of a moorhen, the soft plop of a fish, the plaintive bleat of a lamb – reach his ears without turning his head.

But does he want to be famous?

For there is the prospect that a modicum of such may come his way.

15

Yet surely he can take that in his stride; he has had a taste of minor celebrity.

He might arrive at a pub, where fellow anglers are gathered, to overhear, "It's yon Skelgill that's got the pike record for Bass Lake". And he will grin self-effacingly, or pretend not to notice.

Or, setting the pace to reach a casualty with the mountain rescue team trailing at his heels, there may be such panted protests as, "It's alreet for thee, Skelly, lad – thou set the record for the Warnscale Horseshoe."

No – what troubles him is not so much the recognition – but the idea of being seen to *want* to be recognised. For that is the implication of him being the architect – that his idea will be considered self-serving.

For it is a fell running round that incorporates fishing.

Yet, the more he thinks about it, the more he thinks he must bring it about.

And there exists a precedent. A well-established child of the premier fell-running circuit, the Bob Graham Round, is known as the 'Frog Graham' – an amphibious biathlon that requires swimming across four of the greater lakes.

Though the Frog Graham pays only lip service to the parent round (comprising just 19 of the 42 summits), in the way of 'Envelopegate' or 'Partygate' the libfix 'Graham' serves for ease of understanding. But Skelgill's challenge – as yet innominate – will stay true to the Bob Graham Round: all 42 peaks and – the twist – the 12 wild mountain tarns that lie along the route. From each of these, a fish must be line-caught before further progress is allowed.

He stares across the lake; he squints. The sun has crept around the muscular shoulder of Skiddaw; it is driving the early morning smoke from the water. He picks up his rod and reels purposefully, rapidly retrieving rather than with intent to entice.

The sun tells him it is time to seek out his old mentor.

2. CONSULTATION

Braithwaite – 8.00 a.m. Saturday 18th May

'WHAT DO YOU reckon to it, then, Jim?'
The retired professor has his head bowed over the map that Skelgill has spread upon the cottage kitchen table. It has the Bob Graham Round marked as a red line, its 42 summits highlighted in fluorescent yellow, and further annotations – blue circles, numbered from 1 to 12, and reached by jagged blue detours. A rough chart is taped to the sheet, penned in Skelgill's spiky left-handed italics:

Start – Keswick Moot Hall
1 – Scales Tarn
2 – Red Tarn
3 – Grisedale Tarn
4 – Easedale Tarn
5 – Codale Tarn
6 – Stickle Tarn
7 – Angle Tarn
8 – Sprinkling Tarn
9 – Low Tarn
10 – Scoat Tarn
11 – Styhead Tarn
12 – Dalehead Tarn
Finish – Keswick Moot Hall

Professor Jim Hartley, for a second time, runs his eyes down the list. He gurns mildly, and draws the fingers of both hands through his shock of white hair.

'Daniel, I have never been much of a fellsman, and – good heavens – sixty-odd miles and an ascent close to Everest …'

He sighs. Skelgill strains to read his reaction – is it a wistful sigh, or one of resignation?

He waits.

After a moment more the professor's gaze comes up and meets his.

17

There is a wild look in the pale blue eyes. The elderly man places a hand of long attenuated fingers, spread on the map, in the centre of the round.

'But this makes me want to give it a go!'

Skelgill releases his breath. He wants to punch the air.

'With your angling skill, Jim, you could trounce an elite athlete. What you'd lose on the swings you'd gain on the roundabout.'

The professor grins ruefully.

'I think we are talking more hare and tortoise, Daniel. But I should take it on for the satisfaction, not the time. I would not be able to run – I estimate the walk alone could take me three days.'

'Jim, there's plenty do the Bob Graham over three days, or more – just for the achievement. Some bivvy, wild camp – some folk stop at B&Bs at the crossing points – Threlkeld, Dunmail Raise, Wasdale – even the youth hostel at Honister. Make a little holiday of it.'

The professor is nodding.

'It would be an intriguing assignment. I think you have something here, Daniel. For a wide audience.'

Skelgill is further encouraged.

'Fishing – by a country mile – all the surveys say it's Britain's most popular participation sport.'

For a moment the professor nods reflectively – perhaps weighing the benefits to tourism with the environmental impact; it would not be like Skelgill to want the Lakes any more crowded. But in reality this would likely not affect the overall footprint, just its distribution. And, already, enterprising fisherfolk visit individual tarns.

'Is there a precedent for this?'

'Not as I know of – not in Britain.'

Again Jim Hartley ponders.

'It seems so obvious – but that is often the way of good ideas.'

Skelgill waves a hand over the map, perhaps to distract from any reflex that has him puffing out his chest.

'The beauty is, it's not contrived. These tarns, they're along the Bob Graham route – just asking for a quick detour. There's one or two I've excluded – the likes of Kirkfell Tarn and Beckhead Tarn – they're just little drainage pools with barely any oxygenation. Kept it to a round dozen.'

'How much extra does it add on?'

Skelgill twists his shoulders.

'I reckon about seven miles. Plus six thousand-odd foot in

elevation. About an eighth more distance and a fifth more to climb. I'll cadge a GPS from the rescue when I do a proper recce.'

Something must strike the professor; he leans more studiously over the list.

'Do all these tarns hold fish?'

There is a hint of anxiety in his tone, but Skelgill merely grins.

'Aye – course. If there's not trout there's definitely eels – and sticklebacks as a last resort.'

At this, the professor looks amused. It is many years since they first discussed the delicate challenge of catching a stickleback by means other than a net – though it is not impossible. The line-caught record is a spanking fish of 4½ drams, or about a quarter of an ounce.

Skelgill has diminutive alternatives to add.

'There's likely stone loach, bullhead, minnows.'

Now the professor winks.

'And, of course – in Red Tarn – the schelly.'

A fish almost after his own name, and one that can prompt late-night pub guffaws *("Did thee catch a schelly, Skelly, lad?");* a hint of colour comes to his high cheekbones.

'A nice bonus, Jim – but it might not be your quickest option.'

'Oh, you could award extra points – but …'

The man sees Skelgill's instant reaction – and raises a palm of retraction.

Skelgill has plainly thought this through.

'I shouldn't want it to be like show-jumping, adding apples and oranges. A race should be a race. Run-fish-run-fish. Time only.'

The professor nods.

'No – you are quite right, Daniel. But, as a matter of fact, how do they know when someone has actually reached all the summits – in the Bob Graham Round, today?'

Skelgill frowns ruminatively.

'Mostly they'll accept a GPS trace.'

'But what about fish? That would be on trust.'

Skelgill's expression morphs into something more of a scowl – the idea does not register on his ethical compass. Though it does occur to him that when it comes to competitive angling there is a whole gamut of cheating techniques, ranging from the clandestine pre-baiting of a swim to the up-weighting of a fish by inducing it to swallow lead shot.

He speaks slowly, as if the introduction of doubt has bruised his confidence.

'You could do it on trust. You could film it on your phone. Or – for a record attempt, happen you'd station marshals.'

The professor strokes his chin with his long fingers.

'There is always the DAA. The Bob Graham Round does a neat ring of our upper catchment area.'

Skelgill folds his arms.

Jim Hartley reads his protégé's body language. There is title at stake. He adjusts his tack.

'What kind of time are you thinking, Daniel? I mean, at the sharp end of the spectrum – the opposite of my three-day amble.'

Skelgill shrugs.

'The Bob Graham's down to about half its original record.' He delays his answer, despite that he has rehearsed it in his mind many times, and has even put it on paper, not trusting his mental arithmetic. 'If your luck was in – say, half an hour per fish, per tarn – you could break the 24 hours.'

The professor regards Skelgill with the hint of a smile at the corners of his mouth.

'That would seem a highly notable mark.' He glances away casually, and then back. 'You have a cracking time for the Bob Graham, if I remember rightly.'

'Howay, Jim. I'm not even the fastest fell runner in my family, these days.'

The professor raises an admonishing finger.

'Ah – but you refer to young Jess – she moves like the wind; I have seen her. I hear she even shows the Kenyans a clean pair of heels.'

Skelgill's eyes glisten; he takes a minute to respond.

'Aye – but I'm with you there. The 24 hours would be the mark to aim for.'

Jim Hartley hovers a hand over the map, in a circle that follows the route; it is the action of a sorcerer casting a spell.

'I particularly like that the fishes would have a say in the outcome. I rather feel they would respond best to those who show the greatest empathy with their environs.'

Skelgill has his gaze cast on the map; he understands the oblique reference to himself. He remains silent.

'And thus you, Daniel, with your dual skills and sensibilities – could be a hard man to beat.'

Skelgill shrugs, as if aware already of the weight of expectation that rests upon his shoulders.

The professor is sensitive to his mood, and turns to the pragmatic.

'What gear would you take? Nothing too heavy, I imagine?'

Skelgill shakes his head.

'I reckon a fly rod – telescopic, for speed and lightness. Spools of floating and sinking line. Wet and dry flies, naturals. Plenty of leader – ultrafine. Spare size 32 hooks. Couple of small quill floats. Bit of lead shot. Bread paste. Worms. Bloodworms. Couple of small tobys and spoons. The lot wouldn't even weigh half a stone. I'd start out carrying more weight in Kendal mint cake.'

The professor is listening intently.

'You have thought it through, Daniel.'

Skelgill reacts a little diffidently.

'Keeps my mind off crime.'

The professor chuckles – but he knows to stick to the practicalities.

'Can one small collapsible rod serve effectively for several techniques? It sounds rather like the equivalent of hacking round a golf course with just a six-iron.'

But Skelgill is unperturbed.

'I reckon trout would be the first target – and ninety per cent of what you'd catch. There's not a lot of food in these tarns. Approach with stealth and you can often get a take on your first cast. And most of these species are visual predators – provided you're there in the light. Otherwise it might be an eel off the bottom.'

'Ah – I had not considered the light.'

Skelgill is nodding.

'If you did it in midsummer, you've got three hours pitch dark. Start at the Moot Hall. The first tarn's not until Blencathra – Scales Tarn beneath Sharp Edge. To arrive there at first light you'd want to set off from Keswick at maybe 1 a.m. – bear in mind that's midnight GMT. Then continue on the round to get to the final tarn – Dalehead Tarn – by no later than 10 p.m. Even if it takes an hour to catch a fish – you've got a couple of hours to do the last three tops and run back to Keswick in the dark.'

The professor is intrigued.

'This is genuinely tantalising, Daniel. What say I speak to the secretary and have you put on the agenda for the next committee meeting – next Monday? I really think the DAA would buy into this. We have a month to midsummer.'

Skelgill once again seems doubtful.

The professor doubles down on his logic.

'It would be your round, Daniel. You should set the first time. But held under the aegis of the association – it will give it a gravitas, a protected status. A means of jurisdiction, and a channel for publicity. An honours board in The Partridge.'

Skelgill nods, if a little reluctantly.

'Aye, and one up on the AAA.'

'A silver lining for the club, Daniel. By the way – have you got a name for it?'

Now Skelgill produces in his throat something between a disparaging scoff and a growl of frustration.

'Like, Fish Graham – you mean?'

'Well –'

Skelgill is shaking his head.

A moment's silence ensues.

'You are a Graham, of course. If by patrilineality a Skelgill. That would seem doubly fitting – that you would be the inaugural fell angler. These things work well where dynasties are concerned – just think of the Kennedys, the Churchills, the Redgraves. You're not related by any chance to the legendary Bob?'

Skelgill shrugs – though it is not entirely a negation.

'He were a local – originally from Carlisle, born in the late 1800s. The arl lass don't know. Thing is – Graham's about the 100th commonest surname in England – but the 3rd commonest in Cumbria.'

The professor leans forward with interest, resting his elbows on the map.

'Speaking with my old professional hat on, I should say that makes it more rather than less likely that you share some kinship.'

Skelgill grins ruefully.

'It's generally something I play down. I seem to arrest more Grahams than all the Smiths and Joneses put together.'

'Well – that, too, is surely just a product of statistics.'

Skelgill does not appear entirely convinced.

The professor remains enthused.

'You could simply call it the Daniel Graham. Or the Dan Graham, for short, like Bob for Robert.'

Skelgill is looking pained.

'Well, how about the Trout Graham? Given there's a Frog Graham.'

Now Skelgill shakes his head.

'Except – it's not limited to trout, Jim. Sounds a bit corny, an' all.

Frog Graham – folk think you're winding them up when you first mention it.'

The professor bows to Skelgill's more hands-on knowledge of the matter. But he is undeterred in seeking a solution.

'The Anglers' Graham? No – there's Angle Tarn. Tarn Graham? How about that?'

Skelgill's strength is not the subtle let-down. His features reveal his reaction. But perhaps the older man appreciates such candour.

'I can see I would never have succeeded in advertising. Still, there's time aplenty for a name.'

Skelgill sits back, somewhat relieved; though the conundrum is unresolved.

The professor remains buoyant.

'Nevertheless, the intrigue is tantalising. That a competent angler might walk the route and still beat an elite fell runner. And the planning for each water – knowing what fishes are present, and which species will be most forthcoming at a given time of day – and by what method – and how to minimise the weight of gear carried. And the thought that you, Daniel, could leave a lasting legacy – a record to challenge allcomers for years ahead. Marvellous!'

He inhales deeply, through his nose, and seems to savour the action. In the old stone-flagged kitchen with its antiquated range cooker, there is the faintly alcoholic aroma of fresh-baked bread.

'I don't doubt you'll have eaten your fisherman's breakfast – but I rather feel a celebratory bacon sandwich is in order. What do you say?'

'Don't mind if I do, Jim.'

3. SIXTEEN DAYS LATER

Honister Pass – 7.05 a.m. Monday 3rd June

THE RUNNER, peat-spattered and sweat-stained, hair plastered across features drawn in the way of one getting towards the limits of their endurance – a face that can commonly be seen in the last mile of a marathon – comes down still at a good lick, following the arrow-straight path from Grey Knotts, summit number 39 on the clockwise route.

Honister Pass – or, more accurately, Honister Hause – is the final crossing point of the Bob Graham Round. These are known as the changeovers, where support runners and pacers swap roles, and isotonic drinks and energy gels may be taken on board. At Honister, it is the sunken slate car park behind the youth hostel, a former quarry house that has the look of an old village school about it.

All is quiet.

Steam vents silently from a pipe at the back – maybe the boiler firing up for hot water, or the cook getting going in the kitchen. The day has dawned clear and calm. In the cold morning air the white jet rises vertically.

There are few cars in the car park; it is a little early for day-walkers who take advantage of the high point; and these days it is permissible to arrive at a youth hostel by motor vehicle, a commercial concession made by the organisation when trade was ailing in the 1980s.

The route to Dale Head (summit number 40) strikes up from the road a little to the west of the youth hostel, rather than from opposite the vehicular entrance, which is on the east side of the building. An unofficial rocky shortcut climbs the bank to the road, beside the modern septic tank.

Immediately there is the lane, the narrow and winding B5289 that connects Gatesgarth at the head of Lorton Vale with Seatoller in Borrowdale, reaching an altitude of 1,167 feet; a gradient of 1 in 4 that links the Skelgills at Buttermere to the Hopes at Seathwaite.

The runner gains the road – but now stops.

He turns back and watches the rising fellside to the south, for a good twenty seconds. He scans the path he has descended. His expression is now concerned, or perhaps perplexed.

He turns again to look due north, at the next climb. 1,200 feet in 1¼ miles; not too bad, less of a gradient than the Honister Pass itself.

He steels himself for the effort; he rocks back on his heels in preparation.

Then he hesitates again.

This time he makes a half-turn of the upper body – for a car emerges from the entrance to the car park, no more than 50 yards away.

Curiously, the driver indicates – it must be an old habit – for there are no other motorists to whom to signal.

The car swings out towards the runner.

There is a light *beep-beep* – it is an innocuous toot, of gaining attention, perhaps more than that.

Indeed, almost involuntarily, the runner raises a hand in recognition.

The car rolls unhurriedly towards him.

His features acquire a hint of intrigue, or perhaps even amusement.

And then – when the car is within a few yards, and the engine suddenly roars as if it is out of control, that it has gained a life of its own, and the car leaps forwards – the expression becomes one of disbelief, of horror, of it being too late.

Lower limbs, fatigued and half-paralysed by the halt, cannot react. Upper limbs – the arms, hands splayed – are thrown out in the vain hope of protection.

4. LEAVE TO FISH

Styhead Tarn – 9.00 a.m. Monday 3rd June

IF THERE ARE still faeries in the Lake District, a tarn is surely where to glimpse them. A tarn is a magical place. Even on the busiest Bank Holiday of the year, when the lanes are choked with lines of traffic and the 'leisure' lakes (Derwentwater, Ullswater, Windermere) are a scene of flailing oars and hilarity as first-time rowers from Manchester and Liverpool entertain their families with ineptitude … even on these high days a tarn can be an oasis of tranquillity.

A literal oasis during a dry spell, what sets a tarn aside from any other body of water is its topography. No great scholar, an eleven-year-old Skelgill found his attention piqued when his form mistress dealt out textbooks for a term of physical geography. The cover illustration he instantly recognised as Sprinkling Tarn – and blurted out the fact to the lad at his elbow. Overheard by the schoolmarm, he had been pressed to tell the class what he knew about it.

Crimson-faced and stumbling, his accent raw by comparison to his nowadays modulated enunciation, his response had been along the lines of: *"Yon's a la'al lake up in t' fells, Miss. Twixt Girt End an' Girt Gable. If thee gan skinny-dipping, t' watter's like ice'.*

Not exactly the textbook answer, but evocative nonetheless. Indeed, the implicit admission of nudity had raised a laugh and several jibes – and more colour to Skelgill's cheeks.

The teacher took his side, and praised him – and soon was to notice that, while no star pupil (for reasons not best understood at the time) young Daniel Skelgill demonstrated an unusual affinity for Ordnance Survey maps and the pictorial Wainwright guides employed that semester. His application – and thus his marks – improved beyond measure.

For Skelgill, it had been his first – and perhaps remains his only – experience of schoolwork or academia having a point, a graphic, tangible, topical relevance to everyday life. Here were lessons that taught him not only the names of landforms that were so familiar to him, but also how they came about. The Cumbrian mountains were once as high as the Himalayas. The Ice Ages progressively ground them down. But the ice did not take away; far from obliterate, it etched an intricate legacy, bewildering and tantalising, at once rugged and beautiful.

And then came the Viking farmers. Long assimilated into the Celtic gene pool, and anglicised in their ways, their lasting legacy is woven into the language of the landscape. Describe what you see in the Lakes today and you may find yourself speaking Old Norse. Say "Grisedale Pike" to a Viking farmer and he would know you mean the pointed peak (pike) above the valley (dale) of the wild boar (grise). And so there are the likes of beck (stream), fell (mountain), force (waterfall), gill (ravine), rigg (ridge), scar (cliff), scree (landslip), skel (ledge) ... and, not least, tarn.

The Old Norse *tjörn* in fact means 'small lake' – but size alone is not the qualifier. A handful of the larger tarns have a greater surface area than several of the smaller lakes.

There are generally regarded to be about 200 tarns in the Lakeland fells. But Skelgill knows many more, smaller, obscure, innominate. There is of course the 'actual' Innominate Tarn made famous by Wainwright, close to the summit of Haystacks, and a navigational godsend to the hiker lost in cloud.

Innominate Tarn is diminutive – but it also has one of the key tarn characteristics. Altitude. But being a summit tarn it lacks one other ideal quality, albeit a matter of aesthetics.

To Skelgill's mind the 'classic' tarn nestles in a steep-sided coomb, with a sheer backdrop of towering cliff and sliding scree, the arms of the arêtes sweeping around and down to embrace the elevated amphitheatre. Gouged out by a corrie glacier, it is now flooded, abandoned and silent but for a few essential sounds.

Water percolates in. Water hurries out.

In the rarefied air bird calls resound. The descending crescendo of a meadow pipit parachuting over its patch. The warning *chack* of a wheatear, as if it has struck a pebble against its rock perch. From the shoreline the call of a common sandpiper – locally the willylilt. From the high cliffs the throaty bass *brok* of a raven. Seemingly from the very air itself the urgent keening of a marauding peregrine; beware, each little bird that sings.

And wild flowers.

The bejewelled bankside kaleidoscope of colours: pearl bedstraw, golden tormentil, ruby lousewort, sapphire milkwort. Pale emerald

27

patches of sphagnum moss – where sundew lie in wait for insect prey – at times a deceptively attractive seat, likely to leave the unsuspecting hiker with damp underwear for the rest of the day.

And faeries.

Skelgill has often half expected to poke his nose out of his bivvy bag to see one such being, pulling at a heather briar pipe, or sipping nectar from a harebell – and would never have been surprised to do so.

But perhaps the nose is too much of an early warning, and the faeries hitherto have taken heed, and to their heels.

Still, it is enough to be the only human at a tarn.

Right now he is the only human at Styhead Tarn – though he has not woken here, despite that he waits for bacon to fry over the embers of his Kelly kettle.

He bunked overnight at Buttermere. Home, his Ma's hotpot, and handily placed for a dawn start. Not to mention boarding for his dog. At first light he struck up Buttermere Fell to Littledale Edge, passing just south of the final two Bob Graham tops of Robinson (42) and Hindscarth (41) to reach the summit of Dale Head (40). Thence he took a direct path of under half a mile to Dalehead Tarn. The first tarn for reconnaissance, it will be the last of his round. Within five minutes he caught a small brownie on a self-tied mayfly emerger; and in another twenty a stickleback on a bloodworm; finally – to his surprise – minutes later a small perch took a worm from his Ma's compost heap. Should he just go for perch?

Via an old shepherds' rake, rarely used, he rejoined the Bob Graham route, descending across Honister Pass and up and over the summits of Grey Knotts (39), Brandreth (38) and Green Gable (37). At Windy Gap he left the rollercoaster ridge to descend to his present locus of Styhead Tarn.

Contemplating the 1,000-odd foot return climb (and his intuition sounding alarm bells), it was then that he saw his first fellow fell-wanderers of the day. At about 6:30 a.m. he spied two runners, male, heading east towards Green Gable.

They were several minutes apart, but there was the impression that they were in something together. He had wondered – were they doing the Bob Graham Round? Or maybe training for it? The regular anniversary event is coming up, 12th-13th June – and not many years to the centenary. They seemed to be of about his own age – but too far away to be sure – or to pick out any distinguishing features. Just dark silhouettes.

Skelgill did not linger; he hid his pack and marched on with angling gear only, ascending to Sprinkling Tarn. He fished there, successfully tempting an eel, a brownie and – remarkably – a stocked vendace, grinning ruefully at Jim Hartley's comment about extra points for rare species.

Returning to Styhead Tarn, he had resolved to fish here before breakfast.

Now the fishing is done and the fry-up is ready. Without further ado he loads bacon and tomato onto a torn oven-bottom cake, and wipes the pan clean of fat with the top of the roll, before pressing the halves together.

He chews pensively, holding up his little trophy, comparing look and taste and reminding himself that his Ma's baking takes some beating. Pity he never picked up the skill.

That said, the bacon roll is the sandwich of a thousand variations, and – while some are far superior to others – outdoors, when hungry from exercise, pretty much any flavour will do.

He munches into oblivion – but catches himself doing it – and he hears the chiding of his Caledonian ally, Cameron Findlay. *"Yer in a dwam, Danny, boy."*

He directs his thoughts to the matter that has been troubling him.

He has an Ordnance Survey map spread over a smooth boulder. The bird's-eye view shows the Bob Graham Round to be the shape of a boot, with the toe pointing to the left. He now sits inside the toe.

Sprinkling Tarn and Styhead Tarn also lie enclosed within the toe.

Sprinkling Tarn is 4/10 of a mile from (and 524 feet below) the round at Esk Hause.

Styhead Tarn is 6/10 of a mile from (and 1,026 feet below) the round at Windy Gap.

Additionally, Sprinkling Tarn and Styhead Tarn are 6/10 of a mile apart, the former 528 feet above the latter.

Should he take each tarn from its nearest point on the round, or both tarns together, from either Windy Gap or Esk Hause?

Logic suggests the former of the three options, but a little voice in his head is whispering *"Esk Hause"*.

He continues to scowl at the map.

After more than three decades on these fells his intuition must count for something. As a boy, endless days spent exploring with school pal Jud Hope – not least, the thrice-annual gather – learning the ropes, helping to work the cur dogs to bring down Arthur Hope's

29

hefted flock of 400-odd Herdwicks. Such an introduction to the landscape – later coming up to fish the becks and – yes – tarns. His discovery of blessed lung power, a rangy build and a long, loping stride; junior fell running – breaking records; more latterly, two Bob Graham Rounds to his name. And then the mountain rescue – perhaps the worthiest yet, if occasionally the grimmest of times.

Absently, he scratches two-handed at his temples; midges are biting. He reaches behind to snap off a leafy spring of bog myrtle. He rolls it vigorously between his palms, releasing the warm, musky, sweet aroma. He smears the resinous extract around his face and neck.

Now he curses the impenetrable maths.

He will have to delegate the calculation. DS Jones understands Ordnance Survey maps. Then again, Leyton is tack sharp when it comes to betting odds – and there is a little wager at stake here. Maybe the pair between them.

He sighs – and reminds himself it is okay to relax. Just park the conundrum.

This is Monday and he's off all week.

The weather is set fair, and he has a bivvy bag and ample food.

The DAA have signed off his idea. The professor called him in animated mode. *"Georgina was positively cock-a-hoop, Daniel!"* He had forgotten the club secretary is a Graham by name – if only by dissolved marriage. The committee want him to do the inaugural round over the shortest night, finishing on 21st June, an auspicious date, the summer solstice.

The Chief was surprised and only too happy to approve his holiday request. Skelgill has never yet managed his entitlement, and regularly tarnishes her HR statistics.

No major cases are in the offing. DS Jones is investigating a series of rural shopliftings, and DS Leyton claims to be on the tail of a cat burglar who specialises in stealing ladies' underwear. *Alan Whickers*, in his sergeant's East End parlance.

So, yes, he has all week. He might be following the route of a race – but he is not in one. And certainly not in the rat race.

He finishes the last of his roll, and his tea, and decides he will make another mash. There is ample dry heather, no shortage of water, and unlimited access to restrooms.

A movement above catches his eye. He watches as three walkers inch along the skyline, descending into Windy Gap, these in the westerly direction from Green Gable towards Great Gable.

30

Tiny stick figures. Slightly bent, they carry full packs. Against the bright sky they move ponderously, picking their way with care. Older folks, they all use poles. A tallish chap followed a little way back by two women, one of the latter pair distinctive for her lime-green cagoule and white hair.

They are taking the same route as that which he will resume.

He wonders whence they have come; it is still early – just past nine, by his watch. The hostel at Honister Hause, maybe. He might catch them up.

His plan now, with three tarns and breakfast under his belt, is to take it steady, and to resume the anticlockwise route – back to Windy Gap, over Great Gable (36) to Kirk Fell (35); and on via Pillar (34), Steeple (33) and Red Pike (32) to fish first Scoat Tarn and finally Low Tarn.

Later he will descend to set up camp at the Wasdale Head crossing point.

There, lies a particular attraction, of the pint-sized variety: close at hand, the isolated hostelry.

And always the chance that one might spy a faerie on the twilight walk back.

5. THE INN CROWD

Wasdale Head – 6.25 p.m. Monday 3rd June

IT IS ONE THING to lie zipped into a bivvy bag on the shingle of an isolated tarn, or beside a babbling beck, or in the lee of the tumbledown wall of an ancient shieling, but quite another to do so in an in-bye pasture that doubles as a public campsite. For Skelgill the issue is as much psychological as it is practical. Like the poor down-and-out huddled in a shop doorway, the degree of vulnerability feels extreme – even if the only true threat is from a hungry yowe nosing out breakfast cereal.

To thwart such an ovine exigency Skelgill has chosen a corner of the meadow and is presently rigging up a flysheet, suspended over a line tied hypotenuse-wise across the right-angle of the field walls, the knotted ends snagged in chinks in the dry stone construction. He weights the corners with loose rocks, and steps back to admire his handiwork. He gives a satisfied click of the tongue; not a bad job; at a glance, a half-decent tent.

'Don't they say an Englishman's home is his castle?'

Skelgill spins around.

It takes him a moment to fit the voice to the person – although there is only one of each. The accent is American, soft, with a faint lilt – from somewhere in the middle-to-south? The person is an elderly woman clad in comfortable-looking hiking gear, with shoulder-length white hair, regular features and penetratingly clear pale-blue eyes. She totes a lightweight tripod topped with a small classic Leica camera. She rests the feet of the tripod on the grass before her.

'Mind if I take a shot? I'm making a calendar for my friends. A surprise present for Christmas. A memento of our trip.'

Her manner is at once disarming.

'Be my guest.'

He begins to step back.

'Oh – would you be in it?'

There is the sense that she is feeling for the right words – to the effect that the unkempt traveller will add character to the composition.

He hesitates.

'I can see you're shy. Don't worry – it won't go around the world on social media. It's just two friends.' She pats the camera like a favoured pet. 'Besides – this takes film only; my trusty old companion.'

Skelgill begins to yield – but does not know how to pose. Deftly, she spreadeagles the legs of the tripod.

'What is that – the, er –?'

'Contraption?'

Now he grins.

'Yes.'

'It's a Kelly kettle. Saves you carrying fuel. Works in any weather – some folk call it a storm kettle. Also a volcano kettle.' The device is simmering, and now he kneels and demonstrates, feeding in some pine cones that he has collected into a little heap. Flames begin to lick from the mouth. 'See – the fire comes up the chimney in the middle. The water's inside the double sleeve that makes up the outer body.'

The woman is bent to the viewfinder.

'Would you just carry on, for a few moments?'

'Aye, why not. I was making a mash, anyway. If you'll share a mug, you're welcome to some.'

'Well, thank you, sir – but my friends will be wondering where I am – we have requested dinner at six-thirty.' She glances across to a venerable cream-painted slate-roofed building, beyond the walls that line the lane; painted on its gable end in great capitals, the word INN.

In these digital times Skelgill is ready for a series of takes – but she gets the shot in one. He supposes she cannot waste precious exposures.

She gathers up the legs of the tripod and rests it across her shoulder. Skelgill is still tending the kettle as she approaches and leans to offer a hand.

'I'm Rita.'

'Er ... Dan.'

'Well, thank you, Dan.'

With a faint bow she turns and hurries away. He watches, still kneeling. It is difficult to estimate her age. She moves carefully, economically, but with a certain athletic grace.

As is its wont, the kettle suddenly erupts, and he whips it off the fire base before he loses too much water. He settles on a sit-mat, back to the wall, idly surveying Wasdale. He can just glimpse the black screes that plunge into Wastwater. Closer at hand, the campsite is quiet, just a few folk pottering much the same as he. He pours a tea and methodically sets about his dehydrated rations. In a small pan he makes a packet soup. Then packet noodles. Then packet custard. Finally, another tea, and chocolate digestives.

Three-quarters of an hour pass beneath a clear sky and evening sunlight, and he reflects upon a successful day; though the twin-tarns conundrum still bugs him. There is no signal on his mobile, else he could send a message to DS Jones. Then again, he could phone from the pub.

*

'Let me get that for you.'

For the second time this evening the soft American voice ambushes Skelgill; its white-haired owner is at his shoulder at the bar counter. He turns. If he were in any doubt, he recognises the Leica slung over her shoulder.

'Nay – you're alreet – have you seen the price of ale these days?'

'I must – in return for your kindness over the photograph.' She pats the camera, and then inclines her head slightly. 'Besides – I was telling my friends about your Kelly kettle. Gerry says he must get one. Perhaps you can put him onto the manufacturer?'

Skelgill follows her indication to a corner table. An elderly couple in hiking gear are watching them with interest.

'Please – come and join us for a few minutes.'

Before he can protest further, the woman – Rita – overrides his note proffered to the bar girl and orders another round of the same again, and for Skelgill's beer to be added to the tab.

A little sheepishly, and now indentured, he follows her to the table.

The man rises. He is tall, slightly bowed. He greets Skelgill warmly. The woman remains seated; she is small, elfin, a redhead with a fringe; her smile is mischievous. That they sit close on the settle suggests they are a couple. Maybe late sixties, early seventies, to Skelgill's eye they are in good fettle. Outdoors types, tanned, bright-eyed and just slightly unkempt; a lived-in look. He thinks he detects Yorkshire accents. They are introduced as Gerry and Rosheen.

Rita moves onto the settle; Skelgill is accorded the best chair.

'You sound like a local.'

It is Gerry's question.

'Is it that obvious?'

But Gerry shakes his tousled head.

'My grandfather was from Cockermouth – we used to come up and visit. That's where I caught the Lakes bug – and got the hang of the lingo, lowpin' yats an' all that.'

Skelgill grins.

'So, you're translating?'

Gerry flashes a wry grin at his female companions.

'When I can get a word in. Yatterin' – reet?'

He receives an elbow in the ribs from Rosheen.

'Rita and I have got a lot of catching-up to do.' She turns to address Skelgill. 'Rita's visiting from Missouri. We did teacher training together, many years ago.'

Now Gerry shrugs resignedly.

'And she's had this madcap idea for her 80th to do the Bob Graham Round.'

Skelgill jerks back in amazement.

When it might be assumed it is the coincidence of their undertaking, in fact it is the cited age that wows him. Were he asked to guess, he would have knocked off at least a decade. He glances at Rita but lacks the right words, sensing he might put his foot in it. There is a twinkle in the pale eyes.

He finds a rejoinder, along practical lines.

'You're going anticlockwise.'

Gerry again acts as spokesperson, though he touches Rosheen's arm to indicate her involvement. He does not question Skelgill's assertion.

'Aye – when we set it up, we couldn't get the accommodation to fit the route clockwise. There's only one or two places at most of the crossing points. Surprisingly, it was the youth hostel at Honister that had limited availability. So we stayed overnight at a guest house in Keswick on Saturday, and then Honister last night – very comfortable and friendly. We slept like logs. It took the smell of bacon to rouse us, and tempt Rita away from her photography.'

Skelgill is nodding.

'Were you passing Windy Gap at about nine this morning?'

'Aye, that'd be right. We left Honister just shy of eight. You saw us?'

'I was at Styhead Tarn.'

Gerry is intrigued.

'What took you there?'

Skelgill decides there is no harm in outlining his mission. These are friendly visitors with no stake in its success, or otherwise. Besides, they understand the Bob Graham concept.

'I'm a member of a local angling association. We're launching an alternative version of the round. You complete the Bob Graham, but you must also catch a fish in each of twelve tarns along the way. I'm doing a bit of a recce. Fish wise.'

Gerry is about to drink, but he postpones the pleasure.

'That's a cracking idea. A new twist on the biathlon.'

Now Rosheen pipes up.

'More like an angler's pub crawl.'

Gerry seems to approve.

'That could be the forfeit if you don't catch a fish! You have to down a pint instead.'

Skelgill grins wryly.

'It could get messy towards the end.'

Rita has been listening with interest. She addresses Skelgill.

'Just how do fish get into these tarns? They would seem to have to overcome waterfalls and steep rock faces.'

Skelgill nods over the rim of his glass.

'It's the source of many a late-night pub argument. Discounting eels, which can move across damp ground, the popular theory is the transfer of their sticky eggs on the feet of birds. And some waters must have been stocked by local farmers. It's a sight easier to harvest fish from a little tarn than one of the big lakes.'

He takes a drink, but continues when he realises he has the floor.

'That said, you'll be passing Red Tarn when you climb Helvellyn. There's a rare fish in there called the schelly – it's like an Ice Age relic. It's also found in Ullswater, thick end of 2,000 foot below. Red Tarn and Ullswater being connected by Red Tarn Beck, which runs into Glenridding Beck, it's tempting to believe the schelly pulled off a bit of animal magic.'

Rita is listening with interest.

'You are very knowledgeable – is angling your profession?'

Skelgill might be tempted to milk the compliment, were the question not double-edged. However, it does pave the way for one of his stock replies when he does not want to reveal his occupation. The revelation that he is a police detective can be a dampener or a diversion, depending upon the company.

'I do a bit of fishing guiding.' This is true in that he does occasionally take an acquaintance, though not for payment. He adds a rider, with a vague waft of the hand to the land beyond the pub window. 'I've got a few pals work as shepherds, gamekeepers – keeps me off the streets.'

Gerry is nodding sagely; he seems entirely satisfied. But glancing at Rita Skelgill can see she is not remotely taken in – and there again is the twinkle in her eye. Perhaps she even winks. He supposes he has kept her secret about the photo album calendar.

However, his cover is about to be blown.

The bar girl approaches bearing a tray with the repeat drinks order. As she stoops to place it down she turns to face Skelgill.

'Excuse me, are you Inspector Skelgill? There is a DS Jones – on the landline.'

She glances back to the serving counter, to indicate its location.

Like startled horses, a range of emotions break out across Skelgill's countenance before he is able to rein them in. It is a flick-book of expressions, from surprise to resolve, passing through indignation, embarrassment, apology and resignation.

He rises to leave his companions not annoyed, however, but intrigued and – perhaps more so in Rita's case – amused.

He makes to take his pint, but has second thoughts.

'Shan't be a tick.'

The telephone is of an antiquated variety; however, he contrives to stretch the extending spiral cable round into the corridor that leads to the toilets, to achieve a modicum of privacy.

'Jones?'

'Sorry, Guv – I called your mother – she said you were likely camping at Wasdale Head. I knew you'd have no signal – so it was either the public phone box … or the pub.'

Skelgill makes an ironic growl. Is he so predictable? Then again, it would not have been the first time that he had answered a ringing phone in an isolated rural red kiosk to find the call was for him.

DS Jones continues.

'It's just something I thought you ought to know about – no action needed – but rather than rely on the jungle drums to get it wrong.'

He understands her concern. News can travel fast, even in the fells – but it often arrives as the "send three-and-fourpence" variety.

'Fire away.'

'A runner was struck and killed by a hit-and-run driver at Honister Pass at between six-thirty and eight this morning. The victim was male, aged thirty-five, name Sebastian Sinclair, home address Applethwaite.

He was the owner-director of a design company based in Carlisle. He was carrying ID. He leaves a wife, Morag, and two young children, boys three and five. They've been informed and the family liaison unit are providing support. Her sister is travelling down from Scotland to stay with her.'

Questions vie for prominence in Skelgill's consciousness; others wrestle beneath the surface. He might sound aloof in neglecting the human angle, but his colleague seems to have it covered – and she cannot appreciate his proximal connection.

'The Honister – where?'

'Honister Hause – at the top of the pass, close to the youth hostel. We believe the vehicle was heading towards Gatesgarth.'

'You say between six-thirty and eight. Why such a big window?'

'I know, Guv. Dr Herdwick was there by eight-fifty – six-thirty is his earliest limit. As for eight – that's when he was found.'

Skelgill inhales to reply, but hesitates for a second or two.

'I crossed that stretch of road at about five-thirty. Course – it were all clear. But why would it take an hour and a half for someone to notice him? I know it's not exactly the A66 – but there's a regular trickle of traffic.'

'The body was partly concealed by bracken at the roadside. It wasn't until Jud Hope stopped –'

Skelgill interrupts.

'Jud?'

'Yes, he was towing a trailer of lambs up to Cockermouth. He spotted blood in the road and thought a sheep had been struck. He got out to search – and found the victim. There were faint signs of life – Jud did what he could – but the man was declared dead on arrival at the hospital. Preliminary evidence suggests the cause of death was his skull striking the road, rather than the injuries from the vehicle impact.'

Skelgill tries to picture the scene.

'Hit and run.'

DS Jones takes a moment to answer.

'Obviously, no one has come forward. But – what Jud Hope said – there is the possibility that the driver looked away, perhaps glanced at the youth hostel – and thought they'd clipped a sheep. Jud mentioned that there were sheep on the road.'

DS Jones cannot see – but Skelgill looks like he has bitten into a lemon. He keeps his contrarian counsel, however.

'I take it we've got nowt.'

'We're checking the ANPR cameras on the A66 for suspicious activity – and any local CCTV we can find. It's looking thin on the ground, though. Such a network of uninhabited lanes – I don't have to tell you.'

Skelgill does not press the point; instead, his next question must seem to come from left of field.

'Was he running with another bloke?'

'Ah – well, it's funny you should say that. He's been training with a friend – the husband of a woman, Victoria Lawson, who works for him. The two couples are friendly – similar age and interests. The husband is Frank Lawson. He's thirty-three and has some international sales job – he's away quite a bit. They've been training together to do the upcoming Bob Graham Round anniversary challenge. As far as Morag Sinclair knew they were doing the section this morning from Wasdale to Keswick. They took a cab to Wasdale. We've not been able to contact Frank Lawson yet. Victoria Lawson says he was travelling straight down to Manchester afterwards to catch a flight to Los Angeles. He's not due back until Friday.'

When Skelgill does not respond, DS Jones allows a few seconds before prompting him.

'What is it, Guv?'

'I reckon I saw them. Six-thirty. I was at Styhead Tarn. Two males ran along the ridge – heading for Honister Hause. They were a good couple of minutes apart.'

Now DS Jones grasps his line of thought.

'One could have been run over without the other even knowing.'

Skelgill is nodding grimly.

'If I saw them at six-thirty, happen they wouldn't have made the Honister until seven.'

'It narrows the time window.'

Skelgill makes a pensive tutting sound with his tongue.

'They were definitely running all the way back to the finish at Keswick?'

'As far as we know. I suppose – until we get to speak with Frank Lawson, we can't be sure.'

Skelgill offers a murmur of agreement.

'So – that's it, Guv. Sorry to disturb you.'

'Nay – you were reet. Like you say – there could be an innocent explanation – but maybe not. Hit and run – it's hard to imagine you wouldn't notice.'

'Do you want me to keep you posted? We can cope.'

Skelgill does not reply immediately.

'If I'm up high, there's always the chance of a mobile signal.' Again, he pauses. He is supposed to be on a break. Unfortunate though the incident might be, it is a largely routine matter. But he has that feeling – just like when fishing, having told himself he has had his last cast of the day, his line is in – but out there on the water there is another tempting rise. 'Tell you what – tomorrow night – I'll be in the Dungeon Ghyll Inn at nine.'

There is a smile in DS Jones's voice as she responds.

'Okay. Anything else – that you want me to ask or look into?'

Skelgill suddenly perks up.

'Aye, there is, actually. Get hold of an OS map. Work out the best way to visit Styhead Tarn and Sprinkling Tarn from the Bob Graham Round. Get Leyton to help you.'

Now DS Jones chuckles.

'Righto. Don't we miss you!'

Further words of farewell are exchanged, and Skelgill returns a little pensively to his new-found acquaintances. Too late, he realises he should assume an expression of nonchalance.

It is Rosheen, impishly, who asks if there has been a murder.

Though Rita puts a hand to her mouth, and Gerry reprimands his partner, that it is not for members of the public to be nosy, that the police must be taciturn or fuel wild rumours, Rosheen's audacity in fact serves as an ice-breaker. Skelgill regards her with mock reproach, and takes a sup of his ale.

'Road traffic accident.' He gives a toss of the head, back in the direction of the bar, and the telephone. 'They can take care of it. Just happened to be reported by a farmer friend of mine. That's why they wanted to keep me in the picture.'

This seems to satisfy Gerry and Rosheen, at least – although Skelgill notes that Rita is watching him closely. She might actually be concerned that, below the surface, he is in fact a little rattled. He contrives an additional smile.

But now it seems his occupation is fair game – if only in the general sense, and not the specific. Skelgill does not doubt they have been discussing it in his absence. Gerry continues as spokesperson.

'You must have an interesting life, being a detective inspector in this neck of the woods – the profile of crimes must be entirely different from a metropolitan force?'

Skelgill's demeanour is reasonably forthcoming, though his answer is a tad ambivalent.

'You might be surprised. I'd say we get all the regular crimes, to which you can add stock rustling, fights at market sales, and pitched battles at the Appleby Horse Fair.'

He realises he could hold court, and that they would welcome it – and, after all, the ale is in tip-top condition. But he finishes his pint and makes a show of checking the time on his wristwatch.

'Now, can I get you good folks a drink on my way out? I have to be up with the lark.'

But they still have near-full glasses, and besides they clearly regard him as their guest. Gerry interjects.

'Actually, it's my shout – will you not have one for the road?'

'Thanks, all the same – but no thanks.'

Skelgill can see they are disappointed. He offers a line of compensation.

'Where are you staying tomorrow night?'

Gerry places a large palm on a folded Ordnance Survey map on the settle at his side.

'We're booked in at the Dungeon Ghyll Inn. We thought it would be too much for one day to get all the way to Grasmere.'

Skelgill turns his head briefly in a gesture of respect.

'If you're doing the Scafell Pikes and the Langdales together, that's a big enough ask.'

Gerry is nodding.

'We've got a plan B – escape out of Eskdale. We'll take it steady. See how it goes.'

Skelgill looks at them – now with a certain degree of concern. Though the weather is set fair, and the daylight hours are long. And it strikes him that – while he will be taking detours for tarns – he will never be far away from them. He picks up a beermat from the table and splits it open with his thumbnail. He goes to the bar for a pen, and returns to hand over the item.

'That's my mobile. There's often a signal when you're on the ridge.'

They seem to understand they have a guardian angel. But before any one of them can embarrass him, Skelgill enters a proposition.

'One of my options for tomorrow night is to bivvy below Stickle Tarn – that's just above Dungeon Ghyll. All goes well – we can settle up our rounds in the bar.'

This is well received, and Gerry risks a joke.

'I reckon by then we'll all be needing to murder a pint!'

*

Skelgill is lulled by the *burr-burr* of the ring-tone, an unchanging constant in these days of technological flux. He is conscious of breathing through parted lips – another unchanging constant is the distinctive sickly and acrid smell of the public phone box.

The call is picked up.

'Hello. Seathwaite 234.'

Skelgill grins. Gladis Hope still answers with the number that was very first assigned, back in the mists of time.

'Gladis. It's me.'

'Daniel – is it about the accident?'

'I wondered if your Jud were in?'

'Aye – he's watching the repeat of Ennerdale wi' us.'

'Could I have a quick word?'

When Skelgill emerges from the kiosk his first act is to gulp in a great draught of the cool evening air, and to exhale as though he is purging his lungs of the polluted interior.

He stands for a moment; the birds are stilled by the dusk; only the occasional bleat of a lamb penetrates the deep silence. He stares along the lane, pensive, unblinking; he might almost be waiting for a faerie to scale the wall on one side and cross noiselessly to repeat the feat on the other.

But no such apparition is forthcoming – and a single pint unlikely to produce one.

He turns, his expression severe, and makes for the dubious comfort of his bivvy bag.

6. VICTORIA

Wetheral – 9.25 a.m. Tuesday 4th June

'HOW THE OTHER half live, eh, girl?'
DS Jones nods pensively. There is no note of envy in her colleague's voice; it is merely an observation – if anything DS Leyton sounds admiring of the immaculately painted Georgian property as he swings them between tall pinkish sandstone gateposts and onto the broad gravel driveway. Far from the grandest residence in the affluent commuter village, nevertheless it is a small mansion house in its own right. The colour scheme, fresh white walls with bay windows, central portico and quoins picked out in a smoky duck-egg blue speaks of style-consciousness. The grounds are well stocked and neatly manicured; there is abstract topiary in yew and box, a substantial rustic-poled children's play area beneath a spreading cedar, and a west-facing patio with luxury garden furniture that would break the budget for a best lounge suite in the average household.

A sparkling white new-plate Mercedes sports coupé stands in front of the house. Also, tucked around the side, of lesser pedigree – as though not quite fit for show – a small, dingier white Ford hatchback, with two child seats visible in the rear.

There is congruence in this scene with what they already know. It is the residence of Victoria Lawson, second in command at Sinclair Design, and husband Frank Lawson, erstwhile fell running partner of the late proprietor.

DS Leyton presses a brass bell-push. They hear it ring within the house, and footsteps come quickly across a tiled floor; their call is by appointment and it seems someone has been waiting for them.

The door is opened by a tall, short-haired brunette in her mid-twenties – too young to be Victoria Lawson. She brandishes a smiling (and chewing) toddler – a small boy of under two – his face and hands copiously smeared with tomato ketchup, some of which has transferred to the nanny's pink check blouse.

She is nervy, birdlike, and somewhat distracted – and further so by the action of DS Leyton – who, for a split second, responds instinctively to what might be the proffered child, and begins to reach out to take him, before realising his subconscious error (he is not arriving home) and entering instead into a hurried explanation for their slightly later than scheduled arrival.

The woman listens, rather imperviously, while the boy looks on good-naturedly. But there is a resemblance between the nanny and her charge, a sallowness of skin, and matching large brown eyes.

Now she steps back to admit them, though reluctantly. There is the impression that she is acting upon orders, against her better judgement; a guard dog that under protest has been hushed by its owner; a loyal retainer wilier in the ways of the world than her naïve employer. Of course, there is a natural suspicion of intruders, no matter how friendly they might seem; and the police, like undertakers, always bring an aura of the sinister.

'Victoria is through in her study. If you would follow me.'

The boy playing a silent game of peep-o around her shoulder, she leads them through a capacious vestibule, its décor plain yet stylish, and sparingly adorned with modern art of two and three dimensions.

There are various panelled doors, some closed, some a little ajar. They glimpse a designer kitchen with a large central island; perhaps from there the smell of freshly brewed coffee emanates.

'I expect you have your hands full with the children?'

It is DS Jones that makes conversation.

The nanny half glances back.

'It's easier this morning. Isobel has taken Tommy to nursery.' It seems they are expected to know who Isobel is.

They take a left turn beneath a low beam; a door faces them.

A yard short, the nanny halts and bars their way.

It seems she wants to say something – but that she feels it might be above her station.

She swivels at the hips to turn the child away from them, and leans conspiratorially.

'Isobel lost her husband two months ago.' Her voice is reduced to a whisper, as though only adults will understand. 'Victoria lost her father. They loved their Granddad Beslow.'

The child seems to respond with something that might be *"Jam-jar"*.

The nanny's stare is reproachful – as if to say her mistress has had enough to cope with; and so too the family.

DS Jones nods understandingly.

'Thank you for telling us. We're used to this kind of situation. And you'll appreciate, when there is a sudden unexplained – *event* –' (she places stress on the euphemism) 'we must follow a procedure laid down by the law'.

The nanny is plainly a little conflicted. A trained follower of rules, she cannot gainsay the point.

DS Jones, who is of an age with the woman, reaches to touch her forearm.

'Did you know Mr Sinclair well?'

The dark brown eyes meet the hazel of the detective; for a moment there is perhaps a flicker of understanding.

'Not really, no.'

She turns away and knocks and pushes open the door, and then stands aside as they enter, closing it after them without a word.

The impression of stylish sophistication is continued.

Victoria Lawson is small and dark and slender, blue-eyed with regular features that would be considered attractive. Her chin-length hair is fashionably tousled. She wears a modest amount of make-up and a floral dress and a plain navy cardigan.

She closes a leather bound notebook and places it on the glass table between the two low sofas on which she sits, and rests a black-and-silver Montblanc pen on top.

Her demeanour, however, is of most interest to the detectives, and DS Jones in particular is alert to the smile that is perhaps dutiful, and is performed without a parting of the lips.

She does not rise but indicates they should sit opposite. On the table is a tray with a retro-style percolator, white with a 1970s sunflower motif, and three matching mugs, shallow and squat.

'Have a seat, please. I'll pour you coffee. Help yourselves to milk and sugar.'

She is well spoken, though her accent has a trace of the north, possibly local.

It is always hard to judge a person met for the first time; while she makes them feel at ease, there is the impression of tense anxiety in her speech.

Indeed, as soon as DS Jones has performed introductions, and suitable commiserations, Victoria Lawson interposes a question.

'Have you found anyone? The driver?'

When DS Jones replies in the negative, it is plain that the woman is managing an uneasy equilibrium of distress and resolve. She wrings her hands together.

'Why would they drive off?'

The detectives have planned that DS Jones will lead the interview, but Victoria Lawson directs the question squarely at DS Leyton, as though it is naturally within his ambit. He gestures resignedly, turning up his palms.

'There can be a whole host of reasons, madam. Ranging from not knowing you've actually hit someone, to sheer panic and shock. The commonest reason someone will leave the scene of an accident is because they're over the drink-driving limit.'

'But not at seven in the morning?'

DS Leyton has to agree, that is less likely.

'That's true, madam.'

And she continues to protest the case.

'Surely if you've hit someone hard enough to kill them, you'd know you'd hit something – even if you only thought it was an animal. Surely you'd stop and check? At the very worst – the most selfish – to check damage to your car.'

DS Leyton is nodding, though he feels obliged to present a certain amount of devil's advocacy.

'If it were – say – a large farm vehicle or a lorry, the driver might be unaware of the collision. Not knowing an accident occurred can be offered as a valid defence.'

The woman inhales to speak, but he continues quickly.

'But please be reassured – we are treating this as a crime. Failure to stop or report an accident where there is injury or damage is an offence carrying a six-month jail sentence, disqualification from driving, and an unlimited fine.'

Victoria Lawson now breathes a little rapidly through parted lips. She shakes her head.

'But – *he's dead.*'

The contrast is stark. If there were scales of justice on the table before them, they would be tilted to their limit.

DS Jones recognises the impasse, and now she moves to steer the interview into positive territory.

'Mrs Lawson, we are doing everything within our power to trace the vehicle, but we need to understand every dimension. That is why it's really important that we speak with your husband, urgently.'

Victoria Lawson for a moment stares vacantly at DS Jones. But she seems to rouse herself. She picks up her pen and notebook, though she does not open the latter.

'It's a last-minute trip. I don't have details of where he's staying. A hotel in Los Angeles, near Hollywood Burbank. It's something like two a.m. there just now. I've left him a voicemail and an email. He'll probably get up at six to go to the gym – so he'll get the messages. I didn't say anything about the police – in case he thought something has happened to one of the boys.' She stares at the notebook; it is embossed with the logo of Sinclair Design. 'And I couldn't bring myself to mention Sebastian – I thought it might freak him out – better that I was able to tell him in person.'

She looks up at DS Jones; the officer is nodding.

'Yes. It would be preferable if you could put him directly onto us.'

'I'll do that, certainly.'

DS Jones opens her own notebook.

'Mrs Lawson, can you just reiterate what you know of your husband's movements – what has led to him being in the dark, so to speak?'

Now Victoria Lawson looks at each of the detectives in turn. She is wearing a white gold neck-chain and matching earrings, and the diamond-encrusted pendulum drops of the latter catch the light.

'I think he and Seb met in Keswick, and Frank would have returned to his car and driven straight to Manchester Airport. He phoned me from the lounge but I was in a client meeting and I missed the call. By the time I tried to get back to him he would have been airborne.'

'Did your husband say anything in his voice message?'

She gives a light shake of her head, and the diamonds glint again.

'Not really. I mean – I probably still have it, if you want to hear it. He never mentioned the run. He just said he was in a bit of a hurry and to tell the boys he'll bring them back toys from the latest superhero movie.' She glances about, as if to look for something – but it seems to no avail, and she continues. 'That's his business – he produces POS – you know, point-of-sale material – for the big film studios. The sort of giant cut-outs you see in the foyer at the multiplex.'

DS Leyton seems to show some interest in this revelation, but DS Jones remains focused upon the events unknown.

'Mrs Lawson, we've gathered from what you and Mrs Sinclair explained to the officers who spoke with you yesterday that it's likely that your husband and Mr Sinclair were separated.' (The woman nods, her expression earnest.). 'And in fact we have an eye-witness account from an off-duty officer who did see two runners, fitting their descriptions and at about the right time, a good distance apart.'

Now the woman seems to be staring at the rings on her left hand; a sizeable diamond eclipses those in her other jewellery. She speaks a little introspectively.

'It's the only possible explanation. Otherwise Frank would have ... done something.'

She looks up, but seems unable to speak, as if there is a lump in her throat.

DS Jones introduces a subtle change of tack.

'What is the background to them doing this training together?'

Victoria Lawson takes a sip of her hitherto untouched coffee, and she seems able to continue.

'It was over dinner about a year ago. At Seb and Morag's. There's this endurance challenge – the Bob Graham Round – and an annual event, a race. I think you know about this, yes?' She looks for confirmation and receives nods in return. 'They've both done marathons and Ironman and that sort of thing – and they got it into their heads to take part, this year. Then when they started to practise sections of the route, they realised they might actually do quite well. So they began to take it seriously. That's why they would train at all hours. But I don't think it's like roadwork, where you run side by side. There are different routes. And I think Seb was a lot faster in places.'

DS Jones takes some notes. Perhaps it is by way of creating a small hiatus.

'Mrs Lawson, how long have you known Mr Sinclair?'

Victoria Lawson does not seem surprised by the question.

'It's coming up for ten years. He interviewed me when he was an associate director of Boxtop Design – they're a multi-national with a branch office in Carlisle. After about eighteen months he decided to go it alone – and he asked me to come with him to run the accounts – the clients, that is – you know, account handling?'

DS Jones nods.

'Yes, I'm familiar with marketing agency structure. And I wanted to ask – without alarming you – whether you are aware of any issues or problems with the business.'

The embedded command, however, inevitably has Victoria Lawson looking alarmed.

'What do you mean? Surely not in relation to what has happened to Seb?'

DS Jones raises her left hand as a calming measure. And then she indicates to incorporate her colleague into what she is about to say.

'Mrs Lawson, I'm sure you'll understand – but it would be remiss of us, until we have clear evidence of what took place, not to consider the outside possibility that Mr Sinclair was the victim of a deliberate act.'

Victoria Lawson is plainly shocked – and now, for a moment, speechless. She lowers her gaze and again stares at the company notebook, as though the suggestion has affected her profoundly.

But she shakes her head, quite determinedly.

'I honestly can't think of anything. The firm is successful. And without financial or legal problems – quite the opposite. We're firmly in the black. Staff get good bonuses and creditors are paid ahead of time. Client and supplier relationships are positive.'

DS Jones takes a sympathetic tone.

'I'm sorry to have to put that to you. Given your history, it would seem that you might be the person he would confide in. Obviously we hope to get to the bottom of the matter as quickly as possible. But as a precaution we will need to check Mr Sinclair's admin and communications.'

Victoria Lawson does not respond immediately.

'I wasn't intending to go into the office today. But my deputy, Julie – we all call her Jules – she can show you everything you need.' Again, she hesitates. 'I mean – I actually told everyone to take the day off – but I think they wanted the companionship – and it is what Seb would have wanted – whatever felt best for each individual.'

DS Jones glances at DS Leyton.

'I don't think we need to do it today. We located his car – we have his phone. And we understand he also has a workspace at his home.'

Victoria Lawson nods pensively.

'That's right. He has an attic conversion. He liked the northern light.'

There is a moment's silence – perhaps a collective appreciation of their difficulty in finding the right tense in referring to Sebastian Sinclair.

'What will you do?' DS Jones asks the question with a tone of concern.

Victoria Lawson raises a hand.

'Oh – my mother stayed last night. She only lives in Carlisle, ten minutes away. But when I told her the news she came over later, to put the kids to bed. She's driven Tommy to nursery – she should be back any minute. She's booked lunch at the golf club – she thinks she's helping to take my mind off it.'

DS Jones glances at her colleague; it seems this is a suitable prompt for their purposes. She takes a calling card from her notebook and closes it. She places the card on the table.

'Well, thank you for your assistance under these difficult circumstances. If you would ask Mr Lawson to call my mobile number in the first instance. Or please contact us if anything arises that you feel may be significant.'

The detectives rise and Victoria Lawson steps ahead to show them out. She wears high heels and, while she glides with a certain practised elegance, there is perhaps a numbness in her movements that attracts DS Jones's eye.

As they follow her into the main hallway there comes a squeal of delight from one of the rooms – the door is open and the small boy, face now cleaned, totters out clasping aloft a soft toy.

'William! Come back, you little monkey!'

The nanny appears, half crawling in his wake – it seems to be as much a game as a break for freedom.

The boy heads for DS Leyton, who drops on bended knee to intercept him. The child presents the toy.

'Whoa, little fella! Look at that – he's not even in the cinema, yet!'

It seems DS Leyton recognises the movie character.

The nanny catches up and lifts the toddler, mumbling apologies.

'Don't worry, Ellie.' It is Victoria Lawson that intervenes. She indicates to the two detectives, DS Leyton still clutching his prize. 'Show them the playroom.'

The nanny leads the way. The room is expansive, richly carpeted, something of a cross between a TV lounge and a kindergarten, with its current centrepiece a life-sized cardboard cut-out of the said superhero, and a dump bin full of replicas of the doll.

'It's Frank's latest project. The film release is in the autumn. These are the prototypes.'

DS Leyton is impressed. He makes to hand back the doll to Victoria Lawson.

'No – keep it, please. You obviously have children.'

'Nah – I couldn't possibly, madam – it's not the done thing.'

Victoria Lawson, for just a split second, regards him curiously – but she quickly smiles – for the first time showing her even white teeth – a genuine smile.

'Please – it would bring a little happiness into the day. Look – we've got a hundred of these things. How many do you need? I mean, how many children do you have?'

DS Leyton glances at DS Jones, but she is distracted; she is gazing at a poster-sized colour photograph on the wall just inside the door, an oversized enlargement taken by a professional – the Lawsons, the parents and the two boys, taken quite recently, just head and shoulders, and posed in a rather sentimental 'happy family' mode, complete with wide eyes and cheesy smiles.

DS Leyton is quite easily sold.

'Well, if you really don't mind, madam – it's two, that's operative.'

'You mean there's more?'

'Well, there's a littl'un.'

'Here – take three, then.' And she reaches for two more and presses them upon him. 'They're safety tested for chewability.'

'Very kind of you, madam.'

DS Jones has already stepped out of the room, and now Victoria Lawson follows her into the hallway. DS Leyton waggles his new collection of plush at the little boy as he leaves, a final *peep-o* around the door jamb, and in doing so drops one toy onto the stone tiles. When he stoops to pick it up, and rises with a groan, something above catches his eye. But he does not dwell, and joins DS Jones to cross the threshold and make their farewells.

Victoria Lawson does not wait for them to leave, and they are left alone in the driveway. There is now a fairly new white Volkswagen parked alongside the Mercedes, and while DS Jones gets into her colleague's car, something prompts him to walk to the front of the VW, inspecting its lower parts. DS Jones watches, a little perplexed, as he then performs the same action with the small blue Ford at the side of the building, circling it like a prospective buyer. She sees him glance up at the house as he returns, and recognises something in his expression – a hint of feigned ingenuousness, perhaps.

'What was it?'

DS Leyton huffs as he composes himself in the driver's seat.

'Someone was eavesdropping on us – when we came out in the hall. Upstairs on the balcony – I glimpsed white-gloved hands being withdrawn.' He inclines his head. 'And a curtain just twitched.'

'That must be her mother – it would explain the VW. And what were you looking at – the cars?'

DS Leyton shrugs.

'I noticed a ding in the wheel arch of the VW. And there's a dunt in the bonnet of the nanny's Ford. I assume it's the nanny's.'

DS Jones grins, though she also nods approvingly. DS Leyton

elaborates.

'Nothing like big enough for what we're looking for – and the Mercedes is pristine – but no harm checking, eh, girl?'

DS Jones shakes her head.

'I hope it doesn't come to that – that we need to investigate alibis and motives of everyone who knew him.'

DS Leyton starts up the car. He lowers his window, for the day is warming up. DS Jones does the same. Birdsong, hitherto unnoticed, reaches them, and acts as a reminder of the serene and lush surroundings of the village gardens. DS Leyton selects first gear and lets in the clutch, a little carelessly, and the tyres spit gravel. He makes a guilty face at DS Jones.

'No alarm bells there, though, eh?'

It takes DS Jones a moment to reply.

'No – I don't think so.'

7. FRANK

HQ – 2.15 p.m. Tuesday 4th June

'IT'S HIM.'

DS Jones taps her colleague on the shoulder, and then points to the mobile phone that she brandishes.

'Guvnor's office?'

DS Leyton nods in affirmation, and the pair quickly make their way to the privacy of the hallowed domain. It is strangely tranquil, bereft of their superior's capricious presence.

DS Leyton seals the door, while DS Jones pulls their regular two chairs close to the desk. She places the handset between them, and releases the mute mode.

'Thank you for waiting, Mr Lawson. I'm now with my colleague, DS Leyton. It was the two of us that met with your wife this morning. You said she told you what we discussed.'

DS Jones's statement is by way of catching up for her colleague's benefit.

'I still can't believe it. I don't know what to say. I feel like – I don't know – it's the jet lag, and I'm going to wake up any minute. From a bad dream – you know?'

The line is not particularly clear. But the disembodied voice is still not quite what the detectives might have expected, having gained a certain impression from its owner's sophisticated residence and domestic arrangements. There is a Glasgow accent; and lazy enunciation, almost an uneducated edge. However, there is also a businesslike confidence in the delivery, in contrast to the stilted anxiety of his wife's responses earlier in the day. And now he refers to her.

'Vicky said you've not caught anyone.'

Frank Lawson interposes just as DS Jones is about to set about her own agenda. She glances at her colleague before she replies.

'No. We have not yet identified a vehicle. That is why we want to speak to you, as a possible witness … when you passed the scene –'

In DS Jones's hesitation Frank Lawson has already begun to reply – it would seem to the effect that he saw nothing. But their words cancel

53

out. DS Jones waits for a moment.

'Mr Lawson, there's a delay on the line at our end. I'll try not to interrupt. If you could take us through the sequence of events from your meeting up, to your return to your car at Keswick. With particular reference to Honister Pass.'

The detectives wait for the lag to clear, and find the man forthcoming. He is no doubt accustomed to long-distance communications of this nature.

'Aye. We met on foot at the Moot Hall. You can't park there. We normally park as close as we can get, in residential streets, where there are no time restrictions. I was up past the old picture house. We come from different directions – I didn't ask where Seb had parked. Sometimes he uses the Booths supermarket.'

The detectives exchange a brief nod. This is where they located Sebastian Sinclair's car.

'He'd booked an Uber to take us to Wasdale, and we were going to run back to Keswick. It's the final stretch of the Bob Graham Round. I expect you know – we've been training together for the anniversary event.' He inhales suddenly like a smoker, a sound of regret. 'It's next week.'

There comes a pause, as if he must be thinking about the implications of this. Then he continues.

'Seb wanted to try a different route up to the summit of Great Gable, via Napes Needle. It's shorter but much steeper. There are several points on the round where the best route is disputed. He's more into rock climbing than me – he had a theory that some advantage could be gained. I stayed on the regular route, and after that we lost contact.'

DS Jones has an Ordnance Survey map from Skelgill's collection spread on the desk, and she finds the summit with an index finger. DS Leyton leans to see. She points out Windy Gap – the landmark between Great Gable and Green Gable where Skelgill had spied the separated runners. Frank Lawson's account seems to make sense. DS Jones traces the route over Brandreth and Grey Knotts to where Honister Hause is marked. She gives a little tap with her nail, just as Frank Lawson's commentary kicks back in.

'There was nothing at all at Honister Pass. It was completely deserted. No walkers. No traffic. It was still early. But I was across the road in a matter of seconds – hardly a minute to pass through the area of the youth hostel and the slate mine, and back onto the route.

Obviously, after that –'

What might be an interruption on the line turns out to be that Frank Lawson has stopped speaking.

'Mr Lawson? After that?'

When his voice comes, the tone is patently introspective.

'Well – it doesn't matter after that, does it? Whatever I thought – if Seb would catch me – it was never going to happen. He never got past Honister Hause, did he?'

DS Jones waits until she is sure he has finished speaking.

'What time do you think you passed Honister Hause?'

'I got back to Keswick at about nine – so I think it must have been something like five or ten minutes either side of seven.'

'What were you wearing?'

'Black kit – pretty much the same as Seb. Vicky buys it for me from the same sports shop in Carlisle – she takes Seb's advice.'

'And footwear?'

'Aye. The same brand.'

DS Jones knows from descriptions obtained that the two men are of similar appearance. And that all Skelgill got – it seems their only eye-witness so far – were distant silhouettes on the skyline.

'What was your impression – whether you were ahead or behind?'

Again a delay, but a confident answer also follows.

'Seb took a chance on the diversion. I went pretty quick on that stretch – I wanted to prove him wrong. I'm sure I was ahead.'

'And what did you think when you arrived at the finish?'

'I didn't think much about it. I was knackered and I couldn't hang around, because I'd got the flight to catch. Besides – we've done this before – we set off together, but we don't have to finish together. I didn't know if Seb was still running, or had got back and had driven straight home – or up to Carlisle. They've got showers and changing rooms at the office. I put on a tracksuit and got showered and dressed in the business lounge at Manchester Airport. I wanted my kit here with me, anyway. I tried his mobile a couple of times, but it was off. And I'd got clients calling me – so I had plenty on my plate before the flight took off. I missed Vicky when I tried to call her. Then the time difference meant I wasn't expecting to be in touch – I got her messages when I woke up, half an hour ago – and when I spoke to her she said I must call you straight away.'

The detectives have listened patiently. The account fits the explanation deduced by Victoria Lawson for why her husband has not

55

hitherto been in touch.

DS Jones, however, is regarding her colleague with a small degree of concern.

'Mr Lawson, how long have you known Mr Sinclair?'

'Er – it would be something like five years.'

'How did you meet?'

'Through Vicky. Obviously, he's – he was – her boss.'

'Did you know him well?'

This time the question creates a longer pause for thought.

'I suppose – not really. I'd see him sometimes if I picked up Vicky from work. Then once or twice we went for dinner at theirs – and had them back at ours. That's when the Bob Graham idea came up. Seb was into outdoor stuff – all his life, I think. I got involved more recently – I've always been more of a gym and golf type. We were having a meal – it came up that he was doing the Bob Graham event this year – and his wife Morag said why didn't I do it. As well as the individual event there's team prizes, two and four people, mixed as well, and relays. So it was no skin off Seb's nose for us to enter as a team of two.'

The turn of phrase seems to pique DS Leyton's interest.

'Mr Lawson – why do you say it was no skin off his nose?'

Frank Lawson murmurs, an ironic chuckle almost.

'In case he thought I would hold him back. You can still win the individual, even if you're in a team. And he agreed – having a training partner – it wasn't such a bad idea.'

DS Leyton's nose is for that of the competition.

'Are you saying that Mr Sinclair was in with a chance of winning?'

Again there seems to be a little resistance in the man's delayed reaction.

'You never know, on the day – it could be we both had a chance.'

DS Leyton does not push the matter further. After a moment his colleague resumes.

'Mr Sinclair, before we ring off, can I just ask you once again – about when you passed through Honister Hause. When you think back – is there anything you can remember, or that stands out – even the slightest thing that might be unusual?'

There is a reasonable delay while the man considers.

'I'm afraid nothing that strikes me. I remember what I was thinking – that I'd be there next week, for real – that the families would be there to cheer us on, before they drove to the finish line in Keswick. I pictured the kids with banners and whistles.'

DS Jones accepts the answer, though it does perhaps prompt a related question.

'What about your wife?'

DS Leyton glances at her; for a specific question, it is equally open-ended.

'She sounds like she's bearing up. She's a good organiser – she'll rally the troops and speak to all their key clients. I don't like to sound callous, but there'll be projects to put to bed and everyone's jobs to think of. I've got a full house of meetings at Universal, today and next morning. I doubt if I could get a flight back before tomorrow night if I tried.'

Perhaps that he conflates his own situation, and excuses, with his perspective on his wife causes a raised eyebrow from DS Jones. She glances at her colleague, who shrugs to indicate he has nothing to add. DS Jones brings the call to a conclusion with the standard exhortation that Frank Lawson should get in touch if anything else occurs to him. Further, she advises him that they are likely to require a formal witness statement for the coroner's report when he returns to England.

DS Leyton leans back in his seat, and hunches his shoulders; he has on a white shirt and a multicoloured paisley pattern tie, and the tight collar looks uncomfortable around his heavy jowls.

'What d'you reckon, girl?'

DS Jones gazes musingly at the map. She gives a little shrug.

'He didn't ask how Sebastian's wife is.'

DS Leyton considers the point.

'He sounds a bit full of himself, don't you think – given the circumstances.'

DS Jones nods.

'But his story stacks up.'

'With what the wife told us – and the Guvnor?'

'Yes. It seems plausible that he either ran through Honister Hause ahead of Sebastian Sinclair – or passed a few minutes after the incident, when there was nothing to be seen.'

DS Leyton draws the fingers of one hand through his mop of dark hair.

'Mind you – Guvnor's mate, Jud Hope – didn't he say he noticed blood on the road?'

Again DS Jones nods pensively.

'I suppose it was limited to one spot. If Frank Lawson continued running, he might just have glanced each way to check for traffic. And it does hinge on him being second to arrive.'

Now DS Leyton cranes forward to squint at the map.

'Maybe you should ask the Guvnor about that detour malarkey.'

'Napes Needle? I think I will. He's told me where I can contact him tonight. I know he'll want an update.' She taps the map. 'Which reminds me, he also wants us to calculate a route for him.'

DS Leyton gives an ironic laugh. But he returns to the matter at hand.

'How's DC Watson getting on?'

His question refers to the tracing of vehicles.

DS Jones turns in her seat and folds her hands on her lap.

'I was on my way to update you when Frank Lawson rang. No joy so far, I'm afraid. There are virtually no properties near the road, in the immediate vicinity. And assuming they were travelling north, there's the added complication of the right turn in Buttermere, over the Newlands Pass. Off into wild country with more turn-offs available. When you add into the equation that we don't know what we're looking for, it makes it almost impossible. What we really need is a witness who saw something near Honister Hause at around seven a.m. But we can't find anyone who was up and about. We really need to get a handle on a type of vehicle.'

DS Leyton regards his colleague thoughtfully.

'TV appeal?'

She nods, a little apprehensively.

'I was thinking – I should bounce that off the Chief. The sooner we put something out, the fresher any memories will be.'

DS Leyton makes a contrite face.

'I'd offer to go and do it – but I reckon you're more persuasive than me – and there's definitely only one of us that's photogenic.'

8. THE LANGDALES

Dungeon Ghyll Inn – 8.30 p.m. Tuesday 4 June

SKELGILL IS pretty contented. To sit in peace with a pint and an Ordnance Survey map, in an old beamed bar, the day's doings and dinner safely under the belt is an entirely happy state of affairs. He even has a comfortable secluded pitch to return to, on soft turf beneath an ancient oak beside Stickle Ghyll. There is ample fuel in the form of fallen twigs for his Kelly kettle, fresh water and the last cool scent of late bluebells. He had washed up his aluminium pot and tin mug, and left them to drain on exposed rocks. Even the appetising chalkboard menu *(Today's special – homemade steak-and-ale pie)* does not detract from the satisfaction of his own repast, a reprise of the previous evening's carte du jour: soup-noodles-custard, bookended by a mash of tea. Besides, he has negotiated for his fellside breakfast a packet of smoked streaky bacon and a couple of oven-bottom cakes from the landlady, an acquaintance of longstanding.

As he reflects, he candidly admits he has had an easy day. This recce does not remotely epitomise the intensity of the fell fishing challenge that is to come. Unusually for him he had nodded back off in his field at Wasdale – unbothered by sheep, other than those he counted in his sleep – and had been woken for a second time in his tented bivvy by the sun creeping around the shoulder of Scafell (*Scawfle* in the vernacular, the lesser visited 48-foot shorter but in some ways more august neighbour of the iconic Scafell Pike).

But in fine spring weather, scattered cumulus at 5,000 feet and a light Atlantic breeze to disperse sweat and deter midges, knowing that time was on his side he has enjoyed picking off the old familiar tops, and indeed lingering at the only two tarns on the day's itinerary.

And scenic coomb tarns they both were. First – having traversed the Scafell massif – came Angle Tarn, tucked under the rocky cluster of Esk Pike and Rossett Pike and associated summits and ridges. That was the site of his lunch stop. Later – having crossed the lumpy Langdale Pikes – he had descended to Stickle Tarn.

Here he had enlisted legend and lore, and fished close to the inflow, Bright Beck. In his researches – he is not so proud that he would rely entirely on his own knowledge, especially of waters he has only very occasionally fished, and several of these not since his youth – he had come across an article in the Westmorland Gazette, an old reminiscence of Langdale men who poached at the tarn, at night setting lines with up to 80 hooks baited with earthworms – and, on one occasion, next morning pulling in 57 sparkling wild brown trout, an extraordinary gleaming haul for such a small body of water. With no mains electricity in the dale, and therefore no refrigerators, it was said that the locals feasted on fish and bread for the best part of a week.

He had not quite approached this level of success – though several small trout were forthcoming, on both wet and dry flies. And now, not for the first time, he is pondering the fishing tactics. It is all very good in this weather, when the sun warms the water and hatches occur, piquing the interest of the fish. But it will be no such picnic when conditions are adverse or the hour is unfavourable. The angling really does add an extra and complex dimension of uncertainty. True, the weather can make or break an attempt on the Bob Graham Round, especially if the objective is to set a record time – but, in the main, the tops are there, the paths are there – they have no will of their own, no moods, no idiosyncrasies, no unreadable foibles that will determine whether or not they yield to the runner. Unlike the fish, which may simply not rise to the bait.

Still, that is also the beauty of his idea.

He scrutinises his map. He is not so often down here in the Langdales, the two upland valleys and their eponymous cluster of pikes. Neither is this place a crossing point – though the Bob Graham Round comes within a mile of the B5343 that winds up into Great Langdale, for most practical purposes a dead-end that diminishes to C-status, narrowing and steepening perilously for what by car can in winter be a harrowing drive over the pass beneath Side Pike into Little Langdale.

Therefore, for Bob Graham Round partakers with leisure in mind and time on their side, the detour of under a mile to a homely coaching inn is an appealing prospect, compared to a good 4 miles (and 5 summits) to the next official crossing point at Dunmail Raise, where the A591 cuts south from Thirlmere to Grasmere (and the popular Wayfarer's Rest another two miles). The main downside of Dungeon Ghyll, speaking figuratively, is the steep uphill return to the route next morning.

Skelgill sighs, and makes a guess at the time by the amount of beer in his pint.

They should be through in a few minutes, and he has arranged to return the compliment of buying their first round.

As for his 'guardian-angel-ship', as he has thought of it, he wonders if they were aware of his presence.

His first sighting was at his second waking. At around seven a.m. from beneath his flysheet he had glimpsed Rita with her camera, prospecting for a shot, the early morning rays all the better to delineate the fells of Wasdale with highlight and shadow. Window shopping, she had been a demanding client, and he reckons she snapped only one or two of the many perspectives she tried out.

Later in the day he twice spotted the distinctive trio. The tall, bowed Gerry a little ahead, pathfinding; the two ladies, green-clad Rita her tripod shouldered, spritely Rosheen animated – pointing out features with her walking poles, animatedly gesturing, at times like a semaphore signaller, sending messages he might have decoded had there been flags attached.

He doubts they saw him, but he was able to satisfy himself that they were making safe and steady progress, and that they would indeed arrive at Great Langdale. His most recent sighting was through a window of the dining room, as he rounded the walls of the inn to enter via the public bar.

Now, it seems, they have finished their meal. He hears them coming and signals to the landlady. He has remembered last night's order placed by Rita.

'Ah – the very man!'

It is Gerry that hails him.

Skelgill is suitably humble.

'I thought I felt my ears burning.'

He nods politely to each of the trio in turn. He is at a square table in a corner, facing out from the oak trestle of old church pews. He does not rise but motions that they should sit. The ladies settle accordingly – but Gerry remains standing.

'Ready for a refill, lad?'

But Skelgill indicates towards the bar.

'It's taken care of – see – here it comes.'

The beaming landlady bears a tray with two pints and two half-pints in straight glasses.

'I took the liberty of assuming you'd have the same as last night – for starters.'

Gerry sinks into a chair and smacks his lips approvingly.

'You can't go far wrong with the local brew.'

Skelgill, for a second, looks like he can think of scenarios where you can – but his sentiment is eclipsed by the need to reciprocate a collective motion of cheers.

'How was dinner?'

Gerry again speaks.

'Champion. Happen we've eaten them out of steak-and-ale pie.' He must detect a flicker of a reaction. 'You weren't thinking of it, were you?'

Skelgill holds up a hand and grins. He is tempted to confess that why wouldn't he be thinking of it (of course he has been thinking of it).

'Nay, I'm full. I'm travelling with provisions. I like the feeling as the days go by and your pack gets lighter.'

Now Rita chips in.

'And, you probably feel fitter by the day.'

'Aye, there's that an' all.'

Gerry picks up the point.

'I think we're finding our rhythm.' He gestures loosely at Skelgill's map. 'Another nine peaks ticked off today.'

Rita, however, seems concerned for Skelgill.

'And how was your fishing?'

Skelgill makes a face that perhaps indicates under-achievement.

'A bit too easy for my liking, truth be told. It could lull you into a false sense of security, thinking you'll catch first cast. You know what they say in the army – train hard, fight easy. The reality is, down the years I've had more blank days than I've had hot dinners.'

Skelgill's gaze inadvertently wanders to the specials board – but Gerry brings him back to the conundrum.

'That's the beauty of your idea, though, eh?'

Skelgill is obliged to nod.

'That's exactly what I've been telling myself – more or less word for word.' He draws the fingers of his left hand through his somewhat unkempt hair, exposing more of the craggy countenance. 'And, come to think of it, at Angle Tarn it wasn't so quick – and I was successful with a couple of back-up methods. I just took it a bit easy, that's all.'

Rita is prompted once more.

'I wonder if I got you in my photo – we stopped for lunch on Esk Pike – and there is such a marvellous view of the tarn as you look north into Langstrath. I remember a faint column of smoke rising from beside the water.'

Skelgill nods agreement; he had seen them.

'I must have been just a dot.'

Rita has what looks like a photographer's bag slung over one shoulder; it seems she and her equipment are inseparable. She places a hand on it.

'Of course – I shan't know until I get the films home and develop them. But maybe I can mail you a print?'

She winks at Skelgill – he remembers he is not to say too much about her hobby, and her plans for the calendar.

'Aye – why not?'

Though he feels it forward to offer an address at this juncture; in any event, it seems their paths have intertwined for the week, and there is no urgency.

But perhaps Gerry detects something of Skelgill's reticence, and he reaches to pat Skelgill's forearm.

'You should feel honoured. What you don't know is you're sitting next to one of the USA's most lauded landscape photographers. Think of her as an American Colin Baxter.'

Rita plays down any such suggestion.

'I am long retired – and my equipment has been superseded by technology – we are in an age of drones and artificial enhancement. My efforts today would never pass muster.'

Gerry mutters "nonsense" and folds his arms to emphasise his dissatisfaction with such a state of affairs.

Skelgill has a practical question.

'Do you have trouble getting your films developed?'

She gives a shake of the head.

'There are still places – but I have my own darkroom. I like to stay in control. And I once had half a trip's worth of spools disappear into thin air – I had mailed them to a developing lab as I went along. Now I keep them with me – this is a secure film-guard bag, it protects unprocessed spools from fogging.'

For a man who uses a Kelly kettle, Skelgill can have few objections to the old ways of doing things. He reverts to her suggestion that she may have caught him in her photograph.

'Well – quite likely you did snap me – it's the one downside of the Kelly kettle – it's a bit of a giveaway of your presence. That and the smell of bacon.'

'You weren't tempted to fry a fish?'

It is Rosheen that chips in.

Skelgill grins wryly.

'It wouldn't be the first time – but it would be one less for me to catch when I do the round.'

They chuckle at his joke.

'You should be alright in Angle Tarn.' Rosheen continues. 'The name tells you that.'

Skelgill regards her with a look of curiosity. He is generally well versed in the local nomenclature, but it occurs to him this is one that he has not considered. He does, however, have a rejoinder.

'Now you mention it, there's two Angle Tarns. The other's bigger – over in Patterdale – that's Ullswater way. Funnily enough, folk say it's the shape of a hook.'

Rosheen is smiling in her mischievous style.

'The name probably means fishing pool – and what you say is interesting – *ongull* is the Old Norse word for fish hook.'

Now Gerry resumes his role as blower-of-trumpets for his more modest companions.

'Rosheen was a professor of archaeology. You could write on the back of a postage stamp what she doesn't know about topographical taxonomy in the North of England. She was latterly at Leeds and before that Durham.'

Skelgill is about to quip that the phrase itself hardly fits on the back of a stamp – but the last word spoken by Gerry completely sidetracks him.

'*Durham*. You didn't know a Professor Hartley, did you?' He adds a further descriptor. 'Jim Hartley. He were medieval history – summat like that.'

Rosheen takes a moment to answer.

'I think I do remember a Jim Hartley. It's likely he was at a separate campus.'

There is something in Rosheen's manner that Skelgill finds just slightly disconcerting. Perhaps it is a tiny warning narrowing of the gimlet eyes. It suddenly strikes him that Rosheen and his schoolboy angling mentor, retired Professor Jim Hartley, resident of Braithwaite, would be contemporaries not only in occupation and location, but also in age. And what else?

Rosheen still has that challenging glint in her eye.

Staying his initial exuberance – that he could tell them that on their first morning they passed within a mile of the professor's cottage – he realises this is a subject he ought to raise in Rosheen's company alone.

He is just looking for a way out of the little hole that he has inadvertently dug, when the landlady approaches with a suitable stepladder. She addresses Skelgill in a familiar manner, planting a palm on his shoulder.

'That's the call you were expecting, me love – it's through in t' staff pantry.'

Skelgill's countenance echoes its mea culpa look of the night before, and he excuses himself.

As he leaves the bar he thinks he catches Gerry, remarking along the lines of the inspector having got his teeth into something – either that, or it's his missus checking up on him.

DS Jones teases him along similar lines.

'I hope I've not dragged you away from a wild session?'

Skelgill responds with a resigned groan.

'You might say I've got myself invited to a week-long 80th-birthday pub crawl.'

DS Jones chuckles, in the way of him being his own worst enemy.

'Well – you said you wanted to take it steady.'

Skelgill gives a twitch of the head; he is wrestling with the conundrum. Switching off does not come easily, and Gerry is probably right – not least since last night's call to Jud Hope.

DS Jones detects his wish to move on.

'Top line, as yet, we have no driver – and I honestly think we are going to struggle on that front.' Now she gives a little cough, a contrived prelude to a small controversy. 'I recorded an appeal for witnesses – for dashcam footage in the Honister area. It's going out on the local bulletin, after the Nine O' Clock News.'

Skelgill checks his watch. It will be in not many minutes.

'Fair enough.'

She hesitates for a moment, perhaps surprised by his acquiescence. Then she continues, more confidently.

'We spoke with Frank Lawson. His story fits your sighting. He says he was separated from Sebastian Sinclair at the time he crossed Honister Hause. He doesn't know if he was ahead or behind. But he thinks more likely ahead. He said Sinclair had taken a detour – to climb Great Gable via Napes Needle – '

Skelgill interjects with a scornful exclamation.

'You'd never go that way.'

'It was to check for a possible shortcut – they're signed up for the Bob Graham Round anniversary challenge next week – and it seems they were in with a chance of winning.'

Skelgill's features, unseen by his colleague, remain contorted in doubt.

'It's late in the day to be experimenting.'

DS Jones pauses.

'Okay – but that's his story. He said it wasn't unusual for them to split up, and to drive away without waiting for each other. He says he was unaware of what took place, and was out of contact until this morning, California time.'

Skelgill murmurs, but waits for her to continue.

'The one thing I would say, is that he didn't sound emotionally invested. I think he's just an acquaintance of Sebastian Sinclair, and the relationship is through his wife – she has worked with Sinclair for about a decade. She tried to put on a brace face – but it's the loss of a close colleague. It would be a shock.'

There ensues a silence.

It is a minute before Skelgill asks a seemingly innocuous question.

'What does Leyton reckon?'

DS Jones chuckles, as if she is relieved by the diversion.

'He did check round the cars at the Lawson residence. And he thought we were being stalked by Frank Lawson's mother-in-law. Victoria Lawson's mother, I should say.'

'I take it there was nowt?'

Skelgill's tone is more serious than wry.

His colleague understands he refers to the abstract. Not merely dents in cars – clearly a body-shaped imprint would have been the first news she would have imparted – if not that of an arrest. He means subtle signs of hidden guilt that might hint at foul play.

That he asks her this alerts her to the possibility that he harbours doubts. Moreover, that she finds herself slow to respond tells of some small but as yet unformed suspicion of her own. Accordingly, her answer is uncharacteristically oblique.

'I'm trying not to invent motives. But I realise we might have to go there, if the search for a driver fails. We're seeing Sebastian Sinclair's wife tomorrow, and we'll visit the office. The thing is –'

Skelgill waits determinedly, like he is watching a bobbing float.

It takes a moment for her to admit to conjecture.

'The thing is, Guv – if it were a deliberate act, it's hard to envisage that someone might have lain in wait. Even to have had the opportunity to do so. And the knowledge of timings. It's the middle of nowhere, and to execute the manoeuvre in a couple of seconds ...'

Skelgill allows her musings to hang in the air.

'I phoned Jud Hope last night.'

'Oh, right.'

'He assumed Sinclair had crawled off the road – as you might, to avoid being run over again. But why hide under the bracken?'

DS Jones audibly inhales.

'The cause of death was the head injury. From the impact on the road surface.'

They do not need to speculate further; it is plain that the facts do not quite stack up. If it were a little jigsaw, there would be a piece missing.

DS Jones's voice takes on a tone of resolve.

'I'll revisit the forensic report and the photographs of the crash scene.'

'Aye.'

There is a pause.

'Where can I get you?'

'I'll send you a text – when I've got a signal. Failing that – try the Wayfarer's Rest, same time tomorrow night.'

And now a slightly longer pause.

'Or I could meet you after my yoga class – it's only half an hour down to Grasmere – not like where you are now.'

It must be apparent, to both, that Skelgill does not jump at the opportunity – and perhaps perplexing to him that it is not his instinctive reaction.

'Thing is – I've kind of committed to keeping an eye on this crowd. Just in case there's a change of plan – or an injury or summat. I don't want to mess you around.'

DS Jones opts not to press her point.

'Look – send me a text – I'll do as you say.'

'Reet.'

'By the way – we worked out your puzzle. Want to know the answer?'

Her tone is teasing.

'Is it by much?'

'I should say so.'

Skelgill hesitates, as though this surprises him. Then he stakes his bet.

'Both from Esk Hause.'

'Correct. It's equal to the shortest distance – which is to visit each tarn separately from the route – but it saves over five hundred feet of ascent.'

Skelgill makes an expiration, perhaps a growl of satisfaction. He is not averse to the concept of competitive advantage, provided the means are fair. His smile becomes imbued into his voice.

'Let's keep that one under our hats, eh?'

'Sure.' DS Jones sounds amused. 'But if you don't mind I'd better just ring off – the appeal is about to be broadcast – you know the most likely response is in the first few minutes, and I've promised to be on standby.'

As Skelgill re-enters the bar via a trip to the gents he sees two things. The trio have ordered a new round of drinks. And they are all gazing at a small television set that is broadcasting in silence up in a corner behind the counter.

He turns just in time to glimpse the last few moments of his colleague's appeal, speaking with a female reporter on the steps at headquarters. The ticker tape at the foot of the screen displays the words "Honister Pass Accident" and "Dashcam Footage" and a telephone number.

He lingers a second after her image has faded. Though they did not discuss it, he realises that DS Jones has apparently not revealed to the general public the nature of the accident. There are sound reasons, either way, and he probably errs in the same direction himself. Now the local weather forecast brings further good tidings, and he turns back to the party.

Gerry points past him.

'That's your RTA from last night, eh, lad?'

Skelgill is momentarily taken off guard – not least that Gerry uses the police abbreviation for a road traffic accident. But before he can answer, Gerry sweeps a hand round to indicate he means to include his companions.

'We were wondering if you might want to interview us, as potential witnesses.'

He accompanies his words with a broad grin – as if somehow he knows that Skelgill will long have considered and rejected this idea. Skelgill seems just a hint bashful as he proves the man right.

'Nay. I figured you couldn't have seen owt. The accident took place at the crack of dawn. Then you were well away before it was even discovered.'

It seems that Rita has a contribution to make, for she inhales as if to speak. But Gerry is on something of a roll, and he beats her to the draw.

'Well – we were almost thinking we'd need to call on your services, last night – weren't we, ladies?'

Skelgill regards them perplexedly as he resumes his seat.

Gerry leans in, a little conspiratorially.

'When we got back to our rooms – we thought they'd been rifled.'

Skelgill looks alarmed.

'Was owt missing?'

Gerry shakes his head – though he looks almost disappointed.

Rita interjects.

'I suggest it was just an over-enthusiastic turn-down. Some people have their own views on what constitutes tidiness. And I'd rather that than the lackadaisical sort of maid.'

Gerry gives a little harrumph.

'I'm surprised they even do a turn-down – place, like that, the back of beyond.'

Now Rosheen chips in.

'Whoever it was, I think she was fascinated by my toiletries.'

'Wanted to know how come you're so young-looking!'

It is Gerry's quip. Rosheen looks like she is torn between a reprimand and a commendation.

Skelgill is frowning.

'So long as nowt were gone.' He takes up his pint, but regards it pensively. 'Frankly, I'd be embarrassed – if you were to be robbed. I doubt I'd ever think of locking a bedroom in these parts.'

Rita is nodding. She plainly finds it abhorrent to be suspicious of fellow travellers – and does not wish to countenance the idea.

Gerry is looking at her with a degree of scepticism, however. He reverts to Skelgill.

'I don't suppose there's a local bobby, these days?'

Skelgill inhales through gritted teeth.

'They're thin on the ground, that's for sure.'

Gerry folds his arms, and inclines his head in the direction of the TV set, now broadcasting a repeat of the local soap, *Ennerdale*, with subtitles.

'We were just saying, before you came in – they joke about the police having got shorter – but going by that lass, they're certainly a lot better looking than back in the day.'

There is nothing salacious in Gerry's inflexion, nor does he receive an elbow of reproof from Rosheen – indeed, Skelgill has the sense that they are all looking at him inquiringly. He feels colour rising to his cheekbones – and quickly raises his beer in a gesture of cheers, and quaffs a good mouthful.

For Skelgill, to avoid the foamy head of real ale is never easy, and he surfaces having buried his nose in the pint with a dollop of foam on its tip. Perhaps it is intentional, for it raises a laugh, in which he partakes, and causes a distraction while Rita produces a tissue.

9. MORAG

Applethwaite – 9.45. a.m. Wednesday 5th June

AN ACCUMULATION OF impressions strikes DS Jones as first she and then DS Leyton are shown into the Sinclair home by Morag Sinclair's elder sister, Shona Mackay, and together they add up to the single word, *contrast*. And it is the contrast with the visit they made at a similar time yesterday morning.

Not that the hamlet of Applethwaite is demographically inferior to the affluent Carlisle dormitory village of Wetheral (the latter with its four-star hotel and adjacent golf club) – and indeed almost any settlement within the Lake District national park would be considered desirable – but, heavily wooded and nestled into the dark shadow of Skiddaw, in the northern reaches a long drive from the honeypots and Michelin stars of Ambleside and Windermere – it is certainly off the beaten track.

And the property itself differs by several degrees. Large, certainly, but to the eye a rambling barnacle cluster of a whitewashed farmstead, presumably an original house that has acquired over a couple of centuries extensions and outbuildings for entirely practical purposes, with little regard to aesthetics. The distemper is stained where iron gutters sport flaws, occasional loose slate tiles hang precariously, and paint peels in places from the many irregular window frames.

And, now, upon entering, is further cause for observation. Here is a hotchpotch of belongings old and new, furniture amassed and assembled without a single guiding ambition or even a reference to quality, with many commonplace items that would be found in a much more modest house.

The property they visited yesterday was every inch the home of someone who works in the graphic design business, and who has ruthlessly weeded out aberrations that mar the carefully constructed vision of domestic design perfection. And they met that person in Victoria Lawson.

Yet here is the home belonging to the owner of the business (and, it would be assumed, considerably the wealthier) – a person who by all

71

accounts has carved out his name on the national and indeed international design stage.

Thus the emerging comparison becomes stark.

DS Jones glances back at her colleague as they pass through zigzagging corridors – his expression is not revealing of any machinations within. She wonders if the sentiment is merely something she is erroneously troubled by – another of the shifting shadows in her peripheral vision; influenced by too much time spent with her idiosyncratic superior, who plainly operates by subconscious osmosis when it comes to absorbing external stimuli. It is a far cry from minute Holmesian observation and rational deduction.

The woman they follow is aged around forty, of medium build and height with medium-length straight brown hair, and in possession of the fair skin and greenish-blue eyes of the Celt. She is dressed in denim dungarees and a check lumberjack shirt, and has a purposeful air about her. She has not smiled – or, at best, had forced a smile on opening the door to their arranged visit – and has remained taciturn in delivering them to her sister. Both detectives had responded to such dourness, refraining from making conversation, as if in anticipation of a negative response. What little was spoken, DS Jones felt sure the accent was of the adjacent Scottish Borders.

Like the nanny Ellie the day before she leaves them at the threshold, saying to her sister she will clear away the boys' breakfast things.

The room is a kind of study – it is hard to discern if it were Sebastian Sinclair's alone, or shared. There is the range and randomness of furniture, and an open bureau and a separate desk with a computer, at which Morag Sinclair sits. The fire is not lit, but the hearth contains recent wood ashes. There is a worn English roll-arm sofa and two armchairs.

The woman seems to have been attempting to reconcile papers on the desk with information on the screen, and does not instantly greet the detectives. After a second or two she seems to sigh, as if frustrated or even bored with her task, and only now turns to acknowledge them. She remains seated, and indicates vaguely that they should settle on the suite, and does not offer them refreshments.

To DS Jones's eye she is a younger, slimmer version of the sister; quite similar in all main features – though these more finely chiselled, and more favourably proportioned, such that she would be considered to be attractive. Even the dark half-moons under her eyes – more uniformly blue than her sister's – add to the potential allure, in the cover girl sense of the term. Lacking make-up, however, and dressed in a shapeless reddish-brown cardigan that does not combine well with her turquoise slacks, she offers a further contrast to yesterday morning's interview with the immaculate Victoria Lawson.

DS Jones leads with a reiteration of condolences, and explains – apologises – that at this moment they have no significant further information concerning her husband's death, laying the explanation upon the circumstances – the isolated spot and early hour.

'But – as you may be aware – we have issued a televised appeal for witnesses. It was repeated on the Breakfast Show this morning.'

'Are you optimistic?'

Morag Sinclair's Scots accent is considerably less pronounced than that of her sister, with just the hint of a rolled 'R'.

'Optimistic, yes. Sometimes these things can take time.'

'Can you not tell what car it was? From the paint?'

DS Jones glances briefly at her colleague. This is not something on which they are pinning any hopes.

'Our forensic team is investigating that. But the fatal impact was not from the vehicle itself, but the road surface. In the same way that you hear about someone slipping on ice and hitting their head on the pavement. It looks like the car pushed him – toppled him over backwards, and he fell slightly to one side. But you will be the first to know as soon as we have anything.'

The woman nods rather vacantly.

'Do you feel okay to answer a few questions?'

'What about?'

DS Jones keeps her gaze trained on the woman.

'In case there is something else that we should not overlook. Until we're certain of what happened, we just want to understand the broader context of Mr Sinclair's running activity. We've managed to speak with Mr Lawson in the USA, so we have some details about Monday. Mr Lawson has stated that they had become separated by the time they reached Honister Hause, and that he was completely unaware of what took place.'

DS Jones tries to banish any suggestion of suspicion from her inflexion, but she can see that Morag Sinclair must understand that they are thinking beyond the supposition of an accident.

'Whatever you need to know, I'll try. Though I'm not sure I can tell you much.'

DS Jones continues non-intrusively.

'Had it been your husband's long-term hobby – fell running, and that kind of thing?'

'I don't think he'd ever taken part in any mountain races. But I know he'd completed the Three Peaks and marathons in the past. And he continued to do a lot of hill walking, to keep fit for annual trekking trips with his friends from schooldays.'

DS Jones nods amenably.

'And so the Bob Graham Round – the anniversary event. How did that come about?'

A small frown darkens Morag Sinclair's pale countenance.

'I think you could call it machismo. Male bravado.'

The response is a little surprising – the woman's tone is disparaging, almost as if what she refers to is to blame for the circumstances she now finds herself in. Indeed, she is still holding a sheaf of papers, and she flaps them at her side.

'Could you elaborate?'

'Och – the Lawsons were here for dinner – Victoria, his colleague, and her husband, Frank. He's a bit of a showboat – but unfortunately Sebastian rose to the bait. They'd had too much to drink – and they ended up with neither willing to back down. It was obvious that it was a competitive thing – Sebastian became pretty obsessed with it, and I expect Frank was the same – and they drove one another on – but not in what seemed a collaborative way.'

There is a pause.

DS Leyton seems to appreciate that his colleague has set a certain tone, forming a non-confrontational relationship. He takes it upon himself to interpose what is a more controversial question.

'Madam, did the competitiveness extend to friction – or even that it revealed any animosity between them?'

Morag Sinclair replies evenly, however.

'I wouldn't say animosity – that wasn't in Sebastian's nature. He probably found Frank overbearing. He's a salesman type, full of patter. He thinks you have to keep making jokes for people to think you are interesting. He could have been a bit unbearable if he got the bragging rights. They were supposed to be in a team, but Sebastian wouldn't have wanted to lose to Frank.'

DS Leyton nods, but now holds his peace and DS Jones resumes.

'How well did you know the Lawsons?'

'Me? Obviously, not very well.' It may not be so obvious to the police, though she offers only a partial explanation. 'I only saw them occasionally – hardly every six months. But I think Frank sometimes called into the office to pick up Victoria. In fact I think he might have done work for them, as a sub-contractor.'

The detectives wait, but she has finished.

DS Jones tries not to sound interrogative.

'Your husband was a local man – but you're from Scotland. How did you come to meet? I'm thinking in terms of how long you have known him.'

The woman looks at her for a second or two before she responds.

'We'd been at university in Leicester at the same time. We weren't on similar courses but our friendship circles had some overlap, so we vaguely knew one another. More so towards the end – so probably I first met him about twelve years ago. Then there must have been a gap of five or six years.'

DS Jones recalls the fact of Sinclair Design having been established for some eight years, which would therefore pre-date any reunion.

'And then, what – you met up in this area?'

'I'd been living and teaching in Coventry. I was engaged, but that broke up and I moved to teach in Carlisle. I had the English qualification, so it was the closest I could get to my family in the Borders. Then I met Sebastian by chance at what turned out to be a mutual college friend's New Year's event – it was a big house party at a country hotel near Derwentwater. We were both single, and started seeing each other after that.'

'When were you married?'

There is a fleeting reaction in the woman's eyes – but it is hard to read and so brief that it almost might be imagined. Certainly she would know that any such information is a matter of public record.

'Our wedding would have been six years ago, in March past.'

Morag Sinclair briefly glances at the mantelpiece. There is a modest home-framed triptych of two small children – the boys digging in sand on a beach, the snapshots not all that clear, the light poor and the children well clad in winter conditions.

DS Jones follows her gaze, half expecting to see a wedding photograph in answer to her question – but there is no other.

And now the woman is regarding her with a curious smile; it might be perfunctory, or even ironic – but DS Jones takes the inference to be that this is her priority, her task, her burden – that the small boys have lost their Daddy. And that Morag Sinclair finds herself lumbered with a situation she never asked for.

75

Intuitively, now, DS Jones opts to skirt around this particular personal aspect.

'Have you been in touch with your husband's colleagues?'

The woman looks briefly at each detective in turn – there is the suggestion in her manner that she feels this must be some sort of trick question, to which they already know the answer.

DS Jones moves to reassure her.

'We've spoken with Victoria Lawson. We're planning to visit the office in Carlisle this afternoon. We wanted to make sure you were happy with that, of course.'

Morag Sinclair gives an almost imperceptible lift of her faint brows.

'I think they – er – didn't know whether it would be diplomatic. They have sent flowers and condolences and a note that I am not to worry about anything.' She gives another of her small sighs. 'I suppose I'll need to have a meeting at some stage with the senior team. I haven't really thought about it. I'm not really involved – there aren't matters that only I would know about – that they would need me for.'

DS Jones turns inquiringly to her colleague, as if to indicate she is ready to hand over a pre-arranged point.

DS Leyton produces a mobile phone in a plastic wallet.

'As you know madam, we located your husband's car, and we had it moved to safety in the police pound. Naturally – in view of the children – we didn't want to bring it along – drive it in.'

The woman nods her understanding.

'There were also a change of clothes and other personal possessions – we do have those in a holdall in our car, to give to you.'

Now he raises the handset.

'This is your husband's phone. It was also in the car – we have no reason at the moment to hang onto it. Of course, if he'd been running with it – recording his movements – or possibly even filming – then clearly it would have been of great interest.'

He pauses, though Morag Sinclair listens implacably, and it is hard to know if she is travelling along with him.

'Obviously, while we are still in a position of uncertainty, over what happened, there is the small chance that there is something on his phone that might account for it – or at very least give us a lead.'

Now the small frown has returned.

DS Leyton waits to see if she will speak, and eventually she does.

'You seem to be suggesting that – what? That it might not have been an accident?'

DS Leyton affects a slight recoil.

'It could still have been an accident – most likely it was. But we have to consider the possibility, say, that he liaised with someone he thought he might cross paths with – who could be an important witness.'

DS Leyton's logic is not entirely clear – but he is striving to minimise the cruel transition from the unintentional to the deliberate.

The woman seems sufficiently prepared to move on.

'And, so – his mobile?'

'We wondered if you knew the passcode – or would object to us looking through his activity?'

She gives a slight shake of her head.

'No to both.'

DS Leyton rubs at his hair with one hand.

'Okay. Did he have any regular memorable numbers?'

'I don't think so. He would mention in conversation that he changed passwords regularly. He always said never use your birthday.'

There is a short silence; the detectives exchange a nod – that they are ready to conclude the interview. As they move to gather themselves, DS Jones offers a suggestion.

'Mrs Sinclair, it might be that we can access his communications via the company IT system.'

Morag Sinclair seems unperturbed, verging on disinterested – but she raises the papers she holds, and indicates with them to the desk with the computer.

'If I come across anything – a list of passwords – I'll let you know.'

'That would be appreciated. In the meantime, thank you for your assistance at this difficult time.'

Again there is the enigmatic smile, lips compressed.

'I understand, you need to do this.'

Seated in DS Leyton's car, the detectives share a moment of silent reflection.

It is DS Leyton who is first to iterate their mutual sentiment. He exhales; it is the sound of frustration.

'It's a flippin' sight easier interviewing folk when you suspect them of jiggery-pokery. This malarkey – treading on eggshells – but trying to ask subtle questions just in case there is some smoking gun.'

Despite his colourful words, DS Jones regards him earnestly.

'I know. You almost feel that – in the absence of a sound explanation – we're experiencing an inexorable slide towards the sinister.'

In the back of her mind is the gist of her most recent telephone conversation with Skelgill; it has certainly served to keep the idea of foul play on the agenda.

Ahead in the driveway are parked two vehicles, facing away from them. A four-year-old black Land Cruiser with a local registration, and a small white Vauxhall with an 'S' in its plate, indicative of its Scottish provenance.

DS Leyton shifts in his seat.

Now it is DS Jones who speaks for him.

'Think we should check the cars?'

'Better had, girl.'

10. SINCLAIR DESIGN

Carlisle – 2.40 p.m. Wednesday 5th June

'WHAT'S THE griff, lass?'

DS Jones cannot contain a laugh. DS Leyton has imitated their superior – not so well in accent, but better in turn of phrase. Driving them north on the M6, he employs one of Skelgill's expressions, meaning what has she learned from the telephone call she has just completed to HQ. Perhaps that she has mused silently for a moment has prompted him.

She keeps the reference to Skelgill alive.

'You know I told you about his chat with Jud Hope?'

'About the body being hidden in the verge?'

'I asked DC Watson to do a full review of the forensics.'

She waits while DS Leyton completes a manoeuvre onto the Carlisle off-ramp; it involves a little judicious queue-jumping.

'A key question being, how did Sebastian Sinclair move sideways from where he fell on the road? It was four feet from the bloodstains to the cover of the bracken. Dr Herdwick insists that the fatal head injury from hitting the tarmac would have rendered him unconscious – and therefore incapable of rolling or crawling laterally.'

DS Leyton looks to be forming a question – but DS Jones continues.

'Jud Hope found faint signs of life. He covered him with a blanket and phoned 999. There was a duty ambulance at Buttermere and it arrived within ten minutes. The paramedics placed him on a stretcher and took him away. Jud Hope waited for a police patrol to arrive, and made a statement, and showed them the spot. Obviously, there wasn't much to see – just crushed bracken, and a small amount of drying blood. They took photographs, but with an accident report in mind.'

'There'd have been boots stomping all over the shop.'

'Exactly. As a potential crime scene, it was compromised. DC Watson has had a blood spatter expert examine the photographs. She's certain that the direction of travel was northbound, while the smearing is at right angles. But it can't be ruled out that this was caused by one or more of the first responders. Naturally, their priority was an attempt to save Sebastian Sinclair's life.'

'It's what you'd do.'

'Not least because of the absence of any vehicle. We know now from the injuries that he was struck – but even that wasn't obvious at the time. There was no car, and no skid marks – so he could just as easily have stumbled – or fainted – or, whatever.'

But DS Leyton has visibly stiffened, and DS Jones notices.

'What is it?'

'No skid marks.' He ponders for a moment. 'Ain't that telling us something?'

He waits for her response.

'That the driver didn't brake.' DS Jones answers evenly, trying to resist any questioning inflexion.

'And why would that be?'

DS Leyton's rejoinder, however, is patently rhetorical – that they are both at liberty to opine – but equally in recognition of the opposing forces that they each experience. That Skelgill is always quick to quash unfounded speculation (albeit not necessarily to reject it) is presently counterbalanced by DS Jones's model of the slippery slope to foul play (to navigate which is their job, after all).

DS Leyton reprises the hitherto unspoken scenario.

'Knocked him down – dragged him out of sight. Matter of seconds from normality to driving away. No one to see what you'd done. Took a sharp-eyed farmer to notice something amiss.'

More silence ensues, until DS Jones speaks.

'Do you think that makes it more likely it was an accident? Just someone who wasn't looking, and panicked and tried to cover their tracks?'

They each reflect upon the mores and values of modern society. Acknowledgement of this conundrum has been unavoidable since the outset, and it comes with conjecture attached. An accident is statistically and circumstantially far more likely – but how likely *really* is it that a motorist would have fled the scene? Surely any reasonable person would have stopped to help, or at least attempted to summon assistance. Nearby was the youth hostel, with overnight residents; and the old slate mine might have had staff on an early shift.

A person who would not have stopped – they know from experience – would have done so for one of two reasons. The first, as DS Leyton explained to Victoria Lawson, is that they have something to hide. The second, the reason they have been resisting, the proverbial elephant in the room, is that the act was deliberate.

DS Leyton weighs in on the latter point.

'They didn't actually kill him – or make sure he was dead.'

DS Jones waits a moment.

'Did they want to kill him – or just put him out of action?'

Keeping both hands on the steering wheel, DS Leyton gives a shake of his arms.

'It's a risky way to go about it, girl.'

She nods, and again they are silent.

It takes quite a few moments before DS Leyton yields to the next speculative step.

'What do you reckon to this Frank Lawson character?'

DS Jones nods pensively. She understands that her colleague, given the incomplete picture, is simply joining the dots that are nearest to one another. Frank Lawson is the person they know to have been in closest proximity to Sebastian Sinclair at the time of the incident. And Frank Lawson was in competition with Sebastian Sinclair. Frank Lawson's glib manner – of anybody's encountered to date – raises some doubts.

DS Jones takes her turn.

'Could he feasibly have had his car there?'

DS Leyton tilts his head from side to side.

'We've only got his word for it that he parked in Keswick. What if he left it earlier at Honister Hause and returned to the starting point?'

A small frown creases DS Jones's smooth brow. She reflects upon the intricate checking they might need to do in an effort to identify such activity.

DS Leyton, however, moves the narrative on.

'Got ahead of him on the hillside – he's more or less admitted that – waited in the motor – ran him down. Drove straight to Manchester.'

DS Jones's large hazel eyes widen, causing her pupils to constrict in the bright June sunlight that angles into her side of the car.

'I suppose Sebastian Sinclair might well have stopped if he saw Frank Lawson's car approaching.'

'That would have baffled him, wouldn't it? He'd have been a sitting duck, girl.'

But now DS Jones shakes her head in frustration.

'But if incapacitation were the aim – Frank Lawson would have been identified.'

DS Leyton makes a face.

'A proxy?'

'But – the car. Damage – and other evidentiary traces.'

They lapse into silence, which may just be of a self-reproachful nature – for they have swiftly arrived at the singularity that to Skelgill is anathema – where speculation exhibits a quasi-mathematical quality of exponential growth. One moment the connections seem reassuringly linear, the next they branch in multiple directions, and in turn these branch again – and all ways seem of equal merit.

It is some time before DS Leyton makes a remark.

'Never went there.'

He inclines his head to the right. They are driving into the city on Warwick Road, now passing the football ground, Brunton Park. Carlisle United might not be in their heyday, but it is an impressive stadium with a capacity of 18,000 – just waiting for a plum tie against Liverpool or Manchester United in the FA Cup.

'To a football match?'

DS Leyton pulls his gaze away, for the traffic is steady.

'Used to follow Millwall as a teenager. Travelled all over England, flippin' hours in a coach stuck on motorways – Plymouth, Scunthorpe, Wrexham – that's Wales, mind. Carlisle was the furthest we could go.'

'You must have been dedicated.'

Tch. Kept me out of trouble.'

DS Jones smirks. Keeping out of trouble and being a Millwall fan are not widely recognised bedfellows.

She checks their progress on the maps app on her phone.

'Their office is in Portland Square. Do you know it?'

DS Leyton chuckles.

'Portland Square, now – there, I have been.'

Parked directly outside, they climb broad worn steps to the central portico of an impressive terraced sandstone mansion, its architecture blending Georgian symmetry with more elaborate Victorian gothic, five storeys including its basement and attic rooms. It seems Sinclair Design has the whole place, and they are admitted by intercom to a bright hallway with stylish décor and a centrepiece of an enormous vase of pale cream lilies.

A young person emerges from a room on the right marked Reception; the detectives, in their various ways, react to their tartan-ribboned high bunches and matching tartan skirt, a quirky assemblage finished off with red Doc Martens.

They are asked to take a seat and are offered refreshments, though they decline.

'Jules will be right down.'

Indeed the said person quickly appears, descending a curving staircase.

'I'm Jules – Julie Magnusson, Group Account Director. Vicky asked me to take care of you.'

She halts just out of handshaking range. The soft, well-spoken English accent is perhaps less of a first impression than her visual appearance – and, again, there is a discrepancy in what the detectives see.

To DS Leyton she is a striking young woman, his colleague's age, he would guess – mid-twenties – simply clad in a close-fitting black polo-neck top and a black skirt of respectable knee-length, black tights and mid-heeled black shoes; an elegant pose and slender figure; she might be the stylish manageress of a boutique hotel, or a junior editor of a fashion magazine; but perhaps it is mourning wear.

DS Jones homes in less on the girl's general attributes; she is drawn to the eyes – and not so much their unusual pale grey irises, but the careful yet more-than-ample mascara and eye shadow that create a decidedly sorrowful effect. Is this her regular appearance, or in the undoubtedly attractive features is there a semblance of pained restraint? And against this – and against her whole demeanour – the long, dark hair – a voluminous statement of ringlets that cascades onto her collar bones, a hairdo that cannot have been easy to achieve. It speaks of a certain abandon in the personality, that for now is subdued, if not visually reined in.

'Vicky wanted me to show you Seb's work station. It's the top floor. We can take the lift, if you would follow me, please. It's through at the back.'

The girl turns immediately.

The detectives exchange glances – supplemented by a grin from DS Leyton, which might suggest he is happy to avoid the stairs – though they both know that Skelgill would favour the chance to meander up through the building.

But in fact a feat of contemporary engineering – an external glass elevator – affords views into a variety of studios, office floors – in places open plan – a common room, landings, a glimpse into a gleaming

83

kitchenette. The staff appear pretty much entirely under 30s, trendily dressed, unobtrusively going about their business, either alone at large screens or perhaps consulting with a colleague. Inevitably some stare pensively at their phones. Though it is a soundless vignette, there is the impression that a sombre hush has descended upon a workplace that would customarily be lively and animated. It is a cadre that is shell-shocked, stunned, going through the motions.

The lift disgorges them into an attic suite of interconnected rooms, presently unoccupied. Jules leads them to a studio overlooking Portland Square. There is an L-shaped desk with a large screen at an angle to the dormer window, so as not to obscure the view. They are above treetop level, and beyond the burgeoning limes of the little urban oasis stretches a roofscape that includes one of the crenelated twin barrel towers of the medieval citadel.

'We do quite a bit of hot-desking – but this is where Seb preferred to work when he was in the building.'

She approaches the computer and rouses it from sleep mode; it seems she has it set up ready.

'Vicky mentioned you would want to look at his emails. Here's his dashboard. Our IT guy has a way in – in case of emergency. It requires a second password that we keep here.'

She steps back and indicates to the screen and wheeled chair.

'Should I leave you?'

DS Jones looks inquiringly at her colleague.

'Why don't you wait – in case there's something we need to ask you about?'

There are two sofas in the room, facing over a low table. DS Leyton gestures that they should be seated.

'There's also a couple of general queries – maybe I can ask you about that while my colleague has a look online?'

'Sure.'

But in the girl's hitherto facilitative manner there is perhaps just a slight sense of apprehension.

There is a coffee machine in one corner, and she offers them a cup; but again the detectives state that they are fine.

Now in fact DS Leyton looks like he does not have a list of questions – or even the informal points he has mentioned. But he takes out his notebook and opens it, and gets his pencil poised. He gazes somewhat vacantly at the blank page.

The effect, however, seems to prompt the young woman to voice what she has perhaps been concealing – for there must have been office talk of the police coming in – and in the context of an event – an accident – that surely has little if anything to do with the company. Indeed she poses the question fairly directly.

'Is there something – I mean – connected to Seb's ... *death?*'

She both hesitates over, and stresses, the final word.

DS Leyton's view of his colleague is side-on – but she does not appear to waver in her concentration upon the screen of the iMac.

'Do you know of anything, miss?'

DS Leyton's tone is inquiring – as if her suggestion comes as a surprise.

At the same time, his response serves as a shortcut through what is beginning to feel like a pedantic excuse for the rather obvious fact that they are plainly investigating beyond the event. And his question does produce a flicker of a response from DS Jones, if only in that her fingers hover momentarily over the trackpad.

'No – nothing – why would there be?'

That the ball has come back almost too quickly for proper reflection is notable, along with a slight tremor that shakes through the glossy brunette tresses.

DS Leyton inhales, and lifts and lowers his shoulders; his gaze drops to his notebook – he seems perplexed, as he makes a couple of doodle marks. He releases the breath and now looks up in an avuncular manner.

'The thing is, Miss Magnusson, until we get some concrete evidence relating to the incident, we're having to cast the net much wider. It's all we can do, you see?'

He makes an apologetic face; the girl nods, but she seems to shrink into the sofa; she folds her hands on her lap and lowers her gaze. And she waits for him to continue.

'So if there's anything that you think may be out of the ordinary – concerning Mr Sinclair – no matter how unrelated it might seem – it could help us to understand something we are yet to learn.'

But now the girl looks up imploringly.

'Still – I don't see – how it could be connected?'

DS Leyton grins ruefully.

'You don't have to worry – that's our job, miss.' He glances towards DS Jones – to include her in the challenge.

Jules, however, gives a more purposeful shake of her head.

85

'But aren't you suggesting that there's some extraneous reason for what happened to Seb?'

She inhales sharply, as though it has shocked her to say it – to consider it.

DS Leyton falls back on their stock explanation.

'It may lead us to a witness – someone presently unaware that they have information – for instance if he was communicating with other runners, or exchanging information about his running with a friend or acquaintance or business contact.'

The girl seems relieved. There is a relaxing of her demeanour – she lets go of her hands and smooths out the fabric of her skirt.

But now DS Jones interjects with a question.

'Does this Mac have the iMessage app?'

It takes Jules a moment to register that the query is aimed at her.

'Oh, no. None of the company Macs are hooked up – because of hot-desking – multiple use. It could get confusing – so the Macs are not synched with individuals' iPhones.'

DS Jones proffers a wry smile.

'Okay, thanks.'

But the girl is looking a little flustered. Suddenly she stands up and without a word goes to a small wheeled unit beside the section of the desk that overlooks the square.

She pulls open the top drawer.

She retrieves what is evidently a glossy periodical.

She returns to DS Leyton and offers it.

'You mentioned running – and possible contacts.'

'Aha?'

He squints at what she has handed him. It a fell running magazine, *Fell Running*, no less. He sees it is for the current month, the latest edition. The cover features a rangy athlete silhouetted against a dawn sky, traversing a toothed ridge. A puff calls out a special feature – the Bob Graham Round anniversary challenge – and the question "Will it be a hattrick for The Goat?"

Jules intervenes before DS Leyton can find some words from among his puzzlement.

'When I came in here on Friday afternoon – Seb was reading this. He had it spread out on the desk. He put it away in the drawer – like he was embarrassed that I'd caught him not working.'

DS Leyton waits for a moment; the girl's lips are parted, as though her vital signs are on the up.

Though when she does not speak he starts flicking aimlessly through the pages.

'And that struck you as odd, miss?'

'Just what you said about running contacts.' But now – under scrutiny, perhaps – a note of doubt has crept into her voice. 'And – I suppose – why shouldn't he read a magazine, when it's his company?'

DS Leyton, however, is more encouraging.

'Miss – this is exactly what I'm talking about.' He brandishes the magazine. 'Mind if we hang onto it?'

Now she turns out a full lower lip in a way to suggest she has no power of veto over anything they might want.

DS Jones, a little ostentatiously, closes the mail app on the desktop computer and swivels around in the chair. She gives a nod of having finished to DS Leyton, with no indication that there is anything of concern.

DS Leyton rises.

'We'll leave it there, just now, miss. If anything does occur to you, please let us know.'

Inside the lift, DS Jones positions herself opposite Julie Magnusson. They are of similar height and build, contrasting though, the former honey-blonde and bronzed, the latter dark and fair-skinned. If DS Leyton were asked, he might judge that his colleague is forcing eye-contact upon the other girl.

And, indeed, she has a point to make.

'Mrs Lawson explained that the firm is in good shape – that there are no external conflicts with clients or suppliers.' She pauses, drawing a nod of agreement. 'How about internally? It's not unusual for there to be stresses and strains – in such a dynamic environment there can be complex relationships.'

Jules lowers her gaze. But in the small enclosed space there is little means of escape or distraction. Again, she turns out her bottom lip, this time an almost petulant reaction, it seems.

The question does not specify a connection to Sebastian Sinclair's fate, though it would be implicit – otherwise, why pose it? But the girl, after a moment, contrives to answer in the abstract.

'No more than anywhere else, I should think.' She looks up, certainly apprehensively, and only briefly at DS Jones before turning to address the rest of her reply to DS Leyton. 'Anything like that seems very trivial right now.'

87

DS Leyton's solicitude is plainly sought – and instinctively he provides a sympathetic hearing, both nodding and contriving a suitably hangdog expression. The extended moment sees them to the ground floor – where Jules is efficient in leading them to the exit, and to bid them goodbye.

Out on the pavement they both look up, as if to admire the building. The attic floor is largely hidden from view, recessed into the pitched roof – just the top of the dormer is visible.

DS Leyton jerks a thumb over his shoulder.

'Fancy a turn round the square? Get your steps up. Breath of fresh air.'

DS Jones grins.

'Are you looking for inspiration?'

DS Leyton returns a smile.

'I suppose it's almost the scene of a past triumph. Especially now the sentences have been handed down.'

11. SOUTHWAITE

M6 – 3.45 p.m. Wednesday 5th June

'IF THERE'S NOTHING to speak of in his emails, I reckon we're going to have to crack the code on his phone.'

DS Jones nods pensively.

'And that presupposes we'll find something of note. It does feel like a bit of a long shot.'

DS Leyton taps the hazards to acknowledge a trucker who has flashed him into the crawler lane. He snatches a glance at his colleague.

'I got an inkling you would like to have questioned the girl, Jules. Was that female intuition?'

DS Jones reacts a little awkwardly.

'Oh – I was half listening-in to your conversation – absorbing the vibes. There was something that struck me – a feeling, but I'm not sure I could explain it.'

DS Leyton chuckles.

'You sound like the Guvnor. What I'd say is we spooked her – she looked like a rabbit in the headlights. I even accidentally drew a bunny in my notebook. But she's had a shock – like the rest of them – and then the CID turn up asking questions – she's probably never had anything worse than a parking ticket. And she's young to be left in charge.'

DS Jones perhaps stiffens, as though it does not hold water with her.

'Or should we be concerned that Victoria Lawson has left her to it?'

DS Leyton, however, has more to say about Julie Magnusson.

'I thought she was grasping at straws – giving us that running magazine – but she seemed relieved to do something.'

Now DS Jones murmurs her agreement. She has her shoulder bag at her feet – and now she extracts the publication and peruses the cover.

'It's a week today.' She smiles. 'A bit too late for us to enter a team.'

DS Leyton produces a growl of relief.

'Cor blimey – I wouldn't do that, not for all the tea in China. *Fell running* – that would be me, alright. Fell at the first hurdle. I don't know what makes folks want to punish themselves. And I've never really got me head round these sports that ain't got a ball.'

His colleague regards him with amusement, though she turns her scrutiny back to the cover illustration.

There is, she reflects, certainly something more than usually primordial about fell running. And not least that it has its claimed origins back in the mists of Lakeland time, in name if not in absolute practice.

She thumbs through to the article on the Bob Graham Round anniversary challenge. The page has a diagonal crease, as though it has been folded over to create a bookmark.

She becomes engrossed.

Indeed – so studious is her concentration that DS Leyton is prompted to remark.

'Now, don't get any bright ideas.'

But it seems she has had one.

'Can we stop at Southwaite?'

'Now you *are* sounding like the Guvnor!'

DS Jones smiles wryly – but her tone carries a resolute note.

'Can I explain over a ginger scone?'

DS Leyton shrugs resignedly.

The service station comes up quickly; it is only five miles from the Carlisle South junction.

And when DS Leyton insists it is his round, his colleague splits off to the convenience store. She makes a purchase of a pad of yellow adhesive notelets, and finds him settled at a four-seater table. He has placed her refreshments opposite – but instead she opts to take the seat beside him.

'Before we eat, I'd like to show you something.'

DS Leyton is baffled but does not object.

DS Jones takes out the copy of *Fell Running* and lays it open at the page of the Bob Graham Round feature.

'Look.'

She pushes the magazine in front of him and indicates, but not precisely.

DS Leyton frowns, wondering what he is supposed to see. The double-page spread comprises a large landscape photograph (an extension of the front cover image of the runner silhouetted on the ridge), a main headline and article, and several inlaid items, including a map of the route, with distances and target times.

While he is seeking inspiration DS Jones picks the cellophane off her purchase. She produces a pen, and points with the tip.

'See – this paragraph.'

Now DS Leyton homes in, striving to find a comfortable focal length. DS Jones begins to write upon and peel off a succession of sticky notes, leaning occasionally to refer to the text in front of her colleague.

DS Leyton decides to read out the paragraph. He traces the sentences with an index finger.

' "A particularly punishing stretch lies between Esk Pike and Great End. First, a drop of some 400 feet to Esk Hause, where the paths from Borrowdale and Eskdale meet; catch your breath for a climb of 500 feet; now you will strike out across the rocky plateau, with Ill Crag and Broad Crag to come before – what else! – the agonising sting-in-the-tail of Broad Crag Col, to scale the iconic Scafell Pike itself." '

He clears his throat and reaches for his tea.

Blinking a little, he sees now that DS Jones has eight sticky notes before her, each with a single word, written in capital letters.

He looks back at the page – now more purposefully.

'Someone's underlined those words.'

DS Jones is looking musingly at the notelets.

'Exactly.'

DS Leyton scowls.

'Why would you underline random words? It's not like it's the mountain names or the heights – stuff that might be useful to remember.'

'Mmm.'

There is the suggestion that DS Jones is one step ahead of him.

'Is this a word game, girl?'

She has laid out the words in the order that they appear:

END, DROP, MEET, YOUR, NOW, OUT, ELSE, AGONISING.

'Supposing it's a kind of word anagram – the words are scrambled, rather than the letters. Some of the words are suggestive, don't you think?'

DS Leyton looks doubtful, but finds some agreement.

'*Agonising*, maybe.'

DS Jones brings out the word to create a new line.

DS Leyton jabs a finger.

'*Agonising drop.* If you fall down a mountain.'

DS Jones adds *drop*.

But then she replaces *drop* with *end*.

'*Agonising drop* or *agonising end?* It's one noun or the other to go with the adjective. Though they could both be verbs.'

'Hah – now you're blinding me with science, girl.'

She grins.

DS Leyton glowers, now with renewed determination.

'*Meet your?* What about that – I mean, I know they're already in order …'

But without hesitation she has moved the words.

They have: MEET YOUR AGONISING END.

'Struth.'

DS Leyton curses under his breath.

And it is not only the sudden chilling threat that stirs him – but also the sentence fragment that remains in the line above:

DROP, NOW, OUT, ELSE.

DS Jones casually swaps over *now* and *out*.

DROP OUT NOW ELSE MEET YOUR AGONISING END.

Simultaneously, both sit back and fold their arms.

It is a moment of assessing the reality of what they have just done.

Past the point of expletives, DS Leyton absently reaches for the plate with his scone and begins to eat.

DS Jones is first to speak; her voice is even, unexcited.

'Of course – there must be other combinations. And there could be an innocent explanation.'

But DS Leyton splutters crumbs.

'Come off it, girl – you've just cracked this. It all fits – it's a warning – and the proof of the pudding – it came flamin-well true!'

DS Jones nods, but reluctantly so.

'What if it were him – Sebastian Sinclair?'

'What – like he was going to pass it on – send it to Frank Lawson?'

'Or to another competitor.'

DS Leyton is grimacing unhappily – such that she relents.

'Ok – look – I'm just playing devil's advocate.'

DS Leyton pats her arm.

'I get that, girl – we've got to get it past the Guvnor – he'd only say the same thing.'

DS Jones nods, and now she reaches for her tea.

'I mean – I agree, obviously. It makes far more sense if it were intended for, and received by, Sebastian Sinclair. It appears he was the stronger candidate of the two – and perhaps even in with a chance of winning.'

'And it explains why he stuck it in the drawer when he was interrupted by the girl, Jules. If he'd just worked out what it said.'

They ponder this point in silence.

Now DS Leyton slides the magazine so that it is between them.

'What about this, then?'

He indicates to one of the inset articles, a continuation of the front cover splash: "A TRIPLE FOR THE GOAT?" They both read, DS Jones leaning closer, DS Leyton swaying back and squinting hard. "Will Billy 'The Goat' Higson make it three-in-a-row for the Bob Graham Round anniversary challenge? No fell runner has ever completed a hattrick of wins, but local Cumbrian man Higson is odds-on favourite to make it a first. Nicknamed originally for his extraordinary prowess over steep rocky ground, 'The Goat' will surely merit the dual-purpose epithet 'Greatest of all Time' if he achieves the feat – especially if he sets a new record for the anniversary event – and rumour has it he has been pulling out all the stops in training – even taking time off from his vocation as a Matterdale shepherd, running the course day and night, to gain every possible advantage from the minutest route details and battle-hardened fitness."

They sit back and now both consume their scones in silence.

There is a second small photograph of Billy Higson, aka 'The Goat', toiling up a fellside. He looks to be in his 40s, gnarled and wiry, weatherbeaten and leathery. Grim-faced, shaven-headed, weaselly eyed, he has an ominous appearance.

After a while – looking a little surprised to have finished his food – DS Leyton sighs.

'Reckon we'd better run a check on him.'

DS Jones nods – there is no harm in that – but she shares his discomfort. It is a big leap – an escalation in rivalry that is ordinarily beyond the pale.

Yes – kudos rates highly, humans strive for it – but, face it, this is a comparatively obscure regional English event, one that will be covered at best in a couple of specialist magazines and websites and perhaps a small column near the back of the likes of the Westmorland Gazette.

She speaks.

'The prize money is relatively token.'

But DS Leyton has other ideas.
Now he taps the page – but keeps his finger in place.
'That's what you see. But this is one of my specialist subjects.'
She leans closer – he is highlighting the phrase "odds-on favourite".
'Emma – this is where the money goes round.'
She looks alarmed.
'But that could be anybody.'
'I might be able to find something out – at least, whether there's much of a market been made.'
Now she regards him inquiringly.
'If it's cash, it would be anonymous, right?'
'Yeah. All you need's your little betting slip. No questions asked.'
'And the number one challenger being out of the race – that would skew the odds in your favour?'
DS Leyton chuckles.
'You bet.'
Now DS Jones nods pensively. After a moment she reaches down into her shoulder bag and pulls out a polythene evidence bag. Lifting the magazine by its corner, she inserts it into the latter.
'I think we should get a fingerprint check done.'
DS Leyton grins contritely, and holds up his hands, digits splayed.
'I reckon they'll find ginger scone.'

12. DUNMAIL RAISE

The Wayfarer's Rest, near Grasmere – 9.00 p.m. Wednesday 5 June

IT IS CUSTOMARY for Skelgill upon entering a tavern to scan first the bar counter – for, if there are no handpumps (or handpumps only with their badges' backs turned), then there is no point dwelling further, when an active facility might be found nearby. That said, there are occasions when he is obliged to resort to some packaged equivalent (though in fact there is no such thing as real ale in a bottle or can) – and he is relieved to see that this is not one of them.

A "Hey up, lad" from the far end of the long room confirms the reason why his choice might have been compromised – and now he sees a large hand belonging to Gerry summoning him to where the bluff Yorkshireman sits with his two female companions. The old coaching inn dates back to the sixteenth century, and the low, beamed space probably represents several original salons knocked together, as three hearths with smouldering logs would indicate. They are adjacent to the most distant of these, and Gerry is now pointing urgently to a full pint on their table: that Skelgill need not trouble himself at the bar, where several patrons are waiting to be served. Indeed, the room is pretty well packed, and lively with chatter, and it looks like they have done well to find a table. They appear only just to have begun to make inroads into their own drinks, and the trio incline towards him, it seems, like eager nestlings on the return of a beak-laden parent.

Skelgill waves back, and grins suitably, making eye contact with each of the intrepid crew as he approaches, in a way that suggests he is impressed that they have survived another day on the fells. But, upon reaching them, he turns his attention to getting a seat. There is no empty chair – but, at the adjoining station, a woman in her later middle-age sits facing out from the settle, and tucked under her small round table is a stool. There is only one drink before her, and the woman is perusing the crossword of the Westmorland Gazette.

Skelgill stands for a moment – assuming she will glance up – but she remains engrossed. It gives him the chance to notice that she seems to be a hiker, albeit her outfit is in such mint condition that for a second he feels conscious of his own worn attire (and is reminded of a gentle nudge from DS Jones of there being a summer sale in his favourite outdoor gear store up in Keswick).

He coughs politely.

'Scuse us, madam – mind if I take this stool?'

He reaches for it anyway, which is perhaps what prompts the woman to look up – for she may not have realised he was addressing her – and she seems momentarily flustered, perhaps by his turn of phrase – and then waves an open palm and half-mouths, half-mumbles that he should help himself.

Gerry and Rosheen are seated on the settle, so it is Rita that hotches her chair around to make enough space for Skelgill to squeeze in. He feels a little self-conscious, being more or less shoulder-to-shoulder – but Gerry is quick to break the ice with a forthright inquiry.

'We saw your appeal again, on the telly this morning. Any joy?'

Skelgill, to sit comfortably, has taken his phone from his hip pocket. He lays it on the table surface.

'I've had no signal until now.'

He grins; he might be content with this state of affairs.

Yet he takes a second glance at the handset, frowning briefly, as if in a small way he might also be irked by the absence of communication.

His answer being somewhat obtuse, perhaps Rita senses he is discomfited, and she switches the subject matter.

'How did you get on with your fishing, today?'

At her southern lilt, Skelgill brightens, though he notices that Gerry is regarding him with a hint of concern. Notwithstanding, he begins to hold forth.

'Took my time – tried all the different methods, for practice's sake. Just the two tarns – Codale and then Easedale – one runs into t' other – technically they're part of the Grasmere-Rydal-Windermere system.'

Gerry is engaged by the notion.

'So in theory a fish could swim the entire watercourse?'

'All the way from Morecambe Bay. I don't doubt that eels do it. All the way from America.'

Now Skelgill raises his glass to Rita, and round the trio in acknowledgement of the endowment. After a sup he takes the initiative.

'How about you folks – you all seem to be in one piece.'

Gerry is ready as spokesman.

'Aye – we just took it steady, too. We didn't rush away – I could have gone back to bed, after the Cumbrian sausage at Dungeon Ghyll. Then it's a fair old pull, back up onto the route with the sun pounding down. We had lunch on Sergeant Man. Then we took the direct path down the shoulder from Steel Fell to Ghyll Foot. Unpacked our gear and put our feet up. We were thinking of going into Grasmere so Rita could photograph the old gingerbread shop – but I reckon we all nodded off.'

Now Rita interjects inquiringly of Skelgill.

'I believe it dates from the 1630s. I might have to sneak out before breakfast, tomorrow. It's not too far, is it?'

'It's barely above a mile. It's in an old schoolhouse beside the church. And you're more or less on the flat from here.'

Gerry has a different question of geography.

'And where have you ended up – for your campsite tonight?'

Skelgill glances about – in the way of acting like he would not want anyone to overhear.

'I've half-buried my gear up at Dunmail Raise. No point carting it down, only to lug it back. Thought I might go up from there to Grisedale Tarn. Try a spot of night fishing.' He grins. 'Can't practice enough.'

Now Rosheen, who has been listening with keen interest, chirps up in her impish fashion.

'I hope you've not disturbed the last King of Cumbria?'

Skelgill regards her in a way that shows he understands – when clearly the other two do not – and he waves a hand in the approximate direction of the mountain pass from which he has descended. His response is aimed at Gerry and Rita.

'There's a great pile of rocks at the hause – the road has to split around it. I've always thought it looks more like builder's rubble than an ancient monument.'

Now Rosheen wags a finger, though she knows he is joking.

'It is reputed to be the burial site of Dyfnwal ab Owain, the Brittonic king slain by the Anglo-Saxons.'

Skelgill shrugs, though in a way that respectfully defers to her superior knowledge.

And Rita pipes up, a little breathlessly.

'This sounds like something else I should be photographing.'

Skelgill raises a placatory palm.

'You'll see it soon enough in the morning – it's exactly where you'll pick up the Bob Graham Round to climb Seat Sandal. Dunmail Raise is one of the recognised crossing points.'

Rita regards Gerry inquiringly.

'Gerry likes to keep us moving – I shall have to put in a request stop.'

But Gerry is distracted. He is leaning sideways to see past Skelgill along the length of the bar room.

'Hey up, lad – I reckon you've got company. Unless I'm mistaken, that's your police lass off the telly.'

Skelgill jerks around to see – sure enough – that DS Jones has entered the far end of the room and is surveying its occupants.

He rises abruptly.

'Two minutes – sorry.'

As Skelgill strides away, Gerry calls after him.

'Bring her up for a drink, lad.'

The trio watch with interest as Skelgill approaches the striking-looking young woman – the pair seem to be self-conscious and the most that Skelgill does by way of greeting is to put a palm lightly on her shoulder and dip his head as if to speak in confidence, or to hear what she has to relate amidst the chatter and laughter of the pub.

They see that she glances past him to register their presence – and then it seems she says something along the lines of meeting them – gesturing towards them – and Skelgill, after a moment's hesitation, appears to concede and leads the way back.

The two standing, he makes introductions.

Gerry has risen, and now he indicates to the small table next to them.

'Have a seat lass – look, that woman's away, now. What'll you have?'

Skelgill had not noticed her leave – but certainly the table is vacant and the well-dressed middle-aged crossword-solver and her newspaper are gone – although a half-finished drink has been left behind.

Skelgill for a moment seems to swither – but DS Jones takes the initiative.

'It's very kind of you – but I was just passing. I'm both driving, and on a tight schedule.' She has her bag slung over her shoulder, and now she shifts it round to indicate it has some role in proceedings.

And now Skelgill doubles down on her excuse.

'Sergeant Jones has offered me a lift back up the hill. Two birds with one stone.' He grins a little sheepishly, though his use of the formal title confirms his intent. Then he reaches for his pint and drains the last of the ale. 'My round tomorrow night – the White Mare at Threlkeld, reet?'

Rita reaches to touch his arm.

'Perhaps we'll see you en route?'

And Rosheen chips in.

'You'll be fishing at Red Tarn?'

Skelgill nods obligingly.

'Aye – fair chance you'll be passing just above us. You'll get a cracking view from atop Helvellyn.'

Skelgill and DS Jones are politely backing away, and Gerry recognises the inevitability of their departure.

'Off you go then, you pair – don't let us keep you from your work. A copper's lot, eh?'

And, with a knowing wink at Skelgill, he taps the side of his nose.

13. TÊTE-À-TÊTE

The Dunmail Inn – 9.40 p.m. Wednesday 5 June

'I FEEL GUILTY, dragging you away from your friends.'

Skelgill raises his clear pint of pale ale and stares into it, as though it holds some answer to the conundrum.

But, whatever it is, he decides it speaks for itself, and takes a drink before making any response.

'They're probably more annoyed I've kept you from them. You're quite the little celebrity.'

DS Jones widens her eyes.

'You mean they saw the appeal?'

'Aye. Twice.'

She ponders this statement.

'Still – that's good, isn't it? That it's reached people who are out and about in the fells.'

Skelgill contrives a face that is a little contrary; accordingly, she makes an adjustment.

'True, we don't have much to go on. A couple of hoax callers, and a few genuine drivers who saw nothing – or people who have suggested drivers who might have been going that way. DC Watson is working through them.'

Skelgill, however, is not entirely negative.

'It still tells us summat.'

'In what way?'

He shrugs.

'Despite the isolation and time of day – vehicles use that road every few minutes – I know it well enough. It tells us that whatever happened, it happened quickly. If the driver did stop, they didn't stop for long. If they had, I reckon someone would have noticed – the road's barely wide enough for two cars to pass.'

DS Jones regards him keenly.

'We can't be definite – but Forensics agree there is a clear possibility that Sebastian Sinclair was dragged sideways under the bracken. Except the first responders lifted him out onto the tarmac, when they tried to resuscitate him. And they and others trod everywhere.'

Skelgill nods, accepting the inevitability of this.

DS Jones adds a rider.

'Did I tell you – there were no skid marks?'

Skelgill shows no sign of surprise.

They are silent for a few moments. The Dunmail Inn is merely seventeenth century, though its dividing walls remain intact, unlike those of the earlier-dating hostelry they have left just six miles to the south. They sit at angles, each with a sash window at their back, in the corner of a small end room which conveniently they have to themselves, discovered by DS Jones while Skelgill procured suitable measures of Jennings ale. The only sound is the sporadic swish of tyres that penetrates the old glass as vehicles sweep close by. Long gone are the rattle of stagecoaches and mail, the cries of the ostlers and the hungry whinnies of the teams – though all these and more are preserved in frozen mime in dark and faded pictures that line the walls.

DS Jones seems to gather herself.

'I do have – how can I put it? – an intriguing piece of evidence.'

'Aye?'

She succeeds in extracting a questioning inflexion.

'But can I just fill you in on the other background?'

Skelgill immediately scowls.

'You've seen me eat bangers and mash.'

DS Jones raises her hands appealingly. He eats the sausages first.

'I just think it will distract you.'

'More than not knowing?'

'Can we try?'

Skelgill looks at his beer. It is a good way down.

'If you'll have another half of bitter.'

'That may affect my capacity to drive.'

'I expect you've got your toothbrush.'

She affects an expression of censure.

'I might be open to negotiation. Let me begin with a small aside. DC Watson tracked down the Uber driver who took Sebastian Sinclair and Frank Lawson to Wasdale, to start their run. He positively identified them – but there really is nothing untoward. It seems they both slept most of the way, and hardly exchanged a word, either with him or between themselves.'

Skelgill nods, acceptingly.

101

DS Jones continues.

'Okay. Since we last spoke, DS Leyton and I have interviewed Morag Sinclair at her home, and a girl called Julie Magnusson, who is next in charge after Victoria Lawson at Sinclair Design.'

She suddenly takes a drink – as if something strikes her and she is buying time, wondering whether perhaps to jump the gun. And on this point she decides not to hold back.

'Look – I haven't raised this with anyone – but I think Sebastian and Morag Sinclair's relationship was something of a marriage of convenience.' She purses her lips. 'I know it's taking us into alien territory – but I'm kind of getting the feeling we're going to have to go there.'

Skelgill does not demur. But he waits, all the same.

'They knew one another vaguely at university in Leicester. They hadn't crossed paths for at least five years – but both ended up at a reunion, a New Year's party in Cumbria, a hotel beside Derwentwater.' Now she pauses to take another drink. 'From information gathered, I calculated that it coincided with the date of conception of their eldest child.'

Now Skelgill raises an eyebrow.

'Is shotgun wedding the phrase you're looking for?'

DS Jones gives a light shrug of her shoulders, and brushes away a strand of fair hair that falls across her cheek.

'I've no idea – of the politics at the time – but ...'

Skelgill waits, and finally issues a prompt.

'Aye?'

'Well – she's got an air about her of the willing martyr. I might be doing her an injustice – she obviously has the burden of managing the tragedy with the children – but her reaction and demeanour wasn't what I expected.'

Skelgill pulls slowly from his glass, indicating his willingness to listen.

'I couldn't help drawing the contrast between the Sinclair house at Applethwaite and the Lawsons' at Wetheral. They're both large, high-value homes – but the latter is immaculate, while the Sinclairs' is just an unruly warren, with old and new cheek by jowl.'

'Sounds like my sort of place.'

DS Jones is not deflected.

'One has personality stamped upon it, the other – well – you know some of the rented housing we see – where the occupiers have no vested interest?'

'Could be just that – a different personality. Laid back.'
He is mildly playing devil's advocate.
'Except, she isn't – laid back, I mean. And, then – I know it's a bit corny, a bit lovey-dovey – but the Lawsons have a big portrait – you, know – a staged shot by a professional photographer. The happy family. I didn't see a single picture of Sebastian or Morag Sinclair – just a couple of throwaway snaps of the kids.'

Another silence ensues, and DS Jones reverts to sipping her own drink. She recognises that they are tacitly edging closer to matters of motive – as she has done with more freedom in company with DS Leyton. But Skelgill is less inclined to indulge in conjecture – and will likely not bite at the poor bait she has cast in relation to Morag Sinclair.

She tries an alternative morsel.

'She doesn't hold Frank Lawson in much regard. I'm not sure she wasn't trying to blame him.'

Her choice of words is more suggestive than she intends – and elicits a reaction from Skelgill.

'Put him in the frame?'

'Oh – no – I mean – that she has Frank Lawson down as a loudmouth and a bighead – and that it was his egging-on that caused them to enter for the Bob Graham event. And if they hadn't entered, the mishap wouldn't have occurred.'

Skelgill waits.

'She also said that she didn't think Sebastian had a lot of time for Frank.'

He casts her a quick sideways glance.

'What about t' other way round?'

She opens her palms wide. She does not know. Instead, she reaches again for her drink, and takes a more substantial draught.

Skelgill inclines his head.

'See – I told you it'd grow on you. Natural ingredients, live in the barrel, no pop.'

DS Jones grins wryly.

'You're allowed to be right about some things.'

'What –'

Skelgill seems suddenly distracted – she realises that his gaze is directed past her, at the window behind.

He rises.

'I'll just, er – I'll just nip to the gents.'

'Sure.'

Skelgill leaves the room but turns left into the corridor, where there is an exit door. He steps out and rounds the corner of the long whitewashed building. A car is driving away down the dale, heading north in the direction of Keswick and the A66. It seems to accelerate, although it might be an illusion, or a natural effect of the downslope. It is a small white hatchback; it could be one of a dozen marques, and one of some three million ostensibly similar models on the British roads.

When he returns to their seats he sees that DS Jones has procured fresh drinks; beer for them both.

He smiles but does not comment.

She immediately continues.

'As I said, we also called at Sinclair Design. I wanted to check Sebastian Sinclair's emails – and I was hoping to access his iMessages. I couldn't do the latter, and there was nothing of note among the former.'

Skelgill waits patiently. He knows that she does not generally waste time telling him news that isn't, and that it is merely to lay the ground for what is to come.

'We were chaperoned by the girl I mentioned – Jules, they call her. She was, I would say, both upset and nervy. I don't know if she was under orders from Victoria Lawson – to make sure we didn't stray about – but there was tension in the air.'

Skelgill seems content not to dispute this generality.

'Then – just as we were finishing up, came the interesting bit.'

DS Jones reaches down for the shoulder bag propped against the table leg.

'You're a save-the-best-till-last lass, aren't you?'

But any further debate over their opposing proclivities is pre-empted. Skelgill's attention is piqued when she produces a copy of *Fell Running*.

She holds it just out of his reach.

'I bought this to replace the original that Jules produced from Sebastian Sinclair's desk. But I've marked it in the identical way – for demonstration purposes.'

Skelgill registers the significance of what she says without needing to comment.

Now he accepts the magazine and scrutinises the front cover.

'Latest edition. It's been out a while mind. June comes out in mid-May – so they can sell them for longer.'

DS Jones nods, but otherwise remains silent.

Skelgill, having taken in the front cover message, dutifully turns to the page that is marked by having been folded over from the bottom corner, to create a little ear of a bookmark. He flattens out the crease and presses down along the length of the gutter to keep the spread open.

DS Jones watches as his eyes scan about, quickly taking in the main elements. When she sees that he dwells upon the paragraph with its selected words underlined, she produces a sheet of paper with her yellow sticky notes ready laid out.

DROP OUT NOW ELSE MEET YOUR AGONISING END.

She gives him time to absorb the information. He does not react, other than inscrutably – in the diffuse evening sunlight that refracts over the fells his features seem more than usually craggy, and there is knott and scree in his countenance.

For his part, Skelgill does not question the unjumbled sequence. He takes the view that if this is what DS Jones has come up with, it is the superior combination.

And his first question is incisive.

'How did the lass know about it?'

'Jules? She said she walked into his design studio on Friday afternoon and he stuffed it away in a drawer. We prompted her to remember when we explained that he might have been in contact with other runners. I believe she was entirely unaware of this content.'

'I take it no mention's come up – of any kind of threat?'

Skelgill says this anyway – for he knows also that he would have heard already.

'This came to us pretty much last thing today. I noticed the coded message when we were heading back on the M6. I wanted to show it to you – and keep our powder dry. I've submitted the original magazine for prints.'

Skelgill is nodding pensively.

'What does Leyton reckon?'

DS Jones inhales to speak – but then she hesitates and instead indicates to the inset article on Billy 'The Goat' Higson.

'This was his first reaction. Do you know of the guy?'

Skelgill's expression gives little away, though in the narrowing of his eyes she reads wariness, and perhaps rivalry.

'Aye, I know of him. Word is, he's got sharp elbows. He specialises in endurance events.'

'It says he's odds-on favourite. DS Leyton is going to try to find out if any bets of significance have been placed – on him, or anyone else, come to that. I've asked DC Watson to request a list of entrants to the race.'

Skelgill exhales, his jaw set.

DS Jones slides a manicured finger onto the item.

'What do you think about it – as a possible motive?'

Skelgill is quick to answer.

'It's a long chalk from having sharp elbows to premeditated assassination.'

She gives a half-smile at his economical assessment.

'That's what I said. There's not a lot of prize money in it – betting aside, perhaps.'

'It's customary for the medallists to donate their winnings to the mountain rescue.'

Though Skelgill seems content to close off the financial aspect, it is plain he is not finished. He remains staring at the photograph of the grimacing Billy Higson. Though it takes DS Jones to prompt him again.

'And the kudos?'

Now Skelgill does not answer straight away. He gazes out, his eyes scanning along the undulating skyline high above a darkened Thirlmere, the tops of High Tove, High Seat and Castlerigg Fell in sharp silhouette against the pink dusk.

He casts a hand at nowhere in particular.

'When it's the culmination of a multi-year project – a lifetime, even. Who knows?'

DS Jones scrutinises his expression – he does not appear entirely definitive – but she accepts it is harder to judge what an accolade of such nature means to any given individual.

'So – we shouldn't rule it out?'

'Nay, lass.' At least now he sounds resolute. And he has something to add. He reaches to tap the page with the sticky notes. 'This is just what you've been looking for.'

She feels she half-understands, but regards him quizzically nonetheless.

Skelgill elaborates.

'He received a threat – he died.'

DS Jones nods; he echoes DS Leyton's pragmatic analysis.

'So – you say, show our hand?'

'I don't see what choice you've got, lass. You can only dance round handbags for so long. It's time to step into your alien territory.' He taps the page again, more vigorously. 'Here's an anonymous threat. Turn it to our advantage. Anyone close to him – who cares about him – should be pleased to help us eliminate them from the inquiry.'

DS Jones is perhaps not expecting such free rein.

'And you're okay with that – you being the wandering oracle – and me updating you?'

Skelgill grins ruefully.

'Howay, lass. You know the Chief'll have us guts for garters if I show up – after promising to take a week off.' He folds his arms; plainly there is some underlying frustration. 'Besides, I've not finished my recce – there's a good couple of days left in that.'

Now DS Jones smiles mischievously.

'There's also your little tour party to think of.'

Skelgill scowls, though more out of duty than disparagement.

'Seems like you're an honorary member – if you're going to be turning up like this every night.'

Her smile widens, and she forces upon him eye contact, her hazel to his mainly green.

'I'm sure you'll get used to saving the best till last.'

14. THE GOAT

Matterdale – 9.15 a.m. Thursday 6 June

'IT'S SAYING JUST under half a mile.'

'I'm glad you're on the case.' DS Leyton emits a relieved whistle as he wrestles with the steering wheel. 'I ain't got a clue about this neck of the woods.'

DS Jones is working from a combination of her maps app and advice from Skelgill. They are indeed in a little-known backwater, Matterdale, a designated parish of tree-lined lanes and rough pastures and minor fells that lies in the triangle between the A66 trunk road and the A592 Ullswater road, the busy if slow route from Penrith to Windermere.

But she does have her bearings. To the north she can see Blencathra – it must be a good ten miles away – and even to her moderately trained eye its profile is unmistakable – known colloquially as 'Saddleback' it looks exactly like that – and at its eastern end the early morning sun is casting a crest into stark shadow – a razor arête she knows to be Sharp Edge – Skelgill has pointed it out often enough in passing, reprising its catalogue of perils.

Their immediate area is more benign, rolling rather than precipitous, and less visited perhaps for its sparsity of collectible Wainwrights; although it is home to the three Dodds – Stybarrow Dodd, Watson's Dodd and Great Dodd – notable for their suffixes of uncertain origin, a word that survives today, for the likes of a lump of whipped cream that retains its shape when dispensed from a spoon. There is a scattering of hamlets (fewer than 500 residents in the entire parish), the odd well-concealed caravan park, and mainly small traditional farms, eking out a living from the pasture that is too damp and rush-infested to plant, but in which various hardy breeds of sheep manage to forage.

The lanes, however, are no less challenging to the driver than many of the higher fell roads and passes – single-track in places; undulating straights with deceptively blind summits; and sharply winding curves where the tarmac dives into a densely wooded gill, suddenly dark after bright sunlight. All the more challenging to a driver habitually in a hurry.

DS Jones takes a moment to appreciate such environs. It is another beautiful day; Cumbria shimmers beneath a great cerulean dome. They have the windows down, admitting the wafting scent of creamy meadowsweet in the verges; and birdsong abounds – those she recognises are the chaffinch with its tumbling crescendo of notes, and a distant buzzard, a plaintive mew that drifts on the light breeze. Less quixotic, however, carrion crows at intervals peck at roadkill, flattened pheasant poults that have wandered from their pens, short-circuiting their fate, and their keeper's aspirations of them making it past the end of September when the shooting season opens.

DS Leyton makes an indecipherable warning sound.

They have rounded a bend to meet a steep rise; ahead are two cyclists – a couple, perhaps in their early sixties. First is a man, bent over, off his seat, pedalling like hell in bottom gear. As they give him a wide berth they see he is gasping and red-faced, at the limits of his faculties. Still – he lifts a hand to thank them for their consideration – and wobbles precariously for his trouble.

Fifty yards further is the man's wife or partner. By contrast she pedals steadily; she is poised and upright. With hardly a hair out of place, she gazes about, serenely taking in her surroundings.

'It's electric.'

It is DS Jones that makes the observation.

'Cor – that poor old geezer got the short straw.'

DS Jones ponders.

'Still, he was the one getting the good exercise.'

DS Leyton frowns doubtfully.

'Coronary, more like – and not much of the scenery, by the look of it.'

He inspects his rear-view mirror, but they have already turned a corner, and the couple are no longer in sight.

DS Jones has reverted to tracking their progress.

'We're close by.'

They swing around more sharp bends, then dip to cross a small gill with its tumbling beck briefly glittering; rising again, gnarled hawthorns in bloom cluster around the glimpse of a ruin, close to the road – an old field barn of stone and slate built into the uneven hillside.

'Whoa!'

DS Leyton brakes, but too late – they have passed a narrow entrance. He reverses urgently, crossing his fingers that the battery-powered lady has not caught up.

A rutted track winds up and round the barn to reveal a small single-storey stone cottage in poor repair. There is an entrenchment of moss on the roof slates; the window and door frames are peeling and the exposed wood crumbling with rot.

There are no signs of life – no washing hanging, no woodpile with logs half cut – but at least two dogs are barking from somewhere behind the cottage – and at one side, under a dilapidated lean-to, parked nose-in is an equally dilapidated short wheelbase Land Rover – from its plate, DS Leyton calculates, a model pre-dating the Defender suffix that arrived in 1990 for marketing purposes. The roof rack, rear ladder, sprung step and tow plate are all well rusted.

DS Leyton turns off his engine; they wait.

They have done some homework.

In checking Billy Higson's details – in part to get his address – they know this is his registered vehicle. It is insured and has a valid MOT. Perhaps to their surprise.

For he has a criminal record.

His fingerprints are therefore on file.

Part of the waiting, therefore, concerns such a matter. They hope at any moment for a message. But there has been an unforeseen delay. A computer glitch.

They can only wait so long.

DS Leyton now remarks.

'Suggests he's in. His motor's here. His dogs are here.'

DS Jones unfastens her seatbelt.

'Shall we?'

They climb out, and approach and knock at the door.

There is no answer.

The dogs, which have fallen silent, set up again.

DS Leyton tilts his head to indicate he will look at the Land Rover. Its owner may be elusive, but it remains one of their priorities.

DS Jones hears him moan – it is a squash and a squeeze between the vehicle and the side wall of the cottage.

She tries looking into the left-hand of two small windows placed either side of the door – but she is thwarted by dingy curtains drawn across – a bedroom, perhaps.

She moves to the other side. Now grime and the sun's reflection impair her vision. She activates the torch on her mobile, and presses her forehead to the glass, on tiptoes. Straining, something gains her attention.

'What the hell's thour game?'

She spins about, sliding her handset into her back pocket.

A man is within three yards of her – how long has he been there? He seems to have approached catlike over the dry earth of the farm track.

She recognises him from the photograph in *Fell Running* – there is consistency in distastefully scanty running gear, wiriness, sweat.

His stance is aggressive – when surely this slight girl could pose no possible threat. "Can I help thee, lass?" might have been a more amenable salutation from a local with nothing to hide, and – as is often the case in such encounters – reasons to impress.

But she reads the situation through professional eyes. There is his hostile expression. The provocative words. Not least – that he is a potential suspect in a possible case of unlawful killing.

And, seeing through his eyes – the unmarked car – no uniform to indicate her status – and, for a second no back-up – she has no choice but to brandish her police credentials.

'DS Jones, Cumbria CID.'

The man, leaning forwards as if ready to spring, now goes back on his heels. His dark, close-set eyes survey her; she becomes conscious of her tight jeans and thin woollen top.

But with a grunt, DS Leyton appears – prising himself from between the car and the wall, and looking suitably belligerent – he has overheard the inauspicious welcome.

He gives a sign to her – just a half shake of the head – he is saying his inspection is inconclusive.

'This is my colleague, DS Leyton.'

A momentary standoff.

But DS Jones is frustrated. They have not got off on the best foot. She moves quickly to recover the situation.

'It *is* Mr Higson?'

Now he eyes them both.

'Aye.'

'Is it convenient to speak with you for two minutes?'

Her choice of words is astute – first the suggestion that it is at his option (therefore they are not after him, in which case they would have told him they *intend* to speak with him) – and second that the interview will be brief – which suggests it to be of small importance.

Nonetheless – for the police – it is a potentially critical moment. For the wrongdoer – caught on the hop – an unguarded reaction can be like the apocryphal picture that is worth a thousand words.

They watch him with practised casualness.

He is a little above average height. He is bandy legged, his frame slightly bowed. But the tension in his rangy limbs ebbs. He puts his left hand on his hip and with his right mops perspiration from his brow. He is breathing rapidly, but in the controlled way of an athlete accustomed to recovery, the post-race replenishment of oxygen debt.

'I've got wuk to do. There's a gather at Little Mell Fell.'

DS Jones takes a step forward.

'It is just two minutes.'

He shrugs, faintly.

'Howay, then.'

He has his feet firmly planted, and shows no inclination to conduct the interview anywhere other than on the spot.

DS Jones takes a moment to collect her wits. They have crafted a questioning route – so difficult when they do not want to put a suspect on the defensive. For even an entirely innocent person will incline towards evasion.

'We're looking for possible witnesses to a fatal road accident that occurred at around 7 a.m. on Monday at Honister Hause. A runner was in collision with a passing vehicle. You may have seen or heard our appeal in the local media.'

Thus, they show their hand – but hopefully not that they might suspect him.

Billy Higson perhaps just raises his head – in a faint acknowledgement – as if he is aware.

'Why would I know owt about it?'

DS Jones indicates politely with an open hand towards him.

'I believe you're currently in training for the Bob Graham Round?'

'Aye.'

'We're speaking with people who could have been in the vicinity, route-finding for the anniversary event. Mr Sinclair was also training – and was struck at the crossing point.'

'Well, I weren't.' It seems he refers directly to the location. 'Monday morning I were running with oor Jimmy – he's one of us pacers. We did the three north tops from Threlkeld.'

DS Jones stores the intelligence to relate to Skelgill, though she knows the northern section of the round to be discrete from that which crosses Honister Pass, and Threlkeld a good fifteen miles by road from the latter.

'Jimmy is – your brother?'

'Aye.'

She notes there is no invitation – by way of information – to check this fact. But she opts not to press for such.

'The victim of the accident was a Mr Sebastian Sinclair – did you know him?'

'Nay. Can't say I did.'

But this time the lack of information is accompanied by a brief glance down to one side.

'Do you know of any other runners who might have been there?'

The man's dark eyes return to meet her gaze.

'I plough me own furrow.'

DS Jones nods patiently. She glances at her colleague, and there is the suggestion that their work here is done.

'Well, thank you for your time, sir. We shan't keep you any longer.'

They begin to drift towards DS Leyton's car – but the man stands his ground and DS Jones seems to have an afterthought. 'Mr Higson, given your knowledge of the fells – what do you think about the likelihood of there being witnesses at Honister Hause?'

Billy Higson regards her, his eyes hunted now, as if he doubts the collaborative intent underlying her question.

'Wainwright tickers park there – saves half t' climb up Gable.'

The suggestion is reasonable, albeit one of which they are aware – and it is plain from his tone – he might have as well replied, that's your job, not mine.

As they depart, Billy Higson lingers, watching until their car is out of sight, and listening until it is beyond earshot.

Casually, he strolls over to the window into which DS Jones had peered; he mirrors her actions in looking through the glass.

Next he rounds the end of the cottage and, with a little more ease than DS Leyton, slips between the wall and the Land Rover.

When he emerges he produces a mobile phone from a pouch on the shoulder strap of his camelback.

Scowling, he picks out a number, raising the handset to his ear when it answers.

'Jim? Can thee hear us? Listen on.'

'You go first, girl.'
'Sure?'
'Yeah – I can tell you've got one up on me.'
'Really? Was it that obvious?'
DS Jones seems a little disconcerted that her body language is apparently so easily read.
DS Leyton is concentrating hard upon the curves ahead.
'Not obvious – not to him. But obvious to me – you didn't ask him about the magazine. And you didn't press him on his alibi.'
Now she nods eagerly, as if glad to admit to a small sense of excitement.
'Through the window of the cottage – on a kind of desk – there was a stack of them. *Fell Running.*'
'What – like a collection – back copies?'
She looks across at her colleague, her expression earnest.
'They were all the June edition. I counted five.'
DS Leyton contrives a face of suitable interest – and then a slightly hysterical laugh.
'Cor – reckon the geezer's sending out threats to all his competitors?'
He is not entirely serious, and makes it plain in his tone – but the suggestion is not so much irrational as unlikely, in the sense that Billy Higson is supposedly a shoo-in for the title, and why would he need to do such a thing?
DS Jones presses her palms together in a gesture resembling prayer.
'I've been trying to think of an explanation – devil's advocate. I suppose the obvious thing is that, if a glossy magazine has published a feature about you, you might buy more copies for your own purposes – to keep as trophies, to frame – or to give to relatives or friends.'
DS Leyton is accepting of the argument.
'Yeah, you might do that.' He puts in a minor swerve to avoid a pheasant and checks the success of his manoeuvre in his rear-view mirror. 'But it still don't stop him having sent one to Sinclair.'
DS Jones taps the tips of her fingers together.
'Did you believe him – what he said about not knowing Sebastian Sinclair – and being with his brother?'
'Sly fox like that – you'd never know. Going by his record, he's not a geezer I'd trust any further than I could throw.'

Billy Higson's rap sheet might not set alarm bells ringing in the context of violent crimes against the person – but what they have gleaned is a history of petty deception over livestock exchanged and payments due. In short, theft and fraud. Having met the man, the detectives might be entitled to think him quite capable of backing up his misdemeanours with intimidation, were it to prove necessary.

As for his statements, that DS Jones for good reason left unchallenged, they both know there will be discreet inquiries to make.

After a pause, DS Jones passes over the baton.

'Okay – what about you – the Land Rover?'

DS Leyton performs the characteristic retraction of his head into his broad shoulders that can be a prelude to disappointment. He exhales heavily, before making an intake of breath in order to elaborate.

'It's got a whacking great bull bar on the front. Homemade job, by the look of it – probably illegal, except while it's off the road. Chuck in the flippin' great bumper – and there ain't no bodywork that would be exposed to a dent. There's plenty of marks and rust spots and flaking paint – but I couldn't see any signs of a human impact. I reckon it would knock a geezer over without a scratch on the metal. It would need to go into the lab – under the microscope – before you might find any trace of tissue. And that'd probably be sheep.'

DS Jones nods reflectively.

'And we're some way off from being able to do that.'

DS Leyton shrugs, another from his repertoire – but he sounds a note of optimism.

'Makes those fingerprints on that *Fell Running* magazine all the more vital.'

DS Jones is prompted by the suggestion – and quickly checks her messages.

'I have a signal – but nothing through yet.'

DS Leyton produces a somewhat rueful clicking noise with his tongue.

'It's probably my ginger scone prints what's held them up.' DS Jones does not respond, and he continues reflectively. 'Quite fancy a ginger scone, come to think of it. I wonder if that catering van's back on the A66 – that layby's near the Applethwaite junction.'

He realises DS Jones has her head turned towards him. She has one hand against the back of her neck.

He chuckles, in affected self-reproach.

'I know – now I'm the one sounding like the Guvnor.'

115

But DS Jones seems to grimace, and tips back her head, as if her vertebrae are uncomfortably stiff.

'You alright, girl?'

'Thanks, I'll be fine – I think I slept awkwardly. Nothing a tea break won't cure.'

15. MORAG II

Applethwaite – 11.25 a.m. Thursday 6 June

CONTEMPLATING IN SILENCE, DS Leyton stares at the half-consumed Buttermere biscuit he holds rather fastidiously between chunky forefinger and thumb. Cut in the shape of a sheep (he thinks), just the body is left. By his side, DS Jones scrolls intently through the much-awaited message, forwarded by DC Watson.

DS Leyton is first to utter.

'Just when we thought we were getting somewhere.'

DS Jones compresses her lips; she shares his frustration. The shadow of Billy Higson has loomed large on their horizon since yesterday afternoon, and larger still for the past hour; now it seems they must reconsider.

DS Leyton dips his biscuit in his disposable cup of tea – he holds it perilously poised in order to speak.

'Run that by me again, will you, Emma?'

DS Jones breaks from her concentration.

'Sure. I was just reading the longer version. The crux is that there are two sets of unidentified prints on the outside of the magazine. One set must belong to Jules. None of the identified prints are those of Billy Higson. The only prints on the inside spread about the Bob Graham Round are those of Sebastian Sinclair.'

DS Leyton eats silently for a few moments.

'So, what's that telling us – that Sinclair underlined those words? And Higson didn't have anything to do with it?'

DS Jones does not answer immediately. She gazes, unseeingly now, at her mobile phone. She is conscious of the conflict she suffers – the bald facts versus intuition. Or is the latter simply wishful thinking, when a plausible solution was beginning to present itself? DS Leyton has interpreted the bald facts – but he sounds no more convinced than she feels.

She looks up, and watches as the young couple who run the catering van hand down eagerly anticipated burgers to hungry motorists; they are doing a roaring trade.

'I think we shouldn't jump the gun. If someone knew what they were doing, any explanation is possible. If a person made a threat with serious intent, they would likely know to cover their tracks.'

DS Leyton, crunching the last of his snack undipped, nods until he can speak.

'Right enough, there, girl. After all – if Sinclair was deliberately mown down – then whoever's done it *did* cover their tracks.'

But DS Jones exhales, and hints at hopelessness.

'The unidentified prints on the cover could belong to a member of staff at the wholesaler, or a shop assistant, or a customer who picked it up and put it back on the shelf. Or someone at Sinclair Design, come to that.'

DS Leyton is not discouraged.

'We can ask his missus if he normally got a copy. That might cast some light on it.'

He reaches to tap the small paper bag on the dashboard between them.

'Don't forget your biscuit.'

Returning from the queue she had found the message, and has since been diverted.

Now she grins at her colleague.

'Don't say it, Emma – I sound like *you-know-who*. Except I wasn't angling for leftovers. Got me waistline to consider. Just thinking of the time. I can drive slowly – they're good for dunking.'

DS Jones looks like it might not be her preferred option; she knows the nature of the lanes to come. She foresees thrills and spills of an undesirable kind. Instead she picks up her tea and presses firmly upon the sip lid.

'It's okay – I'll save it. If I don't get round to eating it I'll no doubt find a good home for it later.'

DS Leyton gives her a knowing wink, and sets about getting them moving; Applethwaite lies not far away.

When the detectives arrive at the converted farmhouse they find just Morag Sinclair at home. Indeed, she announces that she is alone and that her sister is grocery shopping, having taken the boys to school. The white Vauxhall is absent from the driveway.

DS Jones notes that her hair is washed and brushed and an outfit of new-looking jeans and a complementary blouse in blue-and-white check is more becoming than the ill-fitting slacks and clashing cardigan of yesterday.

And her demeanour seems a little less dulled. Perhaps one additional day through the cycle of shock and grief. When they were introduced to her, she had been beleaguered by paperwork. Although they could not say she had been unforthcoming. She had opened doors to doubts regarding her marriage, and to the relationship between her husband and Frank Sinclair.

This time they are immediately offered refreshments, but when DS Jones declines she turns to face them beneath the gloom of the untidy hallway, as though any business can be transacted here.

She regards them with a certain neutrality – when she might reasonably expect that their unheralded presence means there is some news of import.

There is the expression 'holding it together' – and DS Jones wonders how much of that is going on beneath the surface. For her part, she is conscious of difficult questions they must ask before they take their leave. And there is no easy way to broach the subject.

'Mrs Sinclair, we have no further news regarding the incident. Therefore, while it is understandable – if reprehensible – that someone may not come forward, it also means we have to take seriously the possibility that your husband was killed by a deliberate act.'

'What?'

Perhaps for the first time in their encounters, here is an unbridled reaction. In her tone and features there seems a genuine expression of disbelief.

DS Jones waits for as long as she feasibly can – and it is just enough to elicit a further question.

'But why would someone do that?'

She stares first at DS Jones and then at DS Leyton – as though one or both of them must bear evidence of their preposterous claim.

DS Leyton carries their spare copy of *Fell Running*. He offers it.

But it is DS Jones who continues the dialogue.

'Mrs Sinclair – did your husband get this magazine?'

Morag Sinclair takes the periodical and holds it before her, two handed.

'Yes. I expect it's in his studio.'

Then, seeming to understand she should return it to DS Leyton, she does so.

'May we see?'

'But – why?'

In turning to the magazine, their response has been oblique at best – but DS Jones deflects further.

'I can explain in a moment – but first it would help if you could show us.'

They are led upstairs, onto a landing with various rooms off, and the same disorder of furniture as the ground floor, and strewn toys and clothing; and then up a small flight that winds into a converted attic area. It is properly floored, but the rafters are exposed and the decking uninsulated. The air is cool, and there is faint smell of mustiness. Much of the space is taken up by the typical contents of any loft, crates, boxes, suitcases, the ubiquitous rocking horse in deep shadow – but in one corner soft light diffuses through a dormer window set into the pitched roof, and here there is a wide desk amidst a cluster of small cabinets and shelves.

As they approach, the view reveals itself: the rising slopes of Skiddaw, wooded in the immediate vicinity, giving way to an open fellside of spring-green bracken that merges into burnt umber heather and grey screes above.

DS Leyton is prompted to remark.

'It's like chalk and cheese from Carlisle city centre. Gets the old creative juices flowing, I shouldn't wonder. He must have worked here a lot.'

'Mainly weekends, actually.'

Morag Sinclair's correction seems to be delivered with a hint of acerbity.

DS Jones has been taking in the more immediate surroundings. The desk is bare, except for an architect lamp, and a cable that trails from a printer at one side, and there is a plug bank with several chargers. On one wall of the dormer a calendar is hung, displaying a landscape photograph that she recognises as the iconic view along Wastwater, with Great Gable at its head, resplendent on a summer's morning; the month is correctly turned to June. On the opposite wall is a framed photograph of about twenty young people posed against a wooded backdrop in a kind of team assembly – they wield weapons, and she realises it is a paintball event – the company, presumably. The faces are daubed with camouflage paint, and the individual images too small to make any easy identifications.

Then she spies the magazine.

It sits on a shelf, on top of a pile of earlier editions. It is still in its clear polythene postal wrap – as are several of the copies in the stack.

She picks it up and reads the addressee details. She displays it to her colleague; he nods.

'So he received it here, by mail.'

DS Leyton's remark is an observation rather than a question, although it prompts a reply from Morag Sinclair.

'He took out a subscription after they decided they were going to do the Bob Graham Round.'

While the detectives are pondering any implications of this, and perhaps thinking what to ask, Morag Sinclair pre-empts them with a simple question.

'Why did you want to know about the magazine?'

DS Jones places the unopened item on the desk surface.

'We have reason to believe it was used to pass a message to your husband. The copy in question was in his office desk.'

They watch her closely – but she is not diverted in pursuit of her goal.

'What kind of message?'

DS Jones flashes a brief glance at her colleague.

'An anonymous suggestion that he should pull out of the race. It could be interpreted as a threat.'

For a second time, a constriction of the woman's features reveals some small internal jolt; it might almost be an expression of fear.

'What did it say?' She looks with trepidation at the copy held by DS Leyton, as though it still bears the warning.

But DS Jones remains composed.

'Just that. That he should drop out, else there would be consequences for him.' Morag Sinclair inhales to speak, but DS Jones anticipates the question. 'The consequences were unspecified.'

Morag Sinclair turns towards the window and gazes out. Standing stiffly, she folds her arms.

'Are you telling me this is connected to what happened to him?'

DS Jones takes half a step sideways, the better to observe her.

'We don't know – but you'll appreciate, given this knowledge – we can't ignore the possibility.'

The woman is staring, almost manically – as if a myriad of images are running amok across her mind's eye.

So much so that DS Jones asks her directly.

'What is coming to mind?'

'What? *Och* – I don't know – I mean – do you have some idea of who it was?'

DS Jones again trades glances with DS Leyton. What they exchange is a recognition that Morag Sinclair is very much to the point – her questioning of them has been far more incisive and linear than theirs of her.

DS Jones, however, is obliged for the time being to prevaricate.

'Naturally there are many competitors in the event – and we have to eliminate each of those. Then there are business and personal contacts.'

'Are you saying you think it wasn't to do with the race?'

The woman's acuity remains undiminished.

'We are in fact exploring a variety of avenues, it is –'

The woman turns to face her, dropping her arms stiffly to her sides.

'You don't think it was me?'

Under such rapid fire, DS Jones has limited options of reply.

'Why would we think that, Mrs Sinclair?'

But DS Jones is conscious that her response is not ideal, and she senses DS Leyton shifting a little awkwardly on his feet. Morag Sinclair continues.

'Then why are you here? Why are you telling me – *questioning* me?'

It is as if the realisation has now fully dawned upon her that she has been the subject of subtle investigation – and now there seems a danger that she will withdraw her co-operation.

DS Leyton steps in to offer some relief to his colleague.

'Madam – I know full well this is a terrible blow for a family to suffer.' Still holding the magazine he folds his hands across his chest, left over right, the former revealing his wedding band. There is the suggestion that in sharing her domestic status he empathises most strongly. 'We're here because you're his wife. And if someone has been making threats against him, you're the person he most likely will have confided in.'

Morag Sinclair's very first reaction – just the hint of a grimace – suggests disagreement with this sentiment. But then perhaps she accepts the argument, and regards him earnestly. She shakes her head, her eyes unblinking.

'I know nothing of it.'

They wait in silence, and she finally has something to add. She casts a hand towards the copy of *Fell Running* held by DS Leyton.

'Are you sure it wasn't Frank Lawson – just playing the fool?'

This time the detectives do not look at one another. The reality is that they have not exactly considered this angle – at least, not the casual interpretation that Morag Sinclair has placed upon it. But DS Jones, rather than fall onto the defensive, takes the opportunity to recover their lost ground.

'We shall of course meet with Mr Lawson on his return from the USA. We have to eliminate him from various aspects of the inquiry. But I'm afraid we have to eliminate everybody who might feasibly be concerned – and not only competitors. Whoever could have sent the message. And whoever may have been present at the time of your husband's death at 7 a.m. on Monday. Otherwise we cannot function. And – to come back to your point – yes, it does include yourself.'

DS Jones's calm words, carefully and professionally enunciated, must sink in – for Morag Sinclair gives a perfunctory nod, an indication that she understands the basic principles of police procedure.

She waves a hand, rather aimlessly.

'Naturally, I was here.' Her tone is one of resignation. 'At that time of day I am preparing the boys' things for nursery and school. Their uniform, PE kit, snacks and packed lunches. Then getting them up – dressed, fed – and taking them to Keswick. They both attend St Catherine's – it has kindergarten and primary up to year two.'

DS Jones nods agreeably. She has no need to provoke the woman by asking questions that can be impartially corroborated elsewhere.

'Did you speak with Mr Sinclair before he left?'

Morag Sinclair looks away from DS Jones before she replies.

'He slept in one of the spare rooms – he was leaving at some ungodly hour and said there was no point in his disturbing me. He said he'd booked a taxi to take them from Keswick to Wasdale. As I told the first officer to whom I spoke, I assumed after the run he would drive up to the office.'

The detectives nod in tandem, in a kind of commiseration – but she does not show any sign of appreciation.

There remains a pressing question, and DS Jones now picks up the thread.

'Mrs Sinclair – speaking of the firm – is there anything of which you are aware that could have caused someone to have a grudge against your husband?'

But the woman merely shakes her head.

'I'm the wrong person to ask. You would have to speak with Victoria Lawson.'

'How about the event – did your husband mention any of the other runners?'

'Only Frank Lawson.'

'Is it possible he would have preferred Mr Lawson not to run?'

'Far from it. As I intimated yesterday – Sebastian would have wanted to beat Frank. That would have been his number one priority.'

DS Jones nods.

'Did they advertise what they were doing? I'm thinking of sponsorship, for example. Or posting their training progress on social media.'

Morag Sinclair gives a terse shake of the head.

'Sebastian didn't want to count any chickens, as he put it. His nature was to be a dark horse. But I can't speak for Frank. I expect he bragged about it to people he met.'

DS Jones looks inquiringly at her colleague, but it appears he has nothing to add. They have more or less exhausted their purpose in coming, and while they have covered the key issues – not least in identifying the magazine subscription – she feels dissatisfied with their more subjective findings. And they will have to wait to ask Frank Lawson whether their running plan for Monday had been announced.

Her gaze wanders to the calendar on the side of the dormer. She notices that in the small section allocated to the grid of weekdays and dates, 12th and 13th June have been ringed in red ink. The dates of the Bob Graham Round anniversary challenge, running overnight from one day into the next. But there is also a red circle around the date of the following Sunday, 16th June.

She realises that Morag Sinclair is watching her – indeed has identified what she is doing – and she finds herself raising the question that has sprung to mind. She points.

'I assume this is the race – but do you know what this refers to – on the sixteenth?'

Morag Sinclair narrows her eyes – it might be an entirely genuine reaction – that this is the first time she has even noticed the annotations. She shakes her head.

'I have no idea.'

'Do you mind if I – ?'

DS Jones reaches for the calendar and unhooks it from its nail without waiting for consent. She lays it on the desk and turns methodically through the pages. Passing the cover sheet, halfway through, she realises it is a company production; it bears the logo of Sinclair Design.

There are no other dates marked.

'Hold on a mo.' It is DS Leyton who chips in. He is flicking through a small pocket diary. 'Yeah – here we go – sixteenth of June – it's Father's Day.'

He makes a self-deprecating clearing of his throat, and a rather sheepish expression captures his features, as if he is embarrassed at having drawn attention to his own station in life. He grins.

'It's never yet got me out of the washing-up – especially after a Sunday roast.'

DS Jones is smiling at him, but when she looks at Morag Sinclair she sees something of a pained expression.

'I'm sorry – did you have something planned?'

The woman may try to answer – but she seems dry-mouthed – and, just as she might respond, her name is called from below. Ascending footsteps quickly follow on the bare boards of the attic staircase, and her sister appears. Seeing the detectives, she stops short.

'Och – here you are – I was worried – the front door was unlocked.'

Morag Sinclair takes a couple of steps towards her. Seeing them together, the shared characteristics of height and hair and carriage leave DS Jones in no doubt of their lineage; though the stockier, elder Shona Mackay at this moment seems the more resolute of the pair. And now she regards the visitors with suspicion, as protective instincts plainly kick in.

However, Morag Sinclair is quick to interject.

'They say Sebastian received a threat – to withdraw from the race – or face consequences. They have to eliminate everyone.'

That Morag Sinclair relays this headline news, without preamble, might seem designed to assuage her sister's apparent antipathy towards the detectives – that they are merely here to do their job – but, if so, it only elicits a more extreme reaction. Shona Mackay steps between her sister and those she plainly regards as interlopers. Her gaze darts about, taking in the magazine and the calendar that lie upon the desk.

'I shall have to ask you to leave. My sister is in no condition to be interrogated.' She turns to Morag Sinclair. 'You know you don't have to answer questions. Not at any time.'

Both officers are somewhat taken aback by the intervention – and even Morag Sinclair looks unsettled by her sister's vehemence. She moves to broker a little truce.

'Shona works as a lawyer. She is only thinking of my best interests.'

DS Jones takes a step forward, the better to engage Shona Mackay with unwavering eye contact.

'That Mr Sinclair may have been threatened is a matter we have to treat extremely seriously. Naturally Mrs Sinclair is the first person we should inform – for reasons that I'm sure I don't need to explain.'

Shona Mackay's lips compress into a fine line. That she is being lectured by the younger woman cannot escape her – but DS Jones succeeds in tone to suggest that she recognises her professional status.

'We will, of course, keep you abreast of any developments – and fully appreciate whatever cooperation you feel able to provide.'

The latter statement is designed to encompass both sisters, in amenable terms – but it is not without some degree of awkwardness that the detectives take their leave, and it is with some relief that they drive away, in silence for the first minute or so.

'That was interesting, Emma.'

DS Jones nods reflectively.

'The trouble is, it's wrapped up in a tragedy, isn't it?'

DS Leyton glances at his colleague.

'You mean Father's Day, and all that? I reckon I put my foot in it, there.'

DS Jones frowns, but she shakes her head.

'If we don't, who will? Her sister knows that. What's the betting she's a defence counsel?'

DS Leyton murmurs in agreement.

'Talk about over-protective. I expect she'll be grilling Morag Sinclair about what we asked her. But she can't think we'd suspect her of being involved.'

When DS Jones does not reply, after a few moments DS Leyton offers a prompt.

'You ain't thinking along those lines, are you?'

Again, there is a pause.

'If you mean could Morag Sinclair have been the person who knocked down Sebastian Sinclair, then I think she could. I haven't detected anything about her manner or their apparent relationship that would make me say definitely not.'

DS Leyton takes a hand off the steering wheel to ruffle his hair.

'I see what you're saying, girl – I get that feeling, too. But – sounds to me like she's got a cast-iron alibi – and it'll be easy enough to check it out.'

Now DS Jones is the one to shoot a quick sideways glance across the car.

'But will it? Sebastian Sinclair was struck at about seven a.m. School drop-off is what, eight-thirty? Honister Pass is only twenty-five minutes from Applethwaite.'

'What about the nippers – she'd have had to leave them in bed?'

'Or strap them in the back. They probably would sleep.'

DS Leyton screws up his features – in part it is a burst of sunlight through a gap in the roadside trees – he reaches to pull down the visor.

'There'd be the crash. The incident. And there was no damage to the car that she uses.'

DS Jones, too, is bothered by the glare of the sun. She lifts a hand to shade her eyes. Her gaze, however, appears to have no particular focus.

'The minor injuries were mainly to his hands and forearms. It's possible he cushioned the impact. There may be no dent.'

DS Leyton gives a little involuntary laugh.

'Cor blimey – you've thought it all through, girl.'

'Actually, I feel like I'm thinking on the hoof. I know it's improbable. I'm just preparing for the interrogation when I pass this information on.'

DS Leyton nods slowly several times. He does not answer immediately, though he lifts an index finger from the steering wheel.

'Tell you what, Emma. What you say about those timings. Right enough, someone could have run him over – and then driven back to get on with their day, without anyone else noticing. But if it wasn't opportunistic – spur of the moment – they'd have to have known Sinclair and Lawson's plans. To lie in wait. It narrows the field, don't you reckon?'

'I do.'

16. SINCLAIR DESIGN II

Carlisle – 2.40 p.m. Thursday 6 June

'RIGHT, THANK YOU, Mrs Lawson. We'll look forward to seeing you and Mr Lawson tomorrow. Please let us know if there's any problem with his flight.'

DS Jones ends the call, but remains staring at the screen of her mobile.

'She's working from home, again.'

DS Leyton, occupied by watching a red traffic light, steals a quick glance at his colleague.

'Don't suppose we should read too much into that, especially not nowadays.'

DS Jones nods and slips the handset into her satchel.

'She's going to call Jules now – and ask her to accommodate us. She said we're welcome to use her office – apparently they've got clients in the main meeting room.'

DS Leyton makes a murmur of assent.

'I didn't quite get the gist of what she said about the training runs.'

DS Jones tilts her head a little from side to side.

'More or less the same as Morag Sinclair. One of Sebastian Sinclair's conditions was that they didn't make a song and dance about it. So they've posted nothing on social media.'

'Not even Frank Lawson?'

'She said he's probably told people in passing – at his golf club, business clients – but just informal chat – to impress, no doubt.'

'Did she sound suspicious – that you were asking?'

DS Jones does not answer immediately. She replays the conversation in her mind. Having previously exchanged numbers, Victoria Lawson could not have been surprised by who was calling – she did not have to take the call. Compared to two days ago she sounded a little more buoyant – but still there was a tremor in her voice, as if underlying distress could break through at any moment. She had asked about their progress and was disappointed when met with ineffectual platitudes. But there will be the chance tomorrow to broach the subject of the threat to Sebastian Sinclair – something the detectives have agreed they want to do in person, and when both the Lawsons are present. She had not questioned DS Jones's request that they would like to speak to the person who handles the mail.

DS Jones now shakes her head in response.

'No – not at all, I'd say. Something, perhaps – but not suspicion.'

But DS Leyton has skidded to a halt in Portland Square, and is now craning over his shoulder, straining the button of his shirt collar as he performs a rapid reverse manoeuvre.

'Handy – that's our private parking space free, again.'

They are shown into Victoria Lawson's ground-floor office by the same flamboyant receptionist (today's ensemble featuring the creative use of brightly patched denim, and the hairstyle a topknot) and invited to sit at an arrangement of minimalistic Bauhaus armchairs that surrounds a matching chrome-framed coffee table, set into the expansive bay window. They accept the offer of refreshments, and are informed that Jules will be down shortly.

The room is immediately off the entrance hall, overlooking the front. It is a grand salon, with a high ceiling and intricate cornices, and an original fireplace; but it is sparsely furnished, with stylish artworks on each of the walls.

'Reminds me of their house.'

It is DS Jones's observation.

'I suppose if she's in charge, she gets to pick the decor.'

DS Jones, rather than respond, rises and crosses to the large desk at the far side of the room. Upon it rests an iMac and keyboard and mouse – but nothing else except a copy of the calendar they have recently viewed at Applethwaite. Evidently its design incorporates a triangular cardboard frame to enable desktop use.

DS Jones picks it up, and her colleague watches as she stares, frowning for a moment, before she begins to turn quickly through the pages. He is about to question her actions when the door swings open – and there is the girl Jules holding it for the receptionist, who carries a tray with coffees as offered, and a jug of water and four glasses. She closes the door and follows the receptionist to the table.

DS Leyton rises and DS Jones replaces the calendar and joins the group.

Once again, a powerful feature is the appearance of Jules – and the contrast of her closely tailored dark outfit and mass of hair, both in itself, and by comparison to the tall and colourful figure of the receptionist, whose seventies-style platforms have the wearer towering above all of them.

But it has not escaped the detectives that there are four glasses on the tray – and now Jules provides an explanation as they sit and drinks are dispensed.

'This is Terri. You met briefly yesterday, of course. Terri deals with the mail.'

Terri forces a nervous smile.

DS Jones moves to ease any tension.

'Excellent. In that case, Terri – could you please tell us how the mail is handled?'

'Aye. I'm usually first in. It's normally here by then.'

Terri's accent is local. A husky voice seems not entirely congruent with red lipstick.

Terri gestures with large hands.

'I separate any junk mail and then drop the rest around to whoever it's addressed to. If they're not in, everyone's got a pigeon hole in the common room. Or if they have an office or a regular desk – I put it there.'

'What about Mr Sinclair, then – what would you do if he weren't in?'

Terri nods, gaining confidence.

'Aye – I would leave that on his desk. Unless it were something marked urgent – I'd probably get Vicky or Jules to look it over.'

DS Jones retrieves a copy of *Fell Running* from her shoulder bag.

'Do you recognise this magazine?'

Before she has even finished speaking, Terri is nodding, with some enthusiasm.

'Aye, I do – I climb myself. I get *Climber*, and *Alpinist* – and *Summit for Nowt* – that's more of a local Lakes newsletter. I don't get *Fell Running*. I'm aware of it – but me, I'm too much of a lummox for running.'

DS Jones smiles politely at the self-deprecation.

'Okay – so, does this magazine arrive here by monthly subscription?'

Now Terri makes a face of puzzlement.

'Not to my knowledge.'

'It would be delivered in a clear polythene wrap. You would still see the cover.'

Terri gives a shake of the head.

'In that case, nay – I would definitely notice, wouldn't I?'

Terri glances at Jules, as if seeking her confirmation.

Jules begins to nod – but DS Jones now addresses her directly. She raises the magazine.

'Have you mentioned this?'

Jules' pale grey eyes regard DS Jones evenly; she understands the question refers to the original incident with the magazine. She gives a shake of the head, the movement passing in a wave through her long tresses.

'No.'

When she does not elaborate, DS Jones turns to Terri.

'Your colleague noticed Mr Sinclair reading a copy – of this, the June edition – on Friday afternoon. He was at his work station on the top floor. We are particularly interested in tracing how he got hold of it. We know he didn't bring it in from his home. It's possible that he bought it from a local newsagent – but we think it may have been delivered.'

It is plain that perplexity is shared between the two being questioned. Why are the police so interested? It seems such a mundane aspect. But they seem to know it is not for them to pry. They should take the inquiry at face value.

And now Terri comes good. The big hands clap together.

'There was a brown C4 envelope for Seb on Friday.' Terri glances briefly at Jules, and then in earnest at each of the detectives. 'That might have had a magazine inside. I remember that – and there was *Design Weekly* and *Creative Review*.'

DS Jones again refers to the copy of *Fell Running*.

'C4 – that holds A4, yes?'

'Aye – unfolded. It might even have been foolscap.'

'So it would be the right size. And it felt about the right weight?'

'Aye.'

'The envelope – was it postmarked? And handwritten or typed?'

Terri's face suddenly falls – and it is clear that this level of detail has not been retained. But then a small renaissance, in the form of a click of the fingers of the right hand.

'It was marked Private & Confidential. That caught my eye.'

DS Jones nods, and she senses her colleague shift beside her. It does not escape them how useful the envelope would be.

'Is there any chance the envelope will have been kept?'

Terri hesitates to answer, and is forestalled by Jules.

131

'Unfortunately not on a Friday.' She turns and indicates to a green-topped bin tucked unobtrusively at one side of Victoria Lawson's desk. 'The cleaners put out all the paper recycling on a Friday night.'

DS Jones ponders for a moment, and then continues to question Jules.

'When you noticed Mr Sinclair with the magazine, was he just reading it, or could he have been writing in it – marking points of interest, for example?'

'No – definitely just reading. He was holding it up, and reading intently. He didn't notice me, at first.'

'And he didn't remark about it?'

'No – nothing at all.'

DS Jones opens the magazine where she has it bookmarked, and lays it out on the coffee table so that the others may see.

'Are you aware – indeed, is it widely known – that Mr Sinclair had entered for this event? It's called the Bob Graham Round anniversary challenge.'

Terri makes a sudden exclamation – the sound of surprise conflated with admiration – and stares somewhat wide-eyed.

DS Jones, however, turns to Jules.

'No, sergeant – I didn't know.'

Her intonation rouses Terri.

'Me neither – I don't reckon anyone did. Someone would've said. That's well massive.'

A silence ensues – but while the detectives perhaps review their options, it seems Terri is becoming increasingly self-assured.

'It might explain a thing, though.'

They look interrogatively.

'Aye.' Terri points across to Victoria Lawson's desk. 'The company calendar – that you were looking at when we came in. Seb asked me a question – a climbing question, like.'

DS Jones regards Terri evenly.

'Could you elaborate?'

Terri now jerks a sizeable thumb in an overhead direction.

'It was the one on the wall in the first-floor common room – I think he might have just flipped the month over to June – and it's Great Gable.' Terri hesitates for a moment – perhaps making an assessment of the rather unfit-looking sergeant with the London accent, and his stylishly dressed colleague. 'Great Gable's one of the popular fells – and I'm fairly sure it's on the route of the Bob Graham.'

DS Jones is nodding.

'What did he ask?'

'It was a bit of a technical point.'

'Try us?'

'Aye – well, there's this climbing spot – a stack called Nape's Needle. It's a pinnacle on the southern flank of Great Gable. Actually it's one of the best-known climbs in England – it's like our version of the Inn Pin on Skye. Seb wanted to know if there was a quick direct route from Nape's Needle to the summit, if you were approaching from the southwest.'

'What did you say?'

'I said direct, aye – but not quick – it's either a rock climb up Arrowhead Ridge or a nasty scramble up Little Hell Gate. The names probably tell you all you need to know.'

Terri regards the detectives a little forebodingly.

'And that was it?'

'Aye.'

'Did you think the question was out of character?'

Terri ponders for a moment before giving a shake of the head.

'Nay – not out of character. I knew he liked outdoors stuff. And he knew I climb. I suppose I thought he was going to do some fell walking at the weekend.'

'And you think that was on the first of June that you spoke?'

Terri looks uncertain in this regard. Quickly, Jules rises and crosses to the desk – she picks up the copy of the calendar.

'The first was Saturday.'

Terri nods.

'Must have been the day before – aye, last Friday. It were in the morning.'

DS Jones banks the information for Skelgill.

She watches Jules, who remains at the desk. The girl has difficulty getting the calendar to stand upright. The integral A-frame seems to lack some backbone in its construction. She becomes a little flustered, perhaps conscious of Victoria Lawson's fastidiousness, and Terri joins her to give a hand.

'Another Frank job.'

The muttered aside that escapes Terri's lips reaches the detectives. But DS Jones is already moving to wrap up the meeting. She stands and returns the magazine to her bag, and thanks them for their help and hospitality. She explains they have things to do, and other cases to move forward.

But outside in the hallway, she asks to visit the restroom.

DS Leyton plies her with an innocent-seeming glance; isn't this one of their Guvnor's tactics?

'I'll get the motor started – touch base with HQ.'

DS Jones is directed to the first floor, and the four go their separate ways.

The restroom proves to be a unisex affair, with private cubicles along one wall and washing facilities at a central island. The decoration, striking and eclectic, consists of many posters – perhaps examples of design work created by the agency.

The theme extends to the interior of DS Jones's cubicle – but now she finds herself face-to-face with a much-enlarged enlarged printout of the paintball team photograph that was framed on the side wall of the dormer in Sebastian Sinclair's attic studio.

With such proximity, and the bigger picture, she can clearly make out the faces – there is a happily smiling Victoria, an enigmatic Jules, and – grinning a little inanely – the towering Terri. Between Victoria and Jules is – she realises – Sebastian Sinclair. He seems to be speaking to the camera – maybe calling out 'cheese' to rouse the group. But what strikes DS Jones most is that, although this is the first time she has seen him – other than at the hospital pathology lab – he seems uncannily familiar.

She finds herself staring into the warm brown eyes that fix her own.

For a few moments she is gripped – she is unsure why – and only breaks from the trance when she reaches for her mobile phone and takes a photograph.

And then suddenly there is the sound of a tap – somebody must have entered the restroom without her hearing.

She emerges to find Jules running water onto the cuff of her sweater. The girl looks up. She smiles self-consciously.

'Oh, hi – I spilt some of the coffee.'

The material is too dark to show a stain.

DS Jones begins to wash her hands. But when Jules may speak further, she does not. DS Jones realises she must break the ice.

'How is Mrs Lawson?'

It is a simple question, intoned to avoid leading the witness or implying secret knowledge. But there is the obvious connotation that Victoria Lawson is not back in the office, when cheerleading might be appreciated.

For a second the inquiry appears to strike a chord – but just as quickly as Jules seems ready to be forthcoming, there is a sense that she holds back.

'Are you aware she lost her father in April? It was rather sudden and she was very upset. Obviously there are the children, grandchildren – and her mother being left alone. We were really busy then, as well. I think it was quite stressful – never mind being disturbing for Vicky. And now I suppose this has brought buried feelings back to the surface.'

DS Jones is nodding to indicate her sympathy and understanding – but she has an intuition – this is all very well, but there is more.

She tackles the girl head on.

'Has something come to mind – what I asked you, yesterday?'

The girl swallows and clears her throat. She is leaning forwards over the sink, and her hair covers her features. But then she turns and addresses DS Jones directly.

'This is really tenuous.'

'It doesn't matter.'

'It's probably nothing.'

DS Jones lifts an open palm; the girl should continue.

She nods, and draws stray locks away from her face with the fingers of both hands.

'It was about a month ago, I suppose. I had worked late and was hurrying for my train. When I looked both ways to cross The Crescent I saw Sebastian. There's a private medical practice over on the other side – and he came out – he was concentrating on fitting an envelope into his inside pocket and he didn't notice me.'

DS Jones waits – but realises a prompt is needed.

'And why did you think it was odd?'

Now the girl raises both hands, to indicate their general surroundings.

'You see – we don't have company medical insurance. Seb didn't agree with private healthcare. Everyone gets paid more instead – so they can choose – it's the same with company cars.'

'So, you don't think he would see a private doctor?'

The girl shakes her head. The grey eyes, hitherto mainly composed, show consternation.

'And then, he – *he died.*'

135

*

'Struth, Emma, you look like you've seen a ghost, girl.'

DS Jones sinks down into the passenger seat and pulls the car door to. She turns to her colleague.

'Really?'

'Yeah – just as you came out of the door there – you had me worried for a mo.'

DS Jones grins an apology. She folds her hands together and now cranes to see back up at the building.

'I suppose I did – see a ghost, I mean. There was a copy of that paintball photo in the loo. I was looking at Sebastian Sinclair. I took a photo of it, actually.'

'What was so spooky about it?'

DS Jones shakes her head.

'I don't know. But there is something else.'

She relays her conversation with Jules.

DS Leyton listens with interest – though it is plain he tries to be objective.

'Maybe there was a gents' problem he didn't want to ask the family GP about.'

'Hm. Could be, I suppose.' DS Jones remains pensive, however. She twirls a lock of hair around an index finger. 'This is going to sound vague, but I feel Jules wants to share a burden – but something's keeping her from doing it.'

DS Leyton grins broadly.

'You're right – that does sound vague. But I'll go with your intuition.' He gives a shrug, holding up his shoulders for a moment before relaxing them. 'Maybe she just had a crush on him – maybe even a bit more than that.'

He leaves the scenario otherwise unexplored.

There is silence for a few moments, until DS Jones springs her second revelation.

'That calendar on Victoria Lawson's desk – there was a scribbled note against 16th June – and no other markings that I could see.'

'What did it say?'

'If I read it correctly, "D-Day" – at least, that's what it looked like.'

DS Leyton does not immediately respond – but then he raises a finger, and smiles to show he cannot be tricked.

'It's *Daddy's Day*, ain't it? That's what she meant.'

DS Jones looks momentarily deflated; it is a simple solution, when there is always the temptation to seek a more sinister explanation. DS Leyton adds a rider.

'I suppose we're gonna meet some coincidences along the way.'

DS Jones nods – and again there is a small hiatus before she speaks.

'What did you make of that jibe about "another Frank job"?'

DS Leyton appears largely ambivalent.

'That's what Morag Sinclair said, didn't she? That he does some work for them. He's got an inside track – but maybe doesn't always come up to scratch.'

DS Jones regards her colleague with a small frown – but if the prospect troubles her, she lets it pass in favour of another question.

'I thought that was interesting – what Terri said about Sebastian Sinclair and Nape's Needle.'

DS Leyton makes a growl of trepidation.

'It was enough to put me off.'

'Exactly. Yet Frank Lawson claims Sebastian Sinclair went that way.'

DS Leyton gives a vigorous rub of his hair, as if he is trying to dislodge an uncooperative memory.

'Remind me, what did the Guvnor say about that?'

'Basically the same thing as Terri – it's not a route you would want to run.'

DS Leyton leans to look at the old Georgian building. Its sandstone frontage is catching the westering sun, its perpendicular lines picked out in highlight and shade. Behind the grand frontage who knows what spectres move.

He reflects more prosaically on their short visit.

'Quite a bit of food for thought, eh, Emma?'

DS Jones nods pensively.

But now DS Leyton rouses himself; he beats out a little rat-a-tat-tat upon the steering wheel.

'On which note – I've promised the Missus – I said next time I'm in Carlisle I'll bring back some of that banana dessert cake. If you recall, the Guvnor ended up eating the last lot I bought.'

17. THRELKELD

The White Mare – 8.35 p.m. Thursday 6 June

'BEFORE YOU SAY IT, kind sir – it's not as bad as it looks.'
Skelgill is forestalled by the soft American drawl.
He has entered what is a small residents' lounge by way of a message left for him at the bar – the detail having taken a few minutes to reach him – hence the partially consumed pint that he bears.

The room is an eclectic mix of smoke-stained oak and tartan upholstery, its walls a mosaic of Lakeland watercolours and old etchings, with various brooding perspectives of Blencathra making a strong showing; there are antique Ordnance Survey maps that would occupy Skelgill were he alone.

But as the hiking group to whom he is becoming attuned shifts into focus (they are the room's only occupants) he begins to understand Rita's words of welcome. She rests on a low recliner with her left leg stretched out and supported on a stool. Where her loose knee-length skirt ends, he sees what might be a makeshift ice pack under her calf.

Gerry interjects.

'She's pulled a muscle dodging some lunatic driver – then not owned up to us – and then she's only gone and walked on it all day long.'

Rita protests.

'Gerry – it wasn't a lunatic driver – it was entirely my fault – and I didn't even feel it at the time.'

Gerry is shaking his head.

'You're your own worst enemy, Rita – you think you're indestructible.' He gestures around with large hands. 'Look at us – we're none of us spring chickens any more. If we ever were!'

Rita waves away what is in fact solicitude on Gerry's part. Skelgill glances at Rosheen – and he reads the look in her smiling eyes – that Gerry is right and Rita is headstrong – and neither will give way.

Skelgill takes the nearest seat and regards the injury with concern.

'What actually happened?'

Gerry is too quick.

'That chuffin' camera'll be the death of her. She insisted on setting up her tripod in the middle of t' road to get a photo of the cairn at Dunmail Raise.'

Skelgill looks suddenly guilty.

'Sounds like if anyone's to blame, it's me. Putting you onto it.'

Rita reaches to place a hand on his arm.

'Don't be silly, Dan.' She wags a finger at Gerry. 'The main thing is, I got the shot. There is only one angle that shows the true scale of the burial mound. And to get Dollywaggon Pike in the background. Most impressive. Such a memorable view. What did you say it means, Rosheen? The risen giant, or fiend?'

Rosheen is nodding.

'Old Norse, yes.'

Rita catches Skelgill's eye – and winks at him – a reminder of their little secret.

'Aye, well – sounds like it'll be another thing to remember.'

She grins approvingly at his retort.

But Gerry has still not entirely unloaded his two pennyworth. He continues to regale Skelgill.

'She's such a perfectionist. I'm surprised she's made it to this age, all the risks she's taken. She once abseiled off a precipice to get a perfect shot of the Grand Canyon. Took four park rangers to haul her back up.'

Now Rosheen interjects.

'Gerry – it did win her a National Geographic prize.'

Gerry huffs.

'They'd just use a drone, nowadays.'

Skelgill still harbours concern over the elderly lady's condition.

'But you walked on, alreet?'

Rita nods vigorously.

'Yes – I soon caught up with these two. The leg only began to stiffen when we stopped for lunch. And then again here.'

Skelgill scrutinises the first-aid arrangement with something of a frown.

'You should ideally ice it every hour straight after the injury. Then every three-to-four hours. But don't do it for more than fifteen minutes at a time. You'll get frostbite. Whatever you came to Cumbria for, it weren't that.'

'I think I'll run the inn out of ice!'

Skelgill shrugs.

'Don't fret – they're used to it. We drop in here – the mountain rescue – to get ice when we need some. There's always incidents up on Saddleback. And then, afterwards, we put plenty of money across the bar – it more than makes up for it.'

Rita addresses her friends.

'Well, that's another thing. When you think about it – any one of us could have twisted an ankle at some point on our walk. We've tackled far more awkward paths and slopes. Besides, it wasn't me that was at risk – just my camera that was a little in the firing line.' She turns to Skelgill. 'I wasn't in the middle of the road – I was at the side in a gateway. I was perfectly safe. I was composing a second shot and I just had some sixth sense about the car I could hear approaching – and I jerked the tripod back off the edge of the tarmac. The sudden movement is how I pulled the muscle.'

Skelgill is nodding.

'Aye, I know where you are. It's a footpath to Steel End. It's more or less at the apex of the pass. The visibility's not good. And where the road splits to go round the cairn – that's probably the first stretch of dual carriageway north of Windermere, if not Kendal. You get impatient motorists flying up there, desperate to overtake. You'd have been better getting behind the stile. I should have told you.'

Rita is shaking her shock of white hair.

'And I'm still not used to the traffic coming from the wrong direction – and we've seen so little during the past few days – you begin to forget about there being any vehicles at all.'

Skelgill regards her sympathetically.

'What kind of car was it, as a matter of interest?'

'Oh, now – all your British automobiles look the same to me. It was dark, maybe brown?'

'Was it an SUV type?'

'Hm. I'd say flatter.'

'It didn't have an aerial like a fish, did it?'

'I don't know, why?'

Skelgill is grinning.

'It's just that you're starting to describe my motor, that's all.'

'It's not much of a description, I'm afraid – I'd be hopeless as a witness.'

Gerry chuckles loudly.

'Good old Rita – she only sees the world through the lens of her camera!' But now he moves to shoulder some of the responsibility.

His voice takes on a contrite tone. 'We were rushing her, lad. Champing at the bit to climb up to Seat Sandal – we thought we might catch you at Grisedale Tarn. We should have waited with her, not been so impatient. We felt we were running a bit late because we walked down into Grasmere for Rita to get her photo of the gingerbread shop.'

Rita trades another glance with Skelgill. She is racking up the sights for her clandestine souvenir calendar. He wonders if he should casually suggest what might be next on her list; there are several landmarks in the vicinity that might qualify as remarkable. But Rita seems to read his thoughts.

'Dan – I must tell you – this pair have convinced me that we should lay up here for a day, and stay a second night. With such a big ascent to come, I don't want to break down in the wilderness and have to summon your team of rescuers.'

There is a certain pathos in Rita's tone that Skelgill finds hard to read – though it seems to send a small ripple of dismay around their little group. It strikes him that they might harbour a concern that this will be the last they shall see of him. He finds a minor point as a diversion.

'And that's alright with your accommodation for tomorrow?'

Gerry waves a casual hand.

'We were able to add an extra night – they're quiet on Sunday. We were too late to cancel tomorrow night – we'll have to swallow that. So instead of Friday and Saturday we'll be staying Saturday and Sunday.'

'This is Keswick, aye?'

'The old hotel in Market Square – The Highwayman.' Gerry holds up both hands, palms outwards. 'And before you say it, lad – I know, it's daylight robbery.'

Skelgill contrives a suitable grin.

'Word is, prices everywhere have doubled since Covid. And it's the perfect spot – not fifty yards from your finish line.'

Gerry is nodding enthusiastically.

'Aye – that's the idea – we thought we could be downing a pint within minutes of touching the Moot Hall. No distance at all, for Rita's gammy leg, eh?'

But now Rita seems to want to steer the conversation away from her own predicament. She reaches to pat Skelgill on the forearm as he puts down his pint glass.

'Enough about us – how did you get on today? Did you catch all the fish that you hoped for?'

Skelgill is taken slightly off guard – he is distracted by a curious sense of disquiet experienced each time he engages with the group. He wonders if it is because he is facilitating a venture that is just a little beyond them, outwith their capabilities. Now there is the prospect that they will head up and over Blencathra and into what is a substantial wilderness, the Skiddaw massif – where the mobile phone signal is not a reliable phenomenon. And Rita is hamstrung – despite her protestations to the contrary. Only the stable clement weather gives him comfort – for to be stranded at least would not represent the threat to life so prevalent at other times, even in this season.

As for his day – it seems a week ago that he fished Grisedale Tarn at dawn. He struck camp long before the trio would have passed the outfall, a tributary of Grisedale Beck, and there would have been no signs of his wild camping – not even a small round circle burnt into the turf by the base of his Kelly kettle, for he had set it on rocks.

Rosheen chips in while he apparently muses over his answer.

'You didn't snag a crown, by any chance?'

Skelgill regards her with bafflement – though her words tug at a half-buried memory. With her impish countenance revealing her enjoyment at teasing him, she obliges.

'That's the legend, isn't it? When the last king of Cumbria was slain his soldiers carried the crown up from Dunmail Raise and made the tarn its safe resting place.'

'Oh, really?' Rita seems enraptured by the idea. 'Heaven knows how they thought they would ever recover it.'

'Happen they didn't.' It is Gerry that pontificates. He crooks an elbow to nudge Skelgill. 'Hey up, lad, you could try magnet fishing.'

Skelgill smiles – but he is picturing the dawn – as he squatted at the shoreline in the cool still air with mist rising from the surface, like mercury evaporating in the first flush of pale light. Sure – he had imagined a Lady-of-the-Lake moment, a desperate yet triumphant hand bursting from the water, dripping glinting gold and jewels in the slanting rays of the rising sun.

The spell had been broken by a metallic clank and a solitary hand waving a tin mug.

Skelgill starts – and finds himself circling back to an earlier juncture in their conversation. He regards them each quickly, but rests his gaze on Rosheen.

'Tomorrow. You should go to Castlerigg. You could get a taxi to take you. It's not much above two miles from here. When you're there at dawn or dusk and there's no other folk – you can imagine you're in a different millennium.'

Rosheen is nodding enthusiastically – though Gerry regards her with a frown.

'What's Castlerigg?'

'A late-Neolithic stone circle.'

It is Rosheen's answer, and Gerry regards her with equanimity. While they exchange nods of mutual interest, Skelgill makes a quick camera motion to Rita, who grins with approval.

But now, Skelgill feels a vibration – a text from his muted phone. He extracts it from his hip pocket.

He scowls as he reads: "Out front. Bring half pint and bag of cheese-and-onion. Tell them you have to see a man about a dog."

DS Jones has hijacked his catchphrase.

He grins ruefully, and looks up to see himself surrounded by knowing smiles.

'Looks like that's your nightly debriefing – no pun intended.' But Gerry's tone is sufficiently thick with innuendo to merit a literal slap on the wrist from Rosheen.

Skelgill drains the last of his pint and promises he'll be back.

Not for the first time, as he leaves the group, he hears Gerry pronounce, more sententiously now.

'That hit-and-run must be troubling them – all this out-of-hours work. Just as well you didn't put a second one on their plate, Rita!'

*

Seen at a distance the White Mare rises like a pale bluff out of the low green fellside, its long, squat frontage facing south, where immediately there are picnic tables on the embankment overlooking the access lane, once the main coaching route between Penrith and the coastal ports; beyond, the busy A66 is concealed in a cutting by trees that baffle the murmur of traffic; further still, directly across the dale, is the rollercoaster ridge ridden today by Skelgill and his charges, comprising a dozen of the Bob Graham summits, not least the three Dodds that divulge the fact that, not so far afield, his colleagues were poking their noses into the business of others.

No sooner has he emerged blinking into the low evening sun – via the comparative gloom of the bar – than the texted catchphrase crystallises as a graphic vision – except it should perhaps have read "see a *girl* about a dog".

Into focus comes first DS Jones – dressed casually in outdoor gear, and seated at one of the benches – and here Skelgill, bearing brim-full drinks and slippery snacks, momentarily flinches – for, coiled at her feet, lies the canine cannonball, Bullboxer Cleopatra. To his relief, he sees the girl has the dog on the leash. The lunge is averted.

'I sprung her from captivity.'

Skelgill gets his precious cargo lowered safely onto the table before wrestling with the explosive welcome beneath.

'It's a cushy number – I reckon she likes it there better than mine – she gets spoiled rotten.'

He pops a packet of potato crisps and his precocious pet is quick to sit to attention.

DS Jones cannot suppress a laugh.

'I can't think how she got such habits in the first place.'

Skelgill scowls unconvincingly.

'Who knows – she was a rescue, mind.'

DS Jones is poised to drink. Her eyes sparkle over the rim of her glass.

'Closer to kidnap – but I shan't split hairs. Cheers.'

'Aye.'

Other formalities are disposed of, and Skelgill opts to squeeze alongside DS Jones to benefit from the view. He lifts his own glass to draw the panorama into its amber-tinted realm, the northern fells in a goldfish bowl.

A strange peace settles upon them; they each comprehend the paradox – that, were there news of sufficient import to convey from one to the other, they would both already know. Equally, they would not – *may* not – be here, were there nothing to consider.

DS Jones begins with a little gentle pitch-rolling.

'How are your hiking friends?'

Skelgill makes a face at the implication – but then obliges.

'Rita – the lady photographer from the States – she had a bit of a near-miss with a car at Dunmail Raise. While she was taking a photo of the cairn.'

'Oh.'

There ensues a longer than needed pause.

However, Skelgill's eventual embellishment is entirely practical.

'She's strained a calf muscle. They're laying up an extra night here.'

'Ah.'

'*Ah?*'

'That takes the pressure off you, a little.'

'Why – what do I need to do?'

'Oh – nothing – just, well – shall I bring you up to speed?'

'I'm all ears.'

'Best first?'

Skelgill casts a reproachful frown over his pint.

DS Jones leans back against the whitewashed wall of the building and stretches out. She is wearing exercise leggings and trail shoes, and looks prepared should a dog walk ensue.

'Okay – well, I think it concerns the magazine. The headline is that there are two sets of unidentified prints on the cover and only Sebastian Sinclair's on the Bob Graham inside spread.' She turns to look at Skelgill, as if to ensure the significant omission sinks in. 'When we called on Billy Higson this morning he wasn't home. There is no discernible damage to his Land Rover, though it has bull bars. Through a window, on a table I could see a pile of five copies of the June edition of *Fell Running*. He suddenly arrived back from a run – I'm pretty sure he'll work out what I saw. So I made no mention of the threat – or the magazine. He claimed not to know Sebastian Sinclair but he was clearly aware of the incident. He said on Monday morning he was training – starting from here in fact, the northern section – running with his brother, Jimmy.'

Skelgill's mouth twists as if he has suddenly experienced a sour taste. Indeed he turns his head away as though he might spit. However, he gestures that she should continue.

'Sebastian Sinclair had a subscription to *Fell Running* sent to his home address. His June copy was still in its clear postal wrap in his attic at Applethwaite. We spoke to the person at Sinclair Design who handles the mail – a Terri – who happens to be a climber. A large brown envelope was amongst the post on Friday, marked Private & Confidential for Sebastian Sinclair. That seems likely to have been the magazine, but the envelope has gone in the recycling.'

Skelgill is nodding. He knows she would convey other essential facts, so these are they. He waits.

DS Jones shifts forward and takes a drink of her beer.

'Unless we are totally wrong – it looks like whoever manufactured the threat – they were being careful – they were forensically aware.'

Skelgill does not answer, and DS Jones bends to check on Cleopatra, who has made short work of the crisps and is tactically snoozing. She casts again.

'I'm trying not to lose sight of the innocent explanation.'

'Looks like a threat to me. And the death remains suspicious.'

DS Jones is encouraged by his words.

'And it just doesn't make sense that Sebastian Sinclair would make the threat. Neither emotively, nor in practical terms.' She turns to look at Skelgill. 'What I'd really like to do is try to match the prints on the outside of the magazine. But it's a radical step – if we have to force it.'

Now Skelgill does produce an inauspicious grimace.

'I can't see the Chief authorising that, not yet.'

DS Jones folds her arms and stares pensively out over the soft lines of the dusky landscape.

'I'm cheered that you say *yet*.'

Skelgill does not elaborate, other than with the raising of an eyebrow.

DS Jones taps the weathered wooden bench.

'We've arranged to see the Lawsons together, tomorrow afternoon. The only person so far to whom we've mentioned the threat is Morag Sinclair.'

Skelgill seems content with this state of affairs.

'To be fair to her, she was shocked – and the opposite of evasive – she was digging, trying to get at our thinking. She even asked directly if she were a suspect.'

'What did you say?'

'Stock answer. Elimination. She told us that at that time of day she gets the boys ready and takes them to St Catherine's in Keswick. DC Watson is checking it out.'

Skelgill takes a silent sup of ale.

'But I don't need to point out to you that Honister Pass is twenty-five minutes from Applethwaite.'

Skelgill grins.

'You just did.'

DS Jones nods reflectively.

'I did. Her sister Shona Mackay was there. It seems she's a lawyer. She was protective, aggressive even. She told Morag Sinclair in front of us that she doesn't have to answer questions.'

Skelgill absorbs this information without comment.

After a suitable pause, DS Jones gathers herself to go again.

'Okay, here's the next thing. Sinclair Design have a corporate calendar of the Lakes. A different view each month. They give it to clients and staff for their desks. I think Frank Lawson might have produced it.'

Skelgill frowns – but it is an introspective moment; there is the coincidence of Rita's calendar. He waits for DS Jones to continue.

'Sebastian Sinclair had a copy hanging beside his desk at Applethwaite. It was completely unmarked apart from the dates of the Bob Graham Round anniversary challenge, and the following Sunday, 16th June, which was also ringed. No words or anything. DS Leyton spotted that it was Father's Day. It prompted a bit of a choked reaction from Morag Sinclair.'

Skelgill throws her a sharp sideways glance.

'Aye – I can get that.'

But DS Jones is reluctant to agree.

'Well, I don't know. I come back to my impression of Morag Sinclair.'

'Which is?'

Well – that's she's detached from the marriage, is I suppose how I would put it.'

'But if it's his calendar – up in his studio?'

'I know – but, well – not that we know much about Sebastian Sinclair – but there's a kind of self-congratulation implied that I feel would be out of character.'

Skelgill, rather than find a further objection, seems to approve of her assessment.

'There's more, reet?'

'Well, in a way, yes. We used Victoria Lawson's office to interview Terri and Jules. There was a copy of the calendar on her desk. I sneaked a look at it – and the only date that was marked was June 16th – and she had written the words "D-Day" – which DS Leyton is translating as Daddy's Day.'

Skelgill is phlegmatic.

'That's more likely, eh?'

DS Jones purses her lips.

'Well, yes – but –'

A silence ensues – she decides to park the point, to put a pin in it.

'There's another thing about this calendar. Unrelated – but related.'

Skelgill plies her with something of an old-fashioned look – but she has a way of winning his interest.

147

'This is up your street. Terri said that on Friday morning in the common room Sebastian Sinclair was turning over the calendar from May to June – and June has a picture of Great Gable. Sinclair asked Terri if there was a running route from Nape's Needle to the summit.'

She looks inquiringly at Skelgill – but he comes back at her.

'What was the answer?'

'Exactly like you said – forget it.'

Skelgill turns to his pint and lifts it musingly.

DS Jones joins more of the dots.

'So Sebastian Sinclair had it from a credible source – *before* Monday morning, when Frank Lawson claimed he went off alone to try the supposed shortcut.'

Skelgill remains silent for a minute.

'Happen he'd just had his fill of running with Lawson.'

DS Jones nods.

'I know – I'm not pinning great hopes on it. But there you are.'

She takes a longer drink – and he reprises her remark.

'What *are* you pinning hopes on, lass?'

She falters – she is reluctant to admit to lack of method.

'I don't know. I hesitate to use the word intuition.'

'There's nowt wrong with intuition – so long as you don't jump to the wrong conclusion.'

She adapts his truism.

'You mean to a *premature* conclusion?'

'Aye – well, that an' all.'

She ponders again.

'It's just, well – when everyone you meet – you know you're not quite getting the full picture – everything is just a little bit hazy. And it's invariably relationships, isn't it? We can only scratch the surface – when these people have known one another for years. Who knows what has been going on between them.'

Skelgill does not respond. When she follows his gaze she realises he is watching a kestrel; it must be hovering above the A66 embankment, it makes a false stoop and disappears for a moment behind the treeline; then it is back up, a little further on, buoyant, bobbing like a float on water, to repeat the manoeuvre – several times indeed, before it finally makes a dive from which it does not reappear, dinner taken care of.

Now she interrupts.

'There is one other fact that I gleaned. Jules – Julie Magnusson, you'll recall – was particularly stirred by it. She hung back to tell me.

About a month ago, leaving work late, she saw Sebastian Sinclair coming out of a private GP's practice near the office. It looked like he'd been given some information – he was slipping an envelope into his pocket. She said he didn't approve of private healthcare – they don't have a company scheme.'

Skelgill inhales and releases the breath slowly.

'I take it she weren't upset for political reasons.'

DS Jones gives a shake of her head and then has to brush away bronzed blonde strands from her prominent cheeks.

'No – it was that he subsequently died.' She returns a sharp glance from Skelgill – that they agree there can be no direct connection. 'I know – all the same – she was troubled. That's what I mean – about the hazy picture.'

They both drink, their movements synchronised.

As the balmy early summer air cools and sinks, swifts are following winged insects that descend; or they might just be socialising, as they come screaming low overhead, the stunt pilots of the avian world, too fast really to be much other than a blur, scything and twisting, driven by an invisible engine that turns flies into rocket fuel.

It is a comparison perhaps not lost on the detectives – their own progress is pedestrian. The pressure will be on Skelgill when he reappears at the Chief's Monday meeting.

DS Jones tentatively speculates.

'I've been wondering if we would get somewhere if we concentrated on the motive.'

'I thought we had one?'

'Well – there's the race, sure – the threat – getting him out of the way …'

'But, what – it's a long chalk from wanting to win to nobbling your opposition?'

DS Jones gestures with an open palm.

'I suppose if it were just nobbling – then maybe not so. But murdering … sure.'

Skelgill squints such that his grey-green irises are all but veiled.

'I agree with all that.'

DS Jones is perhaps a little surprised.

'Look, I realise if you start out with love or lust, or envy or revenge, or greed or gain – you get nowhere. But if you begin with the practical idea that if Sebastian Sinclair had an enemy, they probably came from one of three camps – competitors in the race, his business affairs or his personal life. Arguably, Frank Lawson ticks all those boxes. And he was unequivocally on the spot.'

Skelgill leans back and folds his arms. His expression tells her that he is not more convinced by the man's potential multiplicity of motives.

DS Jones tries a less head-on approach.

'So long as we take the threat seriously, there's a thread running through this, isn't there? Knowledge of the event, knowledge of their training. And the incident on the Bob Graham Round itself.'

Skelgill regards his colleague through still-narrowed eyes.

'Aye, that's what's been mithering us.'

DS Jones tilts her head forward, seeking clarification.

Skelgill complies, if pithily.

'The incident. Knowledge.'

She immediately perks up.

'They didn't put anything on social media. While we can't rule out that an outsider found out where they would be on Monday morning, it's really only the inner circle who apparently knew.'

Skelgill regards her intently for a moment; then he looks away.

'Reet. But let's not go round in too many circles, eh, lass? Not while the view's hazy, like you say.'

DS Jones regards him thoughtfully for a few moments.

'What do you feel about it?'

Skelgill requires a sup of lubricating ale.

'I feel … uneasy.'

'What – that someone might be in jeopardy?'

It is a moment longer before he nods slowly.

18. THE GOAT II

Matterdale – 7.45 a.m. Friday 7 June

SKELGILL is feeling exposed.
But it is a feeling borne out of a misfitting conflation. He is wearing hiking gear whilst riding a motorbike. It is a small incongruity, yet one that, to his mind, would draw the attention of a suspicious observer.

Having earlier secreted his pack beneath dense bracken on the slopes of Blencathra he had hiked home, cross country, hardly two miles, and set out straightaway on the Triumph, eschewing breakfast for a sense of urgency – an expedient he is already beginning to regret. There must have been something in the fridge he might have grabbed.

And now he reflects upon other facets of his circumstances.

There is the practical safety aspect. Though this does not greatly trouble him. Apart from a short blast along the A66 he has not achieved any great speed – the Matterdale lanes preclude such. However, were he now to drop the bike on a slow-motion bend, his lack of protective Kevlar would be telling at the various points of impact.

In the credit column there is anonymity. It is the main reason he has chosen two wheels over four. Few if any folk would recognise the masked rider on the silver-and-blue Legend TT – whereas his car is likely better known, and he would be visible inside it. And, in these narrow lanes, a bike offers the prospect of parking and concealment. Only in approach is it more conspicuous, for it rumbles like thunder each time he is obliged to kick down the gears.

With this in mind, as he nears his destination – following in the tracks of his colleagues yesterday – he coasts in third as best he can – enough torque to deal with the undulations, few enough revs to keep the noise down.

He passes the narrow unmarked opening that leads to Billy Higson's minor farmstead and reviews his strategy – the crux of it being that the exit deserves twice the planning of the entry. As he slows and glances to his right, he takes in the lie of the land. Beyond the boundary wall the ground rises both steadily and unevenly. There is plenty of cover – gnarled hawthorns and self-seeded invasive sycamores – patches of rough herbage that look occasionally grazed – in fact something of a paddock between the wall and the partly obscured stone barn some fifty yards off. The latter structure is sound – although a small section of the roof has caved in. Beyond – Skelgill knows, from the map and DS Jones's description – is an overgrown courtyard and the neglected cottage, with various appended sheds and pens.

As he has anticipated, the lane winds up into a denser copse of oak and birch which extends back to the corner of the barn. The roadside wall recedes and there is a wider verge, overgrown with leggy gorse. This is not a vicinity where sheep roam wild, but grazing animals, probably roe deer have made inroads and there are spaces between the bushes. Cautiously he noses the machine into the spiky shrubs and turns so that it is on the downslope, facing the road but hidden from view. He cuts the engine, but leaves the ignition switched on. The ground is baked hard and dry, but still he finds a slab of exposed rock upon which to heel down the side-stand. The bike tilted but stable, he slips off his helmet and slides it onto the inclined handlebar.

The headgear he replaces with a creased Tilley hat that he pulls from the thigh pocket of his hiking trousers. Slung over his shoulder is an Ordnance Survey map in a clear waterproof case. This is not something Skelgill either regularly uses, or needs in this vicinity, but there is some method in the madness.

His reasoning goes that Billy Higson, though not a man he knows, is a man more his type. *His* type, that is, rather than either of his sergeants'. DS Jones, albeit a local, is not of the land. DS Leyton, albeit of unpretentious origins, is not even of the Lakes – and an urbanite to boot. Skelgill, on the other hand, has earth under his nails and wool in his hair. Jones and Leyton are each sharp in their own ways, alert, shrewd, streetwise – but Skelgill harbours the conviction that if there is a rogue straw in the wind, he might just be the man to recognise it for what it is.

Now he pushes back through the lemon-flowered gorse, inhaling wafts of coconut aroma, and strides along the lane for a good quarter of a mile, continuing in the direction in which he has arrived. In time he heaves himself over a stile, and begins to circle back towards Billy Higson's place. His trajectory is more or less on the level, across an undulating landscape of rough pasture and stone walls. There is little cover – to attempt to take advantage of it commando fashion – run-

crouching behind walls, darting and rolling across gateways – would make one more, not less, conspicuous.

The tactic is to look like a walker. A walker trying to find their way. Skelgill halts at regular intervals, ostentatiously to consult the map and glance haplessly around. Occasionally he surreptitiously sucks a finger and checks the breeze. There is little enough of it, but sufficient to tell him when he is downwind of the farmstead.

He avoids where he can enclosures with sheep (not the best-looking specimens of Swaledales he has seen) – or, where he cannot, he gives them as a wide a berth as the walls allow.

Seventy-five yards short of the rear of the property he gets a clear view of the lean-to where DS Jones has described the Land Rover to be previously parked. It is empty. He stares for a few moments.

Now he casts about on the ground at his feet.

He bends and left-handed selects a pebble and, rising, in more or less the same movement slings it towards the cottage. It cuts a parabola through the crisp morning air and comes down with a crack on the roof. It breaks a slate. The stone rolls until it is halted by moss; the slate shard slithers likewise.

Skelgill waits.

Silence, only subdued birdsong.

No dogs.

Now he approaches directly, and vaults the gate that bars the way into the yard.

Still taking no chances, however, he raps on the front door.

There is no answer. He tries the door. It is locked.

He moves to peer into the window to the right. A little to his surprise, he sees the pile of magazines that DS Jones has reported.

He takes a few paces backwards and surveys the place.

His features reveal cogitation – but a sound behind has him turning on his heel – there are sheep in the barn.

Why would there be sheep in the barn? Lambing is long past; shearing and dipping are yet to come.

He strolls across. The plank door is latched but unbolted.

Its rusted hinges shriek a warning.

He peers into half-darkness – only a shaft of light falls against the far wall from the holed roof. The air is not exactly foetid, but it is ripe with fresh dung and the ammonic tang of urine.

153

On one side, the sheep are penned in by a makeshift arrangement of interlocking galvanised hurdles and a low barrier of bales. They shift about nervously – flight animals with nowhere to run to.

Skelgill ponders their presence – they are muscular Texels – a cut above their scraggy cousins that roam the surrounding paddocks.

As they begin to bleat he suddenly stiffens.

Tyres are crunching up the track – and there comes the distinctive knocking diesel engine of a Land Rover.

And now – barking dogs, closing in.

If they are not already loping ahead of the vehicle, they are hanging out of the windows – in a matter of seconds they will be freed.

Cur dogs are not likely to want to tear him apart – sheep are their thing – but they are territorial enough to set him at bay. To give him away.

It is maybe three hundred yards through the copse to his hidden bike.

And there is a six-foot barbed-wire-topped fence barring his way at the corner of the building.

He slips inside the barn and pulls the door to.

Hardly a moment later, the dogs are baying at the spot he stood.

It is another twenty seconds or so before a harsh voice rings out.

'Leave the beggars be!'

And another twenty seconds elapse before the barn door jerks open by about a foot. Light floods in – a figure is silhouetted in the gap, blocking the yapping dogs from entry.

'Shut it, you devils! There's nowt here for thee.'

But the shepherd remains unmoving – except perhaps for invisible eyes that scan the shadowy interior.

Under his breath, there is a faint hiss of words.

'Yan, tyan, tethera, methera, pimp, sethera, lethera, hovera, dovera, dick.'

And then he is silent – there is only the sporadic canine clamour.

'Get back! Let's get the pair of thee fed.'

The formal command, the dogs obey. *Fed* must also figure in their lexicon, for they fall silent.

The man remains for a few moments longer at the door.

Then it closes, the hinges protesting, restoring the gloom.

There is the scrape of the latch.

But no sound of movement – as if the person has had second thoughts.

Then there comes a heavy clank.

Now footsteps, and the skitter of claws on hard ground, recede from the barn.

Skelgill, prone behind the straw barrier, one eye having watched proceedings through a crack between two bales, releases his grip on the pitchfork that lies at his side.

The dogs are being fed.

He must make his move.

He clambers over the bales, wades through the Texels, and springs over the steel hurdles. As he anticipated, the door is well and truly bolted from the outside. Should push come to shove, he could break out, but not without attracting attention – and certainly not without trace.

He turns to where the shaft of light penetrates the collapsed section of roof.

What was it he told himself about the exit being worth twice the entry?

Now he approaches the back wall. While the stones are squarely dressed on the exterior, such expense was spared inside when this field barn was raised three centuries ago. The interior offers a dozen times more handholds and footholds than the average commercial climbing-wall.

Without hesitation, Skelgill swarms up and hauls himself by means of an exposed rafter onto the top of the wall. A few broken tiles fall noiselessly into the hay below. He gasps a lungful of cool fresh air.

In the fells – walking, scrambling, climbing – down is always more problematic than up. Up, one's eyes are on a level with the next challenge. Down, one's feet have no such sensors. Ask any mountain rescuer, most accidents happen on the descent.

But gravity is an irresistible force, and Skelgill – with only the time it takes a hungry cur dog to gollop a bowl of food on his side – yields to Newton's laws. The barn is the equivalent of two storeys tall. He simply drapes himself, arms fully extended, and lets go.

The landing is not comfortable – but at least the patch of nettles into which he momentarily disappears does not conceal rusted farm equipment – and the thick vegetation has kept the ground damp; it absorbs his momentum more satisfactorily than he might have imagined.

He does not wait to assess any damage.

He sprints down through the rough paddock and scales the wall to the lane. Two hundred and fifty yards uphill and around the corner is the patch of gorse. Remarkably his Tilley hat has remained in place. He slides his right arm through the chin guard of his helmet, mounts the Triumph, kicks back the stand and allows the machine to roll noiselessly out from the bushes onto the narrow tarmac of the lane.

Clutch lever held in, now he coasts downhill, gathering speed and passing the entrance to the farmstead. Downhill still, and faster, he rounds two sharp bends before he toes the gear up into third and releases the clutch.

The machine bucks into life, and Skelgill roars away.

It is probably ten minutes before he makes a temporary stop. He needs to join the A66 – and so, much as he has enjoyed the freedom of riding without a helmet, he yields to the law. He also takes the opportunity to pluck a handful of sorrel leaves from the verge, to administer with vigour to his nettle stings.

To Skelgill's mind, riding a bike is the closest he will ever come to flying. Exposed to the elements (helmet aside, and hindrance discounted), there is the sense of floating motion, of weightlessness despite the paradox of one quarter of a ton of metal; of changing velocity and direction with the minutest of actions – barely actions, it feels more like tiny thoughts that cause rider and machine seamlessly to alter course – much like the swifts he has so recently admired must make the slightest, almost imperceptible changes to their trim, yet they can twist and turn and soar and dive, slow and speed, at will.

And this activity is useful, if not immediately productive. Consciousness subsumed by the physical expedient, the subconscious is freed to its own devices – a kind of not-thinking thinking. Fishing, waiting for a bite – or striding out across the fells, an oft-trodden route – these are other means of achieving the same effect. Showering, ironing, mowing the lawn – these have all been mooted by authorities in creative meditation – but figure less often in Skelgill's repertoire.

Before he knows it, he finds himself dropping down a gear to pass through Rosthwaite. Shortly he swings past the turn to Stonethwaite – and on westwards, towards Seatoller, soon to hang a left up the dead-end track to Seathwaite.

In the farmyard he kills the engine and dismounts, and is hauling off his helmet when a familiar voice has him turning on his heel.

'Sounds like she's misfiring on one, there, lad.'

Arthur Hope has emerged from his smithy-come-workshop.

'I thought – that's a four-stroke triple coming – thought it might be thee. Can't be many of these Legends going about, now. You need to turn her ower regularly, to keep her in decent fettle.'

Skelgill grins a little sheepishly; he hardly ever gets out on the bike. But Arthur does not chide him.

'Up for a fry? Gladis'll be glad to see thee.'

Now Skelgill is genuinely amused. While it might be said he has followed his nose to the farm café on more than one occasion, he assumes Arthur Hope knows about the Honister incident – and must be ribbing him.

'Never say never. But – actually, is your Jud about?'

Arthur Hope is a man of few words. Knowing pale gimlet eyes are set in a hewn countenance. He gives a faint nod of comprehension.

'He's ont' fell. Should be down any minute – he's got to run into Keswick for some raddle powder. Get theesen some grub an' I'll send him through. Leave your keys in – I'll give those plugs a tickle up.'

Skelgill offers his thanks and enters the farmhouse via the kitchen door.

Further greetings and informalities exchanged, he finds himself alone in the parlour – his timing is the lull between early serious fellwalkers and more casual tourists who decide that perhaps a bacon roll is preferable after all to the ascent of Scafell Pike.

'There we go – thou must be fair clemmed, young Daniel.'

It is a phrase Skelgill has heard Gladis Hope utter as many times as he has had hot breakfasts – at least, her legendary Cumbrian Fry. Gladis understanding a man's needs, he is left to his own devices.

But it is only two or three minutes before Jud Hope appears, and slides into a seat.

'Alreet, marra? Thee look like thee've slept int' barn.'

Skelgill grins, but offers no explanation.

There now ensues the rare sight of Skelgill placing a length of Cumberland sausage on a slice of bread-and-butter and offering the sideplate.

'You're alreet – t' arl lass is putting up us bait – I've got to shoot off in five minutes. Couple of errands and a meeting.'

'Aye, your arl fella said.'

Jud Hope does however avail himself of some tea from the pot, turning over an unused mug.

'Are you up about the Honister?'

Skelgill, chewing, nods and responds disjointedly.

157

'Aye – it could be that. I mean – I'm not holding out – it's just a lead we've got. Might be nowt in it.' He takes a swallow of tea. 'Do you know Billy Higson?'

'Shepherd ower Matterdale way? Aye. Mind his younger brother Jimmy were int' year abeun us?'

Now Skelgill recalls. That's right. Knocker Higson. A small-time bully.

Skelgill nods slowly. Jud Hope continues.

'Billy Higson's a runner, aye? They call him t' Goat, don't they? Is that why you're interested? Because that lad as died were a runner – the Sinclair chap?'

'It's what's given us the connection.' Skelgill has no qualms about sharing information with his trusted contemporary. 'Sinclair received a threat – we think – to pull out of the Bob Graham.'

'You reckon from Billy Higson?'

Skelgill grimaces.

'It's a theory.'

'Like – he wouldn't want some upstart spoiling his party?' Jud Hope looks suddenly doubtful. 'It's a drastic step.'

Skelgill contrives a wry smile.

'That's what we've been telling ourselves.'

'Have you asked him? Higson.'

Skelgill finishes another mouthful.

'He knows he's on our radar. We've not let on – about what we know.'

Jud Hope glances away. His gaze rests on the view beyond the small window. Sturdy lambs gambol in-bye.

'I shouldn't trust him – that's for sure. I don't know anyone as would. You know what they say about him – he's never brought a stray yowe to a meet, yet. Though he's laid claim to plenty.'

Skelgill frowns broodingly.

'I were just down there now.'

'What – his place?'

Skelgill regards his old friend earnestly.

'What would he be doing with half a score of Texels in his barn?'

Skelgill had not needed to count. Billy Higson did it for him, using the Borrowdale shepherds' version of the old Celtic numbers.

Jud Hope's expression is one of alarm.

'Were they blue gimmers?'

Skelgill's eyes narrow.

'Aye, they were. In good nick. Especially compared to the rest of his stock.'

Before Skelgill has finished speaking Jud Hope has fished a mobile phone from the breast pocket of his boiler suit.

'Look at this, marra.' He shows a photograph of sheep, tightly bunched. Short-coated, they are blue-black and grey. 'Went missing Monday morning from Jack Thompson's at Stonethwaite – gone by eight o'clock. Ten blue gimmer Texel yowes.'

Skelgill is wishing he had had the presence of mind to steal a photograph of the lug marks or ear tags. But what he recalls of the smit marks, despite the half-light – and the pattern he sees in his friend's photo – is enough of a match.

'Would he keep a rare breed? I thought he were a workaday shepherd.'

Jud Hope certainly does not look convinced.

'It's a tempting pay packet.'

'What would they be worth?'

But now Jud Hope scowls.

'Six, seven hundred guineas apiece to a breeder. But, nay – alive they'd be traceable. Three hundred notes a carcase at retail. You're still talking three grand for a morning's work.'

Skelgill contemplates the suggestion.

'But there'd be margins wanted down the chain.'

Jud Hope is grim faced.

'Not when the reiver and the butcher are all the same thing.'

Skelgill sits back in his seat.

'What are you saying?'

Jud Hope illustratively picks up an unused table knife and makes a slashing motion.

'Jimmy Higson's a butcher. He's got a shop wi' an abattoir out t' back – up at Speatrie.'

Skelgill reaches for his mug of tea and takes a considered drink.

His friend perhaps misinterprets his reaction.

'Trying to solve one crime – find another, eh?'

Skelgill makes to disagree – Jud Hope seems apologetic for bringing the matter to light. He forestalls Skelgill's response.

'I get why you might not want ten sheep to spoil your investigation. You've bigger fish to fry. I can make a couple of calls – we could have it sorted by midnight.'

Though Jud Hope grins with a certain malevolent satisfaction – and Skelgill does not baulk at the sentiment – he considers that village justice is always a dangerous thing. Jud might land himself in trouble – bad enough for him and his family – but with inevitable repercussions for Skelgill, too.

He employs diplomacy.

'It might come to that. But give us a couple of days. And I'll let you know. In the meantime – I'll pay a casual visit to the butcher brother. I'll warn him off – in case they've got any ideas of doing a quick job on the sheep. There's summat I want to ask him, any road.'

*

Later, in the afternoon, and having exchanged two wheels for four, and Gladis's Cumbrian Fry having enabled him to drive past all manner of small and obscure eateries, Skelgill slowly and as unobtrusively as one can in a long, brown and slightly dilapidated shooting-brake with its pike-shaped coat-hanger aerial pulls into the Co-op supermarket car park in the small settlement of Aspatria, "Speatrie" to the locals, and hence the appellation used by Jud Hope.

Skelgill has also swapped hiking gear for what might loosely be considered workwear for a rural Detective Inspector with no great penchant for fashion or fit.

He exits the car and stands facing south, stretching his spine, pressing at its base with the knuckles of both hands. He stares across the unprepossessing farmscape that could be mistaken for many quarters of the United Kingdom. As always it strikes him as incongruous – the sense of *so-near-yet-so-far* – that this is Cumbria but not the Lakes. Some fifteen miles distant, Skiddaw is prominent – together with Blencathra, the great sentinels that guard the northern reaches of the fells.

He casts about.

The early-summer high pressure is holding firm; there is a smattering of light cloud, but nothing organised that portends of an oncoming front. The small car park is something of a sun-trap. Overhead, house martins chatter as they circle and periodically dive in and out of their tiled mud nests hung beneath the eaves. On a vagrant Buddleia that springs from a crack in the wall a small tortoiseshell butterfly flexes its wings. Skelgill starts towards it – an ingrained response, like that of finding a fossil, or fool's gold, or frogspawn or field voles – just some of nature's bounty that is irresistible to a small boy left to his own devices, honing the instincts of a would-be hunter-gatherer.

He is reminded of his task. Now it is perhaps more hunter than gatherer. And it calls for stealth.

Aspatria being a street village, perhaps more characteristic of those across the border in Scotland – its mainly terraced properties crowding the near two-mile stretch of high street – there is no recognised town centre, or obligation for shops to cluster to garner trade. 'James Higson Quality Butcher' is some distance back the way he has come.

Though stealth is required, he has no intention of going incognito.

He enters with his warrant card at the ready, and now he maybe even recognises the man behind the counter – as Jud said, only a year above them at school – though grizzled and careworn in a way that belies his age. Certainly, judging by the photo in *Fell Running* of older brother Billy, there is a family resemblance in the dark sunken eyes, disconcertingly narrowly spaced beneath a primitive brow ridge.

Skelgill waits while he serves an elderly lady with a coil of Cumberland sausage ("made on the premises") and an impulse purchase of sausage rolls, displayed on the counter top, marked with a little flag at "£1 each or 3 for £2".

The lady has a wheeled trolley and Skelgill retreats to see her out of the door.

He returns with his ID at eye level – though he suspects the butcher has already divined something of the nature of his call. While there is no sign of recognition, even when Skelgill enunciates his name and job title, he detects a straightening, a tensing of muscles, the resisting of a step back. Skelgill derives some small satisfaction in seeing the former bully at bay. Knocker knocked.

'Mr Higson, reet?'

'Aye.'

'Just a routine inquiry. We've got a team working on animal thefts. We're checking butchers who've got their own abattoir. Where it's distinctive livestock – it's being offered for slaughter.'

The man glances down at the ID still in Skelgill's hand.

'How come they've sent an inspector – I thought you lot were all supposed to be too busy to attend petty crimes.'

Skelgill could pick three separate arguments with the obdurate retort – but instead he takes encouragement from the apparent diversion.

'Half a score of Texels have been lifted from beside Stonethwaite. Not an easy animal to pass on.'

The man grimaces.

'I know nowt of it. Besides – Stonethwaite – that's Borrowdale. Down int' Lakes. Why would they come this way?'

Skelgill nods contemplatively.

'Mostly it's stock being shipped out of the district – over to the coast by these A-roads,' (he waves a hand at the shop window, indicating the high street beyond) 'and across to Northern Ireland – then on into the EU. But occasionally – it's being sold locally, en route – going for a song.'

Skelgill makes an indeterminate face – in fact to conceal any possible self-doubt that what is an entirely improvised explanation will hold water. But it is not contested. However, when Jimmy Higson indicates neither sympathy nor willingness to co-operate, Skelgill prompts him more directly.

'It were early on Monday morning. You didn't happen to get a speculative visit from a passing hawker chancing their arm?'

There might just be a hint of apprehension in the weaselly eyes.

'I don't open while eleven on a Monday. Besides – I weren't here.'

Skelgill stares in silence.

But now the apprehension seems to melt away – it is almost as if the man recognises an opportunity. Suddenly, he is more forthcoming.

'I were with oor kid – Billy. He's a fell runner – he's in training for an event next week. I do some of his pacing. We parked up at Threlkeld – must have run for a good four hours, started out at five.'

Skelgill makes himself look interested.

'That'd be the Bob Graham, then?'

The man nods.

'Aye. Oor Billy's a bit of a natural.'

Skelgill is thinking on his feet. The unexpected easing – that the man emanates relief – has him wondering what is afoot. It could simply be the welcome change of subject – but he senses it is more than that.

He shrugs, a little resignedly.

'To honest with you – back in the day, I tried it and failed a couple of times. Doubt if I could even walk round it, now.'

Jimmy Higson seems content with his contribution thus far, and does not offer an opinion as to Skelgill's chances.

'Like I say, Billy takes some beating.'

'Aye, well – good luck to him.'

Skelgill makes a show of putting away his warrant card, as if to signify the closing of his visit. And now he looks hungrily at the fare on display, as though the thought of fell running has brought on an appetite. He digs in his pocket and slaps a pound coin on the counter.

'I'll take one of your sausage rolls.'

The butcher responds automatically.

'Like a bag?'

'Aye, if you would. Saves the crumbs.'

While the man bends to separate a small white paper bag from a wad strung on a hook, Skelgill clears his throat and speaks casually, his tone rueful.

'Those three peaks above Threlkeld – I could never decide whether to do Great Calva first or last. You pair must know best – what's the secret?'

Jimmy Higson seems to take a moment longer than is necessary to pick apart the layers of paper – it might almost be that Skelgill's question has momentarily paralysed him, in the way that a fly is immobilised when two swatting hands descend upon it simultaneously from opposite sides.

'First.'

The answer is unquestionably reluctant – and the man's expression distracted – and when the doorbell now tinkles and an elderly couple enter, Jimmy Higson is quick to greet them, handing over Skelgill's snack whilst still engaging with the new arrivals.

Skelgill, however, is ready to depart.

He raises his prize by way of farewell, but Jimmy Higson has turned away. As Skelgill exits, he holds open the door for two more local ladies.

Calculating that these would-be shoppers might occupy the butcher for five minutes, Skelgill ducks into a ginnel just a few doors along. As he suspects it leads to the rear of the row of properties in this section, and joins with an unmetalled lane that provides vehicular access to the various retailer premises and private residences.

Jimmy Higson's abattoir is no grand affair. The back of the shop comprises just a concreted yard with a central drain, and a long brick outhouse, its garage-style door bolted and locked, and a hosepipe coiled next to a wall-mounted tap. There is parked a large van, of the transit type, black in colour and lacking any livery. He circles it. It has seen better days. There are many scrapes and dents, mostly rusted, but he takes some time in perusing these.

Back at his car, the windows wound down and the sound of martins for company, he sits and ponders.

He has spread across the steering wheel his road atlas. The smaller scale – three miles to an inch – gives him a broader perspective than the Ordnance Survey.

It does not, however, show the three peaks to which he has minutes earlier referred. And it does not, therefore, tell the reader that, in the Bob Graham Round, the runner would scale Great Calva *neither* first *nor* last. Clockwise or anticlockwise, until the earth moves, it is always in the middle.

Jimmy Higson took a guess – and no doubt he will be on the phone to his brother just as soon as he can – to tell him which alternative he plumped for. Skelgill grins. He will receive short shrift. Although, no doubt, if pressed they would say it was Jimmy's mistake – he does not know the route that well.

But it is enough for Skelgill – it confirms his six sense – and defies common sense, knowing what he does – that the Higsons were never running round Skiddaw Forest on Monday morning.

The Higsons were at Stonethwaite.

If he were a butcher planning to steal sheep, who would he take with him? Someone he could trust, aye – but what about a shepherd? A man who could do the job in a trice and hide the flock in plain sight.

And, if he were a shepherd planning to steal sheep, who would be his accomplice of choice? Surely a butcher who can launder their booty into convertible currency, used notes sterling.

Now Skelgill regards the map intently.

The hamlet of Stonethwaite nestles high in a dead-end tributary of Borrowdale. The obvious route from there to the holding barn at Matterdale would be due north down into Keswick, then east by means of lanes. Obvious – but perhaps too obvious. The battered black van is conspicuous. Keswick is busy. Keswick has cameras.

Skelgill nods slowly.

If he were leaving Stonethwaite in a hurry, and were trying to avoid being seen … he would turn west … over Honister Pass.

Skelgill stares longer at the map.

His expression remains inscrutable.

After a minute he remembers the sausage roll. One end protrudes from the bag and, without looking, he takes a bite.

Now his features do contort – however, it is not the conundrum, but the pastry that troubles him – and he hurls it from the car.

With desperate cries of alarm two magpies plunge as if from thin air – they must lie in wait for just this kind of dissatisfied customer.

Skelgill watches the noisy contest, no holds barred, pair or not – just a *chacking* flapping blur of black and white.

Then he shakes his head.

It just couldn't be, could it?

Two birds with one stone for Billy Higson? A fifty-fifty share of three grand's worth of prime lamb – and a competitor taken out of the race at Honister Pass.

Skelgill reluctantly swallows his unwanted mouthful; he curses and jams his car into reverse.

'Give us a Haighs, any day of the week.'

19. THE LAWSONS

Wetheral – 5.15 p.m. Friday 7 June

'I T'S LIKE A regular car park.'
DS Jones murmurs in agreement. Her colleague carefully noses his own vehicle into the Wetheral driveway. Three of the cars she has seen before – the modest and rather matt white Ford, apparently used by the nanny, Ellie; the newish white Volkswagen that belongs to the mother of Victoria Lawson; and the latter's own brilliant white Mercedes sports coupé – but now there is a fourth, eclipsing the rest, a muscular oversized turquoise-black Porsche, the sort of supercar that immediately invites judgement about its owner (and perhaps not of the flattering kind that the owner would wish for).

DS Leyton casually circles the monster on foot, affecting admiration, as would be the desired effect – and perhaps doing so in a way that presumes him to be observed. As he pulls himself away he gives a rueful shake of the head to his waiting colleague – it might look like a kind of wishful thinking – but she reads the message that there are no flies on this car's gleaming bodywork, let alone dents. And, suffice to say, tracking data obtained by DC Watson from ANPR and car park cameras has already confirmed that Frank Lawson's car went to Manchester airport and back according to his scheduled journey.

As on their visit three days earlier, they are intercepted at the cautiously opened door by the large, alarmed brown eyes of the tall home-help-come-Praetorian-guard, Ellie. This time, however, they are admitted without the accompanying words of warning; although if not with hostility then certainly suspicion – that here are intruders capable of disrupting a fortress of domestic stability.

It is something upon which DS Jones reflects as they follow the nanny through the hallway.

Passing the playroom both detectives turn to their right, attracted by the sounds of an explosion. A glance reveals the two small boys kneeling transfixed before a huge widescreen TV that plays the latest animated movie. Aged two and four, as is the way with infants, the younger is blonder. Between them, their hands dip rhythmically into a carton of Jolly Time popcorn, perhaps a present from America.

They are conducted into a large modern kitchen, where Victoria and Frank Lawson are waiting at an island bar. Victoria remains seated, but Frank Lawson dismounts theatrically from his stool and comes forward gregariously, just as Ellie dutifully retreats. He engages DS Leyton, who is ahead, with an effusive handshake and greeting – and, in the moment it takes, DS Jones realises there is a further person present – in the background, half turned towards a worktop and sink, an older woman – perhaps in her early sixties – smartly dressed in a coral skirt suit, and neatly coiffured, and wearing white cotton gloves and looking like she may have come from some kind of function. DS Jones makes the assumption that this is Victoria Lawson's mother – though the woman now places two beakers of orange squash on a tray that already bears a mug of perhaps tea, and a folded copy of the Daily Telegraph, and leaves unobtrusively through what looks like a small library or study; there is also an exit to a utility room, and a much wider archway that leads into a stylish extension, a bright conservatory. These rooms must also provide access back to the hallway, and explain some of the many doors.

But Frank Lawson has reached DS Jones before she can make further analysis. He is of medium height and slim build, with short, dark hair cut modishly, with a correspondingly immaculate designer beard. Besuited – in what is clearly a made-to-measure cloth with an expensive sheen – he is casually tieless and just a hint crumpled, in what he pulls off as a slightly heroic state of affairs, the long-distance business traveller. He greets her with an excessive smile.

'Glad I could make it.'

The almost imperceptible innuendo in his tone – a Connery-like slur that he perhaps feels suits his Scots accent – more obvious in his falsely obsequious choice of words – impels DS Jones just for one small split-second to want to punch him between the narrow-set blue eyes.

She resists, and the moment passes – and she realises that Victoria Lawson is now moving to offer them seats – and refreshments – the latter they decline with thanks. They settle opposite the Lawsons, the respective genders directly facing one another.

Frank Lawson now draws direct attention to his attire. He pulls casually at the lapels of his jacket.

'Apologies that I haven't had time to change or shower – I've hit the ground running and I had to spend a few minutes with the boys. They always like to hear about the latest blockbusters I've notched up in business class.'

DS Jones humours him with a perfunctory smile – and perhaps Victoria Lawson detects the young officer's displeasure. She interjects a little breathlessly.

'Have you any news?'

DS Jones makes as if to reply, but first she checks each of the Lawsons with a warning look. It is clear that Frank Lawson is suddenly paying attention; he regards her intently, and slowly twists the expensive timepiece on his left wrist.

'There have been no significant developments as regards the accident itself. Partly for this reason we are widening the inquiry.' She glances at DS Leyton, by way of including him as part of the process to which she refers. 'We will explain more shortly. But first we would like to ask for your help in clarifying a matter. One line of inquiry we are following is that someone knew that Mr Sinclair would be crossing the road at Honister Pass and was waiting for him.'

Victoria Lawson's reaction is immediate – a look of horror grips her features – and she turns to stare at her husband. Frank Lawson, on the other hand, simply seems baffled by the suggestion.

DS Jones could wait – Victoria Lawson seems to have questions ready to burst forth from her lips, whereas Frank Lawson begins to shift a little uneasily as the silence grows – but instead she chooses to control the agenda, speaking evenly and without sinister undertones. She does, however, put the point directly to Frank Lawson.

'We'd like to understand who could have known where you and Mr Sinclair would be on Monday morning.'

Now she does wait.

Frank Lawson puts his hands together and leans forwards on his elbows.

'I don't see how anyone could have known. Even the Uber driver – all we said to him was to take us to Wasdale Head. We didn't discuss the route.'

DS Jones does not press this point.

'Did you tell anybody – neighbours, colleagues, running contacts – where the pair of you were going? Did you make any reference on social media?'

Frank Lawson interprets these questions to be aimed solely at him.

'I couldn't have done.' But now he grins rather obsequiously, and reaches to touch his wife on her upper arm with the back of his hand.

'Remember – at dinner on Sunday night, with Isobel?' He breaks off momentarily to consult with DS Leyton. He contrives a face of fraternal suffering. 'That's the mother-in-law. They were trying to talk me out of going – that I'd never make the flight to LA.'

Frank Lawson looks back at DS Jones.

'I was in bed when I confirmed to Seb that I'd meet him. There was no time to tell anyone.'

DS Jones nods, but does not respond, and the silence prompts some elaboration.

'I figured if I drove straight from Keswick to Manchester I would be fine. So close to the event – I couldn't take the chance on missing a training session. You know – like that Olympic decathlete who trained twice on Christmas Day in case his main rival trained once on Christmas Day. I'm in it to win.' He sprays about him a somewhat inane grin, seeking approbation.

Victoria Lawson has been listening to her husband with a mixture of bewilderment and disquiet, but now she speaks up. As she looks from one detective to the other, there is a welling-up in her cobalt blue eyes.

'You think someone did it – deliberately.'

Rather more so than her husband, who has answered the superficial question, Victoria Lawson speaks to the heart of the matter.

DS Jones glances at DS Leyton. He understands the covert signal, and produces a copy of *Fell Running* from his briefcase. He places it on the island counter, where any one of them may reach it.

DS Jones, however, continues to provide the commentary.

'I said we would explain. Are you familiar with this magazine?'

Frank Lawson takes this as a cue to pick up the periodical. He brandishes it – and turns it towards his wife.

'I buy this. Seb put me onto it.'

Victoria Lawson looks like she wonders what is coming. The detectives have reasoned that quite likely her office staff have relayed the conversations that relate to the magazine – but at this juncture she shows no sign of recognition.

DS Jones turns to Frank Lawson.

'Mr Lawson, do you happen to have your copy to hand? Of the June edition.'

He gives a sideways jerk of the head and slips off his stool.

'It will be through in the conservatory.'

He leaves the detectives' copy but returns a minute later empty-handed. He addresses his wife.

'I can't see any of the magazines?'

Victoria Lawson looks a little puzzled. Then she reaches for her mobile phone.

'Excuse me.'

She dials with the handset lying flat and the speakerphone engaged. The call is instantly answered.

'Hello?'

There are background sounds of television and children's excited voices.

'Ellie – have you got a minute?'

'Sure.'

In a moment the tall figure of the nanny appears at the door. Then she advances a little apprehensively. She joins her hands behind her back.

Victoria Lawson moves to put her at ease.

'It's alright – do you know what happened to all the magazines that were in the conservatory?'

For a moment Ellie appears to think she has committed some mortal sin – but she steels herself to make a confession.

'I took them to Asda on Wednesday when I did the shopping after I dropped Tommy at nursery. With the empty wine bottles. They were in the green recycling box.'

She tilts her head a little, it seems to indicate in the direction of the utility room.

DS Jones now interposes. She picks up *Fell Running*.

'Did you happen to notice if there was a copy of this magazine?'

Ellie's eyes widen, showing their whites, but she shakes her head.

'I didn't sort through them.'

She answers quickly, and looks at Victoria Lawson as though to have done so would have been some breach of trust – the suggestion that she might have extracted any publications that she wanted to keep for herself.

DS Jones is about to speak again – but now the kitchen door, left slightly ajar, bursts open and the smaller of the boys, still a toddler, charges headlong, holding aloft a toy figure and making the *vroom* of a jet engine. As dogs have a sixth sense for the pet-owner in the room, likely to have treats in a pocket, the child makes a beeline for DS Leyton, cannoning into the sergeant's legs as a means of arresting his momentum.

'*Whoa!* – alright, me old china – what've you brought me, this time?'

Hopping and thrusting, the boy gleefully tries to hand the toy to DS Leyton – who protests that he can't accept the most generous offer – though the boy persists, engaging imploringly with great brown eyes. As a compromise DS Leyton lifts the child up onto his lap.

'Now then, little fella – that's Superwoman if I ain't mistaken?'

Just when Ellie seems to recognise that she should intervene, and remove the playroom escapee from the adult meeting, Victoria Lawson's mother Isobel materialises, and swoops in on the boy.

'So, here you are. Up you come, William Lawson.'

She lifts the toddler and without further comment to those present carries him from the room; though they hear her chide him not to disturb Mummy – whose epithet he repeats delightedly, until out of earshot.

There is a momentary hiatus in the kitchen – DS Jones has been watching Frank Lawson – but when she shifts her attention to Victoria Lawson she finds the woman looking at her with consternation. Instinctively, she responds.

'He's very cute.'

Victoria Lawson's expression softens – but her husband pre-empts her further response.

'Like father, like son!'

He affects modesty – but the remark falls flat, even with his wife – and now Ellie speaks up.

'I should go and help Isobel.'

She sways, but her feet remain rooted. DS Jones takes charge of the situation.

'Thank you, Ellie – that was all we wanted to know.'

As the girl turns away Victoria Lawson calls out.

'Ellie – you can leave early if you like – now Mum's here, she can see to the boys.'

The tall nanny nods compliantly – she answers that she will tidy their rooms – and now she wastes no time in making an exit; they hear her double-check that the door to the hall is fastened firmly.

DS Jones can see that Victoria Lawson is discomfited, while her husband – if anything – seems to be exhibiting signs of boredom. She returns to the subject of *Fell Running*, and rotates the magazine so that the cover is the correct way up for the Lawsons to read. She addresses Frank Lawson.

'Mr Lawson, how do you get your copy?'

'I have it delivered – it's an annual subscription.'

DS Jones indicates to the cover story.

'And did you read this article?'

Now Frank Lawson shakes his head.

'I just took it out of the polywrap – threw away the flyers. I've been meaning to come back to it.'

'Do you know any of the other runners – entrants to the Bob Graham challenge?'

He twists again at the wristwatch; he might almost be trying to draw attention to its brand name.

'Seb wanted us to keep a low profile – ambush them with our talent.'

DS Jones has some doubt over the original source of such self-aggrandisement – but she indicates with the tip of her pen the photograph of Billy 'The Goat' Higson.

'What about this chap – he's the favourite, I believe? The record holder.'

But again Frank Lawson shakes his head.

'Anything's possible on the day.'

Now he grins, rather inanely.

But DS Jones picks up on his point.

'If you or Mr Sinclair were among the contenders – there might be someone who would prefer you not to run.'

'My wife, naturally! She wouldn't want me getting injured.'

Frank Lawson's quip is both brash and yet needy – but Victoria Lawson does not seem able to react to either sentiment – she merely regards him with alarm. When Frank Lawson now only shrugs – as though he has exhausted his repertoire of possible answers, DS Jones turns to Victoria Lawson. She speaks in an informative manner.

'We think a message may have been passed to Mr Sinclair, using a copy of the magazine. Your colleague Miss Magnusson brought it to our attention – it was in his desk at your offices.'

'Fingerprints – aye?'

It is Frank Lawson that pre-empts any response from his wife. When he realises that all three of the group are regarding him curiously, he slides the magazine across to the detectives' side of the bar.

'Have mine, for starters!'

Victoria Lawson is looking a little embarrassed – but, casually, DS Leyton seizes upon this opportunity.

He picks the magazine up by its corner, and holds it illustratively.

'I'm sure you can imagine, sir, that any fingerprints we take in the course of an investigation, in order to be admissible as evidence, have to be provided voluntarily.'

Frank Lawson is grinning; he seems to be relishing the limelight.

'I volunteer!'

Now DS Leyton makes a show of consulting his colleague – they do so in unspoken terms – but it is plain to the onlookers that they are in open agreement to this prospect.

DS Leyton resumes.

'Naturally, it will help us to eliminate as many people as possible – however improbable – and we do have a MobileID in the car – it's a scanner, it works in a jiffy. If you have no objection, sir – then we're happy to proceed.'

Frank Lawson gets to his feet.

'Lead the way, officer.' He mockingly offers his wrists for handcuffing. 'I've always wanted my dabs taken.'

'Frank – but –'

Victoria Lawson stifles her protest – and her husband continues unabashed.

'Why not? After all – I was the one with him on Monday morning.'

'And so you couldn't have run him over.'

Frank Lawson raises a hand as he follows DS Leyton out of the kitchen.

'Exactly.'

It takes a few moments for Victoria Lawson to gather her wits. She refers meekly to DS Jones.

'What about me – do you want my fingerprints? I was here – I overslept – because Frank disturbed me in the early hours.'

DS Jones regards her evenly.

'Were you aware of the copy of *Fell Running* that arrived at your offices?'

Victoria Lawson shakes her head.

'I had no idea – but I guess this is why you were asking about who handles the mail?'

DS Jones nods.

'Your team are evidently doing their best to shelter you from unnecessary hassle. But – no, is the answer to your question about fingerprints.'

Victoria Lawson seems to ponder the implications for a moment, and she folds her hands together on her lap.

'I realise – that when you came on Tuesday – you were careful to skirt around the idea that something had been done deliberately to Seb – but – now – it's hard to believe that you have to consider the worst.'

She hesitates, and DS Jones responds, her tone sympathetic.

'You can be sure that the police – unfortunately – are trained to think of every eventuality, from the outset. But we're not quite at that stage, yet.'

Victoria Lawson nods reluctantly.

Then suddenly she rises.

'Would you mind if I had a glass of wine? Can I give you one?'

'It's no to both.'

Victoria Lawson walks around to an imposing American refrigerator that broods in the corner behind DS Jones. She tugs at the right-hand door where several uncorked bottles stand in a shelf. DS Jones slips off her stool and approaches. The left-hand door is stickered with family photographs. She peruses them while the woman pours herself a small measure of Chablis in a large-bowl glass. She replaces the bottle and closes the door – and now she makes reference to the picture that seems to hold DS Jones's interest.

'That's my Dad – Granddad Beslow, with the boys.'

A man who seems only to be in late middle-age is sitting or perhaps leaning lightly against the bonnet of a large car, a classic Mercedes perhaps, its navy or black bodywork gleaming like a freshly waxed wedding limousine, reflecting a bright sky. The man squints in the sunshine, and has a hand each around the shoulders of the two small boys; they are perched happily on the bonnet, one either side of him, sucking red ice lollies. Behind, out of focus, is what might be a maritime horizon.

DS Jones draws a conclusion from the children's appearances.

'This must have been quite recent.'

Victoria Lawson takes a sip of her drink; DS Jones suspects it is to stifle a tremor in her voice.

'It was taken about a month before he died. In March – it was William's second birthday – Dad took them to the seaside.'

There is a respectful pause.

'I'm sorry for your loss.'

'Thank you.'

Victoria Lawson takes a more substantial drink.

They stand for a moment; it is hard to tell if Victoria Lawson is reprising memories captured by the photographs. DS Jones, for her part, scans them – they are mostly of the children, as would be expected – though it looks like Frank Lawson has interposed himself into several of the shots, clowning at the camera – and there is one of the two grandparents, in walking gear, seated outside a pub. But there is none, DS Jones notes, that features Victoria Lawson with her partner.

'There *is* something.'

'I'm sorry?'

DS Jones is jolted from her thoughts.

Victoria Lawson begins to step back towards the island bar. She puts down the glass and reaches to touch the magazine. Now she begins to speak rapidly.

'I didn't like to say in front of Frank. A couple of weeks ago – Sebastian had given me a lift home. My Mum was in here preparing the boys' tea, so we went into the conservatory to finish discussing a project. Frank's copy of the magazine was there – it was still in its clear wrapper. Sebastian noticed it – and he said, that's the man I need to beat.'

Now she points to the image of Billy Higson, his features contorted by the gruelling climb.

DS Jones waits a little longer.

'Was that all he said?'

It takes a moment before Victoria Lawson replies.

'I can't remember exactly – I think he might have said something like, the guy doesn't take any prisoners. Perhaps along those lines. I didn't think much of it – it's not like it's gladiators – or even a contact sport.'

DS Jones nods pensively.

'Sounds like he thought he may have been able to beat him.'

Victoria Lawson seems uncertain.

'Well – I don't know – but I didn't like to say – I mean, Frank obviously thinks *he's* got a chance.'

The two exchange glances, and there is a certain amount of unspoken female intuition in lieu of further explanation.

'And there has been no suggestion – from either – that one of them should drop out?'

The older woman shakes her head.

'Frank wouldn't be able to keep something like that to himself.'

'What about Mr Sinclair?'

'Well – he would be more likely to.'

DS Jones nods.

But just now there comes the sound of a sudden disturbance. It is from the little library room. Its connecting door from the hallway must have been opened and the person entering has bumped into someone inside. The profuse apology being in DS Leyton's East London lingo, it seems he has done the bumping. There is also a woman's voice, spoken quietly in answer. A moment later, he emerges into the kitchen.

'Whoops-a-daisy.' He grins sheepishly at Victoria Lawson. 'Almost flattened your Ma there – she was on a step trying to get a book down. No harm done – Roger's Thesaurus safely obtained.' He looks about the kitchen, as though he is still a little disoriented. 'Lost me bearings – you've got so many doors out there in the hall – I took the wrong one.'

Victoria Lawson rises and steps over to peer around into the study – but evidently her mother has taken her book and gone; she closes the door and turns back to the detectives. She regards them inquiringly, and it is DS Leyton who responds – first to his colleague.

'That's all done.' He turns to Victoria Lawson. 'Your husband's been showing me his motor – under the bonnet. He's got a spot of oil on his hands – he's gone upstairs to clean up and shower.'

DS Jones puts away her notebook and slings her satchel over her shoulder.

'Mrs Lawson – thank you – I'm sorry we have disturbed your domestic routine.' Victoria Lawson begins to protest, that it is no trouble – but DS Jones cuts her off. 'Just one small thing – could we borrow the photograph – of your father? I would like to show it to someone.'

It is hard to say if Victoria Lawson is perturbed – not least that DS Jones does not offer a proper explanation – but she does not seem able to summon up the energy either to question why or outright object. She walks over to the fridge and begins to unpick the print of her parents seated outside the pub. DS Jones follows her.

'Actually – would you mind if we took this one.' She indicates the shot of the trio seated on the car bonnet.

'Of course – here – take them both, why don't you?'

DS Jones makes a play of taking out her notebook and carefully inserting the slightly curling prints between its covers. When she looks up at Victoria Lawson, who has watched in silence, she is sure she reads in the deep blue eyes an entreaty of hope.

*

Some two hundred yards out of the Lawsons' driveway, DS Leyton brings the car to an abrupt halt.

'There's the nanny.'

He has spotted the young woman, marked out by her distinctive height and upright bearing, standing sentry at a bus stop in their own direction of travel. He lowers the passenger window, and calls across.

'Miss Ellie – hop in – I expect we're going your way.'

The young woman is plainly torn – the opposing sentiments being, one, that these are the enemy, and two, she must obey orders.

DS Jones, meanwhile, pressed back against her seat to facilitate the exchange, is wondering what her colleague is up to. They do not even know the girl's address, let alone where she might be going. However, she plays along with such opportunism, and looks reassuringly at the swithering nanny.

'I'm meeting my mother at Asda. We're having tea in the café. I'm helping her with the shopping. Then she's giving me a lift home.'

Ellie's response smacks more of explanation than excuse, and DS Leyton capitalises upon the nuance.

'Spot on, girl – we're going for cheap petrol. Jump in – and we'll save your fare – if your bus ever comes.'

These points all carry weight, and it seems the scales have tipped. Rather to the chagrin of several other would-be passengers, Ellie makes a dart for the car and folds her long-limbed form into the rear nearside seat.

'I don't know what Victoria would say about me getting a lift from you.'

It is an ingenuous remark – but it is clearly the nature of the girl – she wears her colours on her sleeve. DS Jones offers some mitigation.

'She's obviously a considerate employer – she was keen that you got away early – why wouldn't she want you to have a lift, as well? It's not like it's a marked squad car, and people would wonder if you'd been arrested.'

Now Ellie does think the better of saying what comes to mind, for she mumbles something to herself, a sentence that finally materialises with a not-entirely-convincing thank you.

DS Leyton is quick to make conversation.

'So, they don't let you take the little Ford home with you? That would be really handy.'

He can see in his rear-view mirror that Ellie is shaking her head.

'It's got the child seats. Sometimes they need it.'

177

DS Leyton is nodding. He doubts Frank Lawson would want a kiddie seat anywhere near his pristine Porsche, let alone a toddler armed with an explosive packet of Quavers. And Victoria Lawson's coupé is hardly suitable – lacking adequate space in the rear. A second child brings unseen challenges for a two-flash-car household.

He makes a noise of exasperation – it is an abstract expression, that he empathises with her predicament – and perhaps she senses this. He continues, his tone sympathetic.

'Sounds like they have you working evenings, an' all?'

Ellie gives a considered shake of the head.

'Not so much, lately. Isobel has been staying over a lot since – well – since her husband passed away – and I suppose it distracts her, to mind the boys. She goes to bridge on Tuesdays and book club on Thursdays – so that's when I normally work late, now. But I can get the boys bathed and in bed for seven.'

'That is impressive.'

DS Leyton nods ruefully – a nanny, and seven o'clock bedtime – paradise. Ellie seems to appreciate the compliment – and perhaps relaxing a little now, and after having observed her employers' co-operation with the police, she leans forward, almost conspiratorially.

'You need to make allowances for Victoria, you know. She was very upset when her father died. And now this is bringing it back. I think it's affecting her memory. I didn't like to say in front of Frank – but you can see how she likes the house tidy – and she'd asked me to collect up all the magazines from the conservatory, for the recycling.'

The detectives are nodding. They have seen enough of the immaculate property – it has the permanent look of a home staged for an interior design photoshoot. And, perhaps not surprisingly, it seems the girl's loyalties lie with Victoria rather than Frank Lawson.

DS Jones remains unsure whether her colleague has some plan in mind – indeed, as time passes it seems more likely that he merely acted on impulse. As they cross the M6 roundabout – from where the Asda superstore is just a two-minute drive – she raises a question that lingers vaguely in her own thoughts.

'Mrs Lawson said that Mr Sinclair sometimes gave her a lift home – and that on occasion they might carry on a meeting or a discussion. She mentioned that they'd seen that running magazine in the conservatory a couple of weeks ago.'

Ellie does not respond, and DS Jones draws out her seatbelt so that she may twist around. She sees that the girl is looking disconcerted.

'Don't worry about the magazine. We'll take care of that. I was just wondering – you mentioned previously that you didn't know Mr Sinclair very well – but can you think of anything out of the ordinary? Especially recently.'

Ellie's expression shifts a little, perhaps from worry to puzzlement.

'About Sebastian – Mr Sinclair – you mean?'

'Aha.'

DS Jones regards Ellie encouragingly, but offers no further guidance.

It takes a few moments for the girl to respond.

'Not really, no. I mean – perhaps he's been round more often, lately – but I supposed that was to do with him feeling sorry for Victoria – over her father. Taking some of the work pressure off her.'

DS Jones waits.

'Anything else?'

The nanny shakes her head. But then she adopts a more forthright manner – as if she feels that in return for the lift she ought to come up with something in kind.

'Oh – they took the boys out a couple of times. With a picnic tea, down to the river. Victoria doesn't let me take them down there – unless there's two adults. I wouldn't anyway – it's too dangerous – and they're live wires – up to mischief the second you let them out of your sight.'

DS Leyton makes another involuntary groan – identifying with the predicament. But they have reached their destination, and it is plain that despite her softening towards them, the nanny is eager to escape her present company. They watch her stride briskly into the store.

DS Jones is distracted as they drive away – but as they pass the petrol pumps she starts.

'What about fuel?'

DS Leyton chuckles.

'Nah – I've got three-quarters of a tank – much as it's a decent price.'

DS Jones nods, but remains silent until they have joined the southbound motorway, a process requiring a frustrating sequence of lane and traffic light manoeuvres that provides her colleague with an excuse to let off steam.

'Did you buy all that about the magazine?'

DS Leyton shoots her a sideways glance.

'Didn't you?'

DS Jones hesitates.

'Well, I think I did – it would be a bit much for them all to be wrapped into a conspiracy.'

DS Leyton is nodding.

'Mind – did you make that up – about Victoria Lawson and Sinclair seeing the magazine? To get the nanny talking about them?'

DS Jones turns in surprise.

'Actually, no – she told me while you were admiring the status symbol in the driveway.'

Now DS Leyton scoffs.

'He thinks he's flamin' James Bond – either that or some comedian – and there's his pal who's hardly cold. Sounds like he's still planning to run, an' all. Show some respect, eh?'

DS Jones regards her colleague reflectively. Plainly he is no more enamoured by Frank Lawson's personality than she. However, she suspects that insecurity rather than guilt lies at the root of his manners. Indeed, there is a small paradox at play, and she shares her thoughts.

'He could hardly pay attention, could he? You know – I doubt he ever reads a magazine, a book – or whatever.'

'What are you saying?'

'Oh, well – just the coded message – the threat to Sebastian Sinclair – would Frank Lawson really come up with something like that?'

DS Leyton screws up his features; he concentrates for a moment on passing a van that has been hogging the middle lane – though its driver sails blithely onwards, oblivious of the black looks he is garnering.

'Maybe you're right, girl. It didn't occur to me – I ain't much of a reader, myself – just to the nippers. The 101 Dalmatians, they like. Plus, that stuff's more my reading age.'

DS Jones grins charitably.

'I suppose those prints could settle it.'

DS Leyton nods.

'Well – he ain't on the national database – but I don't suppose we expected him to be. Here's hoping Forensics get back to us in the morning with a match to the magazine.'

'Agreed. I'll reserve judgement.'

She inhales deeply, unexpectedly.

'What is it, Emma?'

'Oh – nothing really. Just this magazine threat. Without it, we'd have nowhere to go – but I keep worrying that it's a – well – a red herring, I suppose.'

180

'You mean, to throw us off the scent?'

Now DS Jones turns to regard her colleague – as if his commonplace remark is somehow perspicacious.

'Oh – well – I suppose – I meant, more of our own making. That's it's just a hoax for its own sake.'

But now she falls silent, and DS Leyton goes along with the situation; for those capable of it, the monotony of the motorway can be a good time for abstract reflection. Indeed, they are approaching the sign for Wigton before DS Jones speaks again.

'Victoria Lawson was shocked at the suggestion of Sebastian Sinclair being targeted.'

'Yeah – I thought that, too. And we didn't even mention the wording of the threat. Mind you – she obviously didn't think her Frank could have had anything to do with it.'

DS Leyton glances at his colleague – she does not appear entirely convinced. He clears his throat.

'Look – I'm as game as you are to play devil's advocate – we should of course allow for good acting. Seems to me that any one of these folk could have got to Honister Pass and back on Monday morning. Even Victoria Lawson – okay, she's got the nippers to take care of – but her old Ma stays over, remember?'

DS Jones hesitates – but then avoids being sidetracked.

'She didn't want Frank Lawson to know that she and Sebastian Sinclair had seen the magazine, and were discussing the race. She told me that Sinclair picked out Billy Higson as the man he would have to beat.'

DS Leyton makes a growl in his throat.

'*Hah* – that would definitely have narked Frank Lawson.'

DS Jones nods pensively, as though that is not all.

After a moment, she intones reflectively.

'He can't be an easy person to live with – high maintenance, they call it, don't they? It must be like having an extra child. But when it's an adult, more tiresome.'

DS Leyton seems to be checking the play in his steering rack, making tiny rapid movements of the wheel, without the vehicle showing any signs of deviation.

'He'll definitely be peeved if he don't get his chocolates on Father's Day.'

DS Jones turns to regard her colleague; she inhales, giving the impression that something is remiss of her.

'I wanted to mention that – but, you know, when I was with Victoria Lawson on her own – and we were looking at the photographs of her Dad – I couldn't bring myself to raise it.'

DS Leyton shrugs.

'Nah – it's probably something and nothing. There'll be folk all over the shop who've marked Father's Day on their calendars. But I did wonder why you asked to borrow the photo. Is it to show the Guvnor – that he might know the geezer?'

DS Jones makes a face of some disquiet – that DS Leyton has perhaps hit the nail on the head – but that she has not yet got her ducks in a row on this matter. Skelgill, in giving her free rein, in his absence has doubly allowed her to speculate unchecked – moreover, his assertion – gut feel or not – that someone else may be in jeopardy has spurred her along. But much of this she has kept from DS Leyton; she has no wish to rope him into some hairbrained theory of the case. She gives a non-committal nod of the head.

'Something like that.'

'A hunch?'

'Hmm. I'm still thinking it through.'

DS Leyton turns and plies her with a grin – then he checks the time on the console.

'Then you'd better get your thinking cap on, girl.'

20. THRELKELD II

The White Mare – 8.45 p.m. Friday 7 June

IN WHAT SEEMS a small Groundhog Day moment, Skelgill enters the secluded residents' lounge to find his friends again have the small, cosy room to themselves, despite it being a Friday night and the inn accordingly busier. On this occasion, however, Rita no longer has her left leg stretched out and supported on a stool. Instead, she sits normally.

'How's the walking wounded?'

'Much better, thank you, sir. We took it easy – and Rosheen has kindly massaged the muscle. I believe I'll be fighting fit by first thing tomorrow morning. Right as rain, as Gerry likes to say.'

Gerry groans. He casts a despairing hand up at a dark landscape painting that looms above the two ladies.

'She only wants us to climb Blencathra by Sharp Edge.'

Rita protests.

'Just think – what a memory it will be!'

Now Gerry harrumphs.

'You just want the most dangerous photo you can think of. As if dangling above the Grand Canyon wasn't good enough for you.' He addresses Skelgill, who places the pint he has carried through from the bar on their table and takes the seat reserved for him. 'What do you think to that, lad?'

Skelgill imbibes a considered pull of ale. He is conscious of the three sets of eyes upon him, and their conflicting preferences that hang upon his answer.

'Sharp Edge? In damp, fog and wind I wouldn't recommend you went within a mile of it. But in dry, clear and calm conditions like these – if you've got a head for heights and are sound of foot – you can do it and barely put a hand to the rock. It's only classed as a Grade 1 scramble – that tells you it's not physically challenging. But the exposure, particularly on the south side into the coomb – it's proper rock-climbing exposure.'

Skelgill's exposition provides equal ammunition for the warring factions – while it seems Rosheen is ambivalent, and she mediates in the small argument which now ensues between her companions.

When it seems like neither side will give way, Skelgill offers the basis for a truce.

'You can always start out – and, if you're not sure – take the lower path on the easier slope under the ridge on the north side. At least a slip there won't be life-threatening.'

Gerry sees the opportunity to close the matter. But still he wants the last word.

'We'll talk her out of it over breakfast.'

Rita winks at Skelgill. He is pretty sure he knows what is going to happen. He moves the conversation on.

'How did you folks get on today?'

Gerry comes straight back in.

'Aye – we went to Castlerigg, like you suggested. Rita got her photo. We tried counting the standing stones and all got different answers. And Rosheen was in her element – she even gave an impromptu lecture to a group of foreign students – in French!'

The red-headed Rosheen grins rather coyly beneath Skelgill's gaze, employing her fringe to modest effect.

Gerry continues.

'What was that phrase that wowed them – about the Druids?'

Rosheen reluctantly recites.

'Sorciers en gilet blanc.'

Skelgill frowns. Though he plays along, as though he is expected to make a stab at the translation.

'Jelly and blancmange with sauce?'

His effort raises a collective laugh.

Rosheen reaches to tap him consolingly on the forearm.

'I can't claim it as mine – it was Coleridge – his original words were *white-vested wizards.*'

Skelgill looks suitably impressed.

But again Gerry interposes.

'Speaking of dessert, lad – Rita's bought you some parkin. On the driver's recommendation we spent the afternoon at Rheged – watched a wonderful film about Mallory and Irvine. I'm still convinced they were the first to climb Everest. Where else would Mallory have left that photograph of his wife, but the summit?'

Skelgill regards Gerry reflectively. While in other company he would enter into the debate – but with Sharp Edge beckoning, the terrible fate of the two British explorers might not be the best subject.

'So you didn't pop into the town, after Castlerigg, then?'

Gerry grins.

'We thought we'd save the flesh pots of Keswick until after our trek.'

Skelgill reciprocates with a smile.

'There's some decent local shops and cafés there. It's not so touristy as down Windermere way.'

But Gerry raises a cautionary finger.

'Now you mention Keswick – here's a funny thing. When we returned earlier this evening, before we went in for dinner, I thought I'd ring The Highwayman – just to make sure they'd got the arrangements right, in case the staff had changed over and they hadn't got the message – and they were wondering why we hadn't turned up.'

Skelgill nods.

'Any rate, lad – I spoke to the landlady and she said it was just as well we were coming a day late. There's been some vandalism and they've damaged the door of one of the rooms we've got booked – so it wouldn't be usable until they can get a joiner in tomorrow morning.'

Skelgill now makes a face of suitable commiseration.

Gerry, meanwhile, regards Rita with affected concern.

'Story of our trip – seems like we don't have to look for our troubles.'

Skelgill finishes a draft of beer and inhales to speak. He jerks a thumb over his shoulder, in the direction where Blencathra rises unseen behind the inn.

'Are you sure you want to go by Sharp Edge? I'm thinking maybe I should give you a lesson in alpine-style roping.'

'That's quite enough, young man.'

It is Rita that rises and presses an admonishing hand upon Skelgill's shoulder. She excuses herself, and states that she will order a round of drinks. She places her camera bag carefully on her seat. They watch her go.

Skelgill is first to remark.

'She does seem to be moving freely.'

Rosheen responds with a complimentary murmur – but now that Rita has left the room, Gerry leans forwards in conspiratorial fashion.

'Truth be told, lad – I told a little white lie, there. The reason I phoned The Highwayman was that we've arranged to get a pricey bottle of bubbly put on ice in Rita's room tomorrow before we arrive – this is her special trip – and we wanted to give her a little surprise and congratulate her for the achievement. I was just checking up for that reason.'

Skelgill nods in approval.

Gerry continues.

'The landlady was right upset. It was actually the single room for Rita that was broken into. But she assured us they'll have it all shipshape by the time we get there.'

Skelgill ponders for a moment.

'It was definitely broken into? Or was it just random vandalism?'

Gerry seems to understand the nuance, and that he has not been clear.

'It was the only incident she mentioned. Seems it had not long happened. I mean – if someone were out to steal the champagne – thinking we were coming as originally planned – well, who would know that?' He glances at Rosheen, seeking affirmation. 'It'd have to be one of the staff, wouldn't it? I didn't like to press the owner – I thought it might embarrass her.'

Rosheen offers a caveat.

'Mind – you'd think if it were staff, they'd have a skeleton key – a master key.'

Skelgill is regarding Rosheen thoughtfully when Rita returns, and they must change the subject.

Gerry taps the side of his nose. Skelgill is now the repository of secrets for both sides.

'What about thee – how did you get on, lad? Did you go up to Scales Tarn?'

Skelgill shakes his head.

'You might say I did a spot of prospecting around the area. It's a while since I took on the Bob Graham Round – there's always little shortcuts to be found – you can chisel away a minute here, a minute there.'

It seems one white lie begets another.

'I saved the tarn until tomorrow – since it's the last one.'

His companions look relieved. Rita is first to speak.

'So we might see something of you?'

'I don't see why not.'

Now Gerry chips in.

'It'd be first on the clockwise route, of course – I suppose you'll do it that way, when you make your record-setting attempt? You'll want a fast start – get that first fish under your belt.'

Skelgill is taking a drink. He nods over the rim of his pint glass. It crosses his mind that Scales Tarn will not be a walkover. His previous experience is that the Blencathra brownies are not easy to coax from their mountain pool.

Rosheen has a question.

'How will the catches be verified?'

Skelgill nods.

'The local angling club is taking ownership. They'll be providing marshals.'

'*Ha-hah.*' Gerry finds some amusement. 'Can't have folk trotting round with a bag of sprats. If you see someone running in chest waders, you'll know what they've got down the legs!'

Skelgill responds with a knowing look. To a degree, Gerry is correct about waders – they are the time-honoured repository for fish caught over the bag limit.

But Rosheen begs to differ.

'You couldn't run in waders, though, could you? You'd probably get heat exhaustion.'

While a little interchange takes place on the matter, Skelgill zones out – and when he comes to, he realises he is being observed rather uncharacteristically checking his mobile phone.

'No peace for the wicked, eh, lad?'

Again, Gerry is shrewd in his assessment. It is past the time for DS Jones's arrival – based on an earlier text message – and certainly not characteristic of her, either.

Skelgill grins – but he rises, and explains he will just "have a deek" along the lane.

'I expect they're closing in on a suspect.'

Gerry's regular quips seem half designed for him to overhear. But on this occasion, as he departs, he gleans more of the conversation. First there is Rita's response.

'Do British police always work when they're supposed to be on vacation?'

And Gerry's rejoinder.

'If I were a young inspector and I had a sergeant like that one, I'd be working round t' clock!'

While Gerry is being elbowed by Rosheen, Skelgill exits via a side door from the passage – and he spies, facing him, DS Jones's car parked a little way along from the front of the inn. She is behind the wheel, and he guesses that tonight she has come unaccompanied. Head bowed, she appears deep in thought and does not notice his approach. He opens the passenger door and slides into the vacant seat. She hurriedly snaps shut the case of her phone, and lays it on the dashboard. A more proprietorial sort might wonder what – or rather whom – she is communicating with.

'Summat up?'

It seems she is not quite ready to tell him – though she does her best to conceal the sentiment beneath a welcoming smile.

But Skelgill is not fooled.

'While you get your head straight, let me just chuck another spanner in the works.'

'Oh, really?'

'Aye. About your friendly neighbourhood shepherd and fell runner, Billy 'The Goat' Higson.'

Skelgill opts to dispense with possibilities and launches into a definite account.

'Billy Higson's got ten prize blue Texels in his barn that were stolen from Jack Thompson's at Stonethwaite. He's holding them for Jimmy Higson who's a butcher at Aspatria. The pair of them did the job in Jimmy's van early on Monday morning.'

DS Jones regards him, wide-eyed.

'So, they weren't running, north of Threlkeld.'

'Did we ever think they were?'

'No, I suppose not. But it would be hard to disprove.'

She sounds a little dejected – as if she has failed in this regard.

'Don't fret, lass. I caught out Jimmy Higson with a trick question about the fells – he'd obviously been briefed by Billy – but not well enough.'

DS Jones thinks for a moment. She might be wondering what exactly is the encumbering spanner that this information represents.

'Do they know we know this?'

Skelgill contrives a sly grin to accompany a shake of his head. But then he turns to regard her intently.

'The best quiet route away from Stonethwaite is over the Honister.'

She widens her eyes again – more deliberately now.

Skelgill adds a rider.

'The timing fits. The sheep were gone afore eight.'

'The vehicle?'

'I checked it. It's an old nail, banged to bits. It would take some detailed testing.'

DS Jones presses her hands together and touches her fingertips to her lips.

'We've consistently said – to target Sebastian Sinclair you would need to know he was going to be at Honister Hause. Therefore an accident was far more likely. But – after an accident – who wouldn't stop? *A pair of crooks with a stolen cargo.*'

Skelgill remains silent – there is the hint that he may not concur entirely with the scenario she paints.

Now DS Jones raises her hands and begins massaging her scalp, as though it is a process of rearranging and recalibrating the information within. With spread fingers she combs higher and gradually her hair falls like fine streams of golden sand in the low evening sunlight that penetrates the car's interior.

She shakes her tousled head.

'What I just said – it seems perfectly plausible, doesn't it? But – you know – paradoxically, that Billy Higson could in one fell swoop steal sheep and take out his main rival, whom he claims not to know …'

She gazes at Skelgill. He is plainly not champing at the bit to advocate his finding.

'Guv?'

Skelgill starts.

'Aye – I tend to agree with you. It would be the coincidence to beat all coincidences. Plus I'm assuming his brother was driving. To identify Sinclair in the two seconds it took him to cross the road – and then go for him – it's a tall order.'

Now both sit in silence for a while. DS Jones is still processing this new information. She is first to speak, however.

'There are a couple of things I should mention in this context. First, that some big bets have been placed with local bookmakers on Billy Higson to win the race. They've been laid off with one of the big firms, where DS Leyton has a contact. But to all intents and purposes, the bets are anonymous.

'Second, Sebastian Sinclair knew about Billy Higson. He told Victoria Lawson that Higson was the man he had to beat, and that he took no prisoners – words to that effect.'

Skelgill rubs a knuckle against the stubble on his chin, exaggerating his prominent jaw. DS Jones continues.

'This came up when the pair of them were having a chat at the Lawson's house after work. Frank Lawson's copy of *Fell Running* was in the conservatory. The magazine – by the way – has disappeared – apparently the nanny put it in the recycling. I should also say that Frank Lawson virtually forced his fingerprints upon us.'

Now Skelgill does raise an eyebrow.

'Is that what's been mithering you?' He nods towards her phone.

He refers to her state of preoccupation when he arrived.

DS Jones grimaces reluctantly.

'Indirectly, I suppose.'

Skelgill waits for a moment.

'Are you going to tell us, then, lass?'

DS Jones nods – but she does not reach for her mobile. She composes herself, and delays a few moments before responding.

'Is it your friend Alice that coined the metaphor about how single strands of evidence don't carry much weight, but when you wind them together they make an unbreakable cable?'

Skelgill looks puzzled.

'As I recall, she used hangman – but, knowing Alice, she could have been winding us up.'

That Skelgill says this, without having really thought about it, for a moment sidetracks him. Was he really so gullible to think that a High Court judge would employ the hangman game for decision making? But now he realises that DS Jones has stopped, when she has hardly begun.

'Any road – go on.'

She seems pained, as though finding a starting point is problematic.

'Well – you said I could look for a motive, right?'

'Did I?'

'In your roundabout way.'

'Reet.'

'So, I suppose I've been tuned in – more and more as I've met the various parties, and met them again – to relationships. It's kind of like – ' She makes obscure shapes in air with her delicate fingers. 'A Venn diagram with various interlocking circles.'

It is plain this does not advance her explanation in Skelgill's mind – it prompts her to shift tack.

'Okay, look – let me take a prosecutorial point of view – and give you my impressions accordingly.'

Skelgill shrugs more amenably; they are trying to solve a crime, after all. She takes his cue.

'Morag and Sebastian Sinclair – I'd say their relationship was one of going through the motions. From the beginning it looks like it was a marriage of convenience – even happenstance. Their home life, and Morag Sinclair's entire reaction bears that out. If anyone is badly wounded by Sebastian Sinclair's death it's Victoria Lawson. There are times when she can hardly speak. She's stayed off work. She's confused. And remember they've been in a close business partnership far longer than either of them has been married. Meanwhile – if you were to ask me – Victoria Lawson finds her husband tiresome, and he knows it. He must be like having another kid – a man-child – and his insecurity is palpable. He even competes when the children get attention ahead of him. And we know that Sebastian Sinclair only tolerated him for practical purposes.'

She has been gazing ahead, but now she checks for Skelgill's reaction.

'Don't pull your punches, lass.' He grins sarcastically.

'I mentioned about Victoria Lawson and Sebastian Sinclair looking at *Fell Running*. She only told me that when Frank Lawson was outside with DS Leyton. She pretended it was because she didn't want to embarrass Frank – because it was about how Sebastian and not Frank was the one who might beat Billy Higson. But – I don't think so.'

'You don't?'

'The nanny, Ellie, we gave her a lift to Asda – she let her guard drop. She's squarely in Victoria's camp – not Frank's. She let slip that Sebastian Sinclair was a regular visitor after work. They'd have long chats in the conservatory – and sometimes they even took the boys out for a picnic, down to the Eden. I think that is what Victoria Lawson is hiding from her husband. I think it's what's bubbling under the surface at Sinclair Design, that the staff are too loyal to mention.'

At this Skelgill shifts a little uneasily. While he is getting the gist of the case she is building, what she describes may not be so unusual: for close work colleagues to give lifts, continue business discussions, and in the process to get to know one another's families. There can be an innocent explanation.

DS Jones perhaps detects his reticence – now she does reach for her phone.

191

She taps, scrolls, and manipulates an image.

Holding the handset determinedly, she leans across, close to Skelgill. He can smell her deodorant; a person cannot always hide their rising pulse.

Obligingly, he concentrates upon the screen.

'Look – this is zoomed in – it's Sebastian Sinclair.' The image is a close-up of the man's animated face, the photograph she took of the firm's paintball event.

Keeping the handset in place, from the central console she picks up the two prints she has borrowed from Victoria Lawson's fridge. The shot with the children uppermost, she holds them alongside the phone.

'And here – with Victoria Lawson's late father – are the Lawson boys.'

Her position in the car, twisted forwards and around, is not easy to hold, and there is a slight tremor in her hands.

Skelgill's eyes flick to-and-fro.

He does not speak – but though he relieves her of the items, she remains in close proximity.

'Okay.'

He flips shut the phone case and hands it back; now DS Jones relents and sinks into her seat.

Skelgill minutely examines both photographic prints: the trio on the car bonnet and the couple outside the pub. He might almost be trying to identify the locations. It would be typical of him.

DS Jones remains silent, when it might be tempting to press for an opinion, or at least pose a leading question. Instead, she reverts to her handset.

Skelgill finishes his perusal of the prints; perhaps a little reluctantly, he places them on the dash.

Now DS Jones has something else on her screen to show him.

'And this is what I was looking at when you took me by surprise.'

Skelgill squints and instantly recoils.

'Steady on, lass!'

For a second she is shocked – until she understands his joke – she tuts and jabs him with a reprimanding knuckle – but immediately reverts to the serious matter at hand.

'This is on the website of the private medical practice – from where Sebastian Sinclair was seen to emerge by the girl Jules a few weeks ago. One of the main services they advertise is paternity testing.'

Now she does pause and look intently at Skelgill.

But he merely nods to encourage her to continue.

'As a rule, blue-eyed parents have blue-eyed children. Victoria Lawson has blue eyes and so does Frank Lawson. Yet I kind of knew there was something odd the second I noticed a family photograph at the Lawsons' house.' She gestures towards the prints. 'As you just saw – their youngest child William has brown eyes.' And she raises her phone. 'And, as you also just saw, so does Sebastian Sinclair.'

Now inquiring hazel irises meet inscrutable grey-green.

Skelgill shrugs; it is not a battle of wills he needs to win.

'The bairn's the spit of Sinclair.'

She is fooled by his nonchalance – and it takes her a moment for his words to sink in – before she appreciates his tolerance of her theory.

But now she seems a little lost for where to go.

'Like I say – you said I could look for a motive.'

Skelgill nods contemplatively.

'Reckon it gets us any nearer *who?*'

DS Jones inhales sharply.

'Well – you might say that's where I'm up to. But – you see – this business with the calendar. Father's Day. Or D-Day. I think Sebastian Sinclair was planning to go public. So, time was running out.'

'DNA Day.'

His quip prompts her to stifle a nervous laugh.

'So it becomes a question of who knew – and who would want to stop him? Who had the most to lose? You can make a strong case for each of Morag Sinclair, Victoria Lawson and Frank Lawson. They all knew where Sebastian Sinclair would be – and they each could have been there. DC Watson found that Morag Sinclair signed the children into school late on Monday morning. Victoria Lawson claims to have slept in. And we know that Frank Lawson was on the spot.'

Skelgill grins broadly, but does not immediately respond.

DS Jones knows to wait, however, and eventually he intones.

'Okay – you've found a motive, self-preservation maybe – in fact, you can double it to retribution in the case of Morag Sinclair and Frank Lawson. And, like you say, there was the opportunity. But what about means? We haven't identified the murder weapon – and the best bet for that's looking like Jimmy Higson's butcher's van – despite that you've nearly kyboshed my little piece of work. Seems like I ran the gauntlet of the Higsons for nowt.'

Skelgill's tone, notwithstanding his objection, is somewhat plaintive, and DS Jones feels obliged to offer a compromise.

'It could still have been that, Guv – the Higsons could have hit him. Perhaps there's a connection we don't yet know about.'

But Skelgill is slowly shaking his head.

'If there is, it needs to explain the threat.'

DS Jones raises the fingers of her left hand to her temple, as though she has suffered a sudden stabbing pain. Skelgill regards her sympathetically. He grins.

'I'm glad you're trying to work this out, and not me.'

'What are you doing, then?'

He shrugs. He ducks his head so that he can see the state of the evening light; he checks his wristwatch and then gazes at the old inn.

'I'm suggesting we should probably sleep on it.' He begins to open the door. 'Howay, Miss Marple – I'll buy thee a pint.'

21. ON EDGE

Scales Tarn – 8.45 a.m. Saturday 8 June

SKELGILL HAS BEEN fishing for some time. It is slightly worrying to him that he has so far drawn a blank. But he excuses himself on the grounds that his mind has not been on the job. Equally, his mind has drawn a blank, so there are also grounds for frustration.

Try a mash.

He props his flimsy fly rod against his rucksack and returns to the water's edge with his Kelly kettle. Stooping, he takes care not to disturb the sediment as he dunks the vessel in the shallows – but curses as what looks like a pond skater is drawn into the spout. He grimaces; perhaps it was just a fragment of vegetation.

The site is barren for a would-be firebug, but Skelgill has brought a fresh supply of newspaper and chopped kindling from his garage, and soon has a decent little blaze going beneath the battered aluminium chimney.

While he waits, settled on the dry shoreline, he ponders again DS Jones's theory. As a tapestry, it is faded, and incomplete in parts. And yet, that its circumstantial fragments are stitched together by her conviction has a certain appeal to him. When it comes to such matters of the heart, he trusts her intuition.

Was Sebastian Sinclair about to tell all? If so, it looks like Victoria Lawson knew of his intention: they both had the date on their calendars. And she can hardly have been in the dark about the child's paternity – or, at the very least, his probable paternity. (And, perhaps, one degree of certainty removed, Frank Lawson may doubt that he is the father. And one further degree of certainty removed, Morag Sinclair may have reason to suspect the same. Or maybe she even knows – perhaps her husband has already told her?)

The kettle boils and Skelgill is not ready for it. His second oath of the morning is uttered. Erupting water puts out the fire in the base. If he wants another brew he'll need to start again. Growling, he fills his tin mug, and stirs the teabag together with milk powder and a dollop of sugar, and sets the mug on a rock beside him. He pulls up his knees and gazes across the calm surface of the tarn. There are no rises to distract him.

Were Sebastian Sinclair and Victoria Lawson in it together? Was it a joint plan? That they would make a synchronised announcement. That's why they needed a DNA test – not to prove paternity to themselves, but to prove it to those who would ... who would what ... who would *object?*

For sure, he still wrestles with the conundrum that DS Jones has contrived.

In their further discussions last night, they had rather danced around the crux of the matter. DS Jones's view is that the pivotal relationship is – was – between Sebastian Sinclair and Victoria Lawson. Through misfortune and misguided decision-making it was interrupted by their respective marriages. And then, each hitched to an unsuitable spouse, they had contrived to produce a child of their own.

"Why not let sleeping dogs lie?" Skelgill had instinctively floated the question. And he had alluded to – guessed reasonably accurately – the statistic that one child in fifty is raised by a man who wrongly believes himself to be the biological father.

But DS Jones would not countenance his ill-considered suggestion. And, now that he reflects, he is glad she did not. Indeed, he feels a pang of guilt for making it. But – enough hypotheticals – he refrains from following the sentiment to any personal conclusion.

Instead he reprises their discussion, their wide-eyed debate – over just where Victoria Lawson's loyalties would lie. She would be in a cleft stick, an impossible predicament. Unite herself with father and child. Wrench herself from father and child. Leaving Frank Lawson might be only a small wrench, but perhaps less so the affluent domestic situation – never mind the elder child, and the havoc it would wreak in his cosy world.

Similar arguments could be made in the case of Sebastian Sinclair. His wife, Morag, and his two elder children. Their home.

Skelgill shakes his head. Small wonder, really, that his reflex had been *don't rock the boat*. And, yet, as he gazes unseeingly across the millpond surface of the tarn, if the boy William were *his* son, what would he do?

The same as Sebastian Sinclair had decided? Go public, come hell or high water?

DS Jones had not pressed for his opinion in this regard – nor had he posed the equivalent question.

Besides, it looks like a decision had been made.

Somebody found out. Somebody put a stop to it.

DS Jones had asked, however, whether he still felt that someone was at risk.

He had not been able to say no. Indeed he is still unable to shake off the feeling of trepidation. But it has struck him since that there is a kind of double jeopardy at play – in the shape of the somewhat accident-prone trio of elderly fellwalkers who have fallen under his wing. And now he has given them tacit permission to tackle Sharp Edge – and he is sure they will. He winces.

He stares again across the water. He is reminded he needs to catch a fish. He has a swim-feeder that he might resort to. Although he does not consider it the fairest method of fishing for trout, it might be a necessary exigency and he should at least test it. Gerry's words were apt – if Scales Tarn is the first water on his round, he does not want it to hold him up. He should make sure he has every method taped.

In the preternatural silence of the coomb, with its static pocket of resonant air, any noise is amplified. He can hear an airliner 30,000 feet in up the blue. The bass bark of a raven seems to reply to its own echo. Slipping low across the water, like skimmed stones, the swingy notes of a sandpiper, the willylilt, indeed.

A ping.

For a moment he is baffled – he knows no natural equivalent against which to calibrate the alien sound. Then he realises it is from his mobile. Last time he checked his phone there was steadfastly no service, here deep in the rock-walled amphitheatre. But it is his experience that it can mysteriously wax and wane – and a queued text can slip through, even when there is the most attenuated of signals.

He extracts his handset from his pack. No bars. But there is a text.

It is from DS Jones.

"Calls diverting to your voicemail. Forensics confirm Frank Lawson's prints on outside of 'threat' copy of *Fell Running*. Please respond to discuss bringing him in for questioning."

Skelgill stands up and stalks about.

What does he think about this? Somehow it jars with whatever his subconscious is onto – and, yet – could it fit with that?

Why are Frank Lawson's prints outside but not inside?

He knows it is an important question – despite that no immediate answer springs to mind.

And now, another sound – more alarming to his instincts.

It is a stone, dislodged – it skitters down the steeply angled scree beneath Sharp Edge.

Skelgill looks up; he squints into the dazzling azure sky.

He spies Rita – she must be four hundred feet above him. If he can see her, she can see him. She is setting up her tripod. It occurs to him that she seems to be quietly collecting shots of where he fishes.

He sees no sign of her companions. He guesses they will be ahead – perhaps gentleman Gerry is chaperoning Rosheen across the razor arête – and will return for Rita.

But, if so, they have not yet reached the rise where they might come into view, at the base of Foule Crag, from where there is a steep, if unexposed scramble up to Atkinson Pike. He scans from left to right, his gaze crossing Rita – and he spies another walker.

But it is an unfamiliar blue cagoule – well to the right, low on the broad rise before Sharp Edge asserts itself in name and tapered form. And certainly it is neither the tall, bowed, slightly ponderous gait of Gerry nor the small, elfin, sprightly Rosheen. Details are indeterminate; a medium, stocky figure, hood raised, gender uncertain. They move in short bursts – stopping to check ahead – yet purposefully, almost remorselessly.

The path must take the person to their right, and they disappear from Skelgill's sight.

He looks back at Rita – and thinks again just how distinctive she is with her shock of white hair, the lime-green cagoule, and the tripod, the photographer's pose.

'*Rita!*'

Suddenly Skelgill is on the move.

'*Rita!*'

Bellowing her name every few seconds, he first runs then hits the point of inflexion – a rapid increase in gradient, approaching eighty degrees at its most severe – a dangerous slope, almost worthy of a rock climb. He swarms up – clambering, shouting, sweating, dislodging loose rocks ... cursing.

When he reaches her, he has no breath to speak. He pulls himself astride the ridge and, gasping, mops his brow on his sleeve and makes indeterminate gestures with his long-fingered, scree-scarred hands.

'Good heavens, Dan – what on earth is going on?'

When he is unable to reply, Rita speaks again.

'I didn't know what to do when you kept calling my name.'

His breathing rate subsides – and now he seems a little abashed – as though he has comprehensively overreacted.

He gasps, and forces a grin.

'It weren't entirely for your benefit.'

He casts about.

Ahead, in the upwards direction, now he sees Gerry and Rosheen – they are waiting at the foot of Foule Crag. He gives a loose wave, and they reciprocate. He turns – but down the ridge there is no one to be seen.

He stares, intently – indeed, his features take on qualities of the surrounding landscape – craggy, foreboding, omniscient.

Rita clears her throat.

'Dan – I may as well photograph you, while you're here.'

Skelgill starts – and though he smiles – in his eyes there is a look of intense resolve.

'Actually, I need to ask you about one of the photos you've taken.'

*

Skelgill skips his way expertly along and down Sharp Edge.

He has his phone on speaker. His call is promptly answered.

'Guv?'

It is DS Jones. She sounds a little breathless.

'Hark. I may not have a signal for long.'

'Sure.'

'Meet me at Scales Farm in –' (he assesses the route ahead) 'twenty minutes. Speak to Forensics – the photographic unit. Tell them we're going to need a priority turnaround – developing and enlargement.'

He waits only to hear that she has absorbed the message before he terminates the call; he would rather have his hands free, and he slips the mobile into his hip pocket.

He pats his zipped breast pocket. And he keeps patting it, every so often.

He does make an exception, however, to eat the parkin, the little packet pressed upon him by Rita – he had seen her safely across to Gerry and Rosheen, and left them with no other explanation than that he would see them later.

He jogs down the broad shoulder beneath Sharp Edge and stops to drink at the outfall of Scales Beck. But he eschews his gear, trusting it will remain unseen and undisturbed for the time it will take him to return.

But he does linger for a moment, and gazes ruefully at the tarn.

He has not caught that fish.

He turns, and breaks into a trot. It is the thick end of two miles down the path to Scales Farm, and he does not want to keep his colleague waiting.

He scans ahead. There is no trace of the walker in the blue cagoule, nor had he crossed with them on his descent from the arête. But his mind turns back to Rita and her companions.

Rita had taken some persuading, in what he had asked of her. And, yet, he sensed she has an inkling of what he is up to.

Indeed, all of them – he saw it in their eyes – they knew something was afoot.

And Gerry's regulation parting observation, ostensibly aimed at his friends, was this time couched in the second person: "You look like you're on the scent of summat, lad."

Skelgill had merely raised a hand, part affirmation, part au revoir.

His timing proves to be perfect. DS Jones is just waiting for a gap in the traffic, to turn off the A66 into Scales, as he comes trotting along the verge. He pats his breast pocket for one final time.

She pulls in, and he jumps in beside her. She is wearing gym gear – trainers, yoga pants and a top that reveals her tanned midriff. Her hair is drawn tightly by a band at her nape. He takes a moment to recover his breath; in the interlude she poses the question that has no doubt been vexing her.

'Is this to do with Frank Lawson's prints?'

Skelgill plies her with a long look; he seems a little perplexed by the question.

He tilts his head – it is neither a shake nor a nod.

'Critical mass. Penny dropped.'

However, she regards him a little doubtfully.

'I'd convinced myself it wouldn't be Frank Lawson's MO – a clever coded message. Despite him being in the proximity of Honister Hause. And – playing devil's advocate – his prints on the cover don't prove he made the threat.'

It seems DS Jones would willingly talk herself out of the inference that stems from the shock news from Forensics. She continues.

'I've been running through in my mind, everything Victoria Lawson has said – and how she has behaved. She said she slept in. But what if she went out and was back in bed before the house got up? Her mother was there at dinner – if she stayed overnight the kids would have been safe. Ellie would have turned up. And it would have been easiest for her of all people to smuggle the magazine into the offices, to Sebastian Sinclair's desk.'

Skelgill listens inscrutably.

Indeed, she has to prompt him.

'Guv?'

He nods, calmly.

'Don't fret. Hark at this.'

He relays two sets of terse instructions.

The first is for her, the second is for DS Leyton.

And, without further ado, he climbs out of the car.

Holding open the door, he leans back in.

'I'll be in the fells for a good few hours. Let's the three of us get on a conference call at one o'clock – I'll make sure I'm up on a top with a signal. I'll wait somewhere if necessary. Then – depending upon what you pair find by then – we'll make a plan.'

He closes the door, and strides away at a ferocious pace.

22. LEG WORK

To Honister – 10 a.m. Saturday 8 June

IT WAS ONLY twelve miles back along the A66 from Scales to police headquarters. Her initial task, its wheels in motion, DS Jones is returning in a westerly direction, passing the spot where she had rendezvoused with Skelgill half an hour earlier. The Saturday morning traffic is light, and she does not pay too much heed to the speed limits; time may be of the essence.

Upon leaving Skelgill she had made two brief phone calls. The first was to discover – to her relief – that the lab was open (in part because they have some big project on, and a skeleton staff is working over the weekend). The second was to DS Leyton – who was not supposed to be working over the weekend, but who accepted the instructions relayed from their superior with his usual phlegmatic stoicism. It was not in his nature to shoot the messenger; and he had not baulked at Skelgill's arguably shameless delegation of the same to his colleague. "Right enough, Emma – if the Guvnor's gone back into the hills, there's no telling when he might lose the signal, just at the crucial point."

It had sounded like her fellow sergeant was poolside at the leisure centre – a background cacophony of chaotic echoing excited children's cries – and perhaps there was a small silver lining in being recalled to duty.

Less malleable had been the self-assigned gatekeeper at the reprographics reception counter. A young man a couple of years her junior, whom she recognised but was unacquainted with, had appeared after a long delay, and casually sized her up, in a way with which she was not entirely enamoured. She was glad, at least, that she had donned a sweat-top.

But she was there to jump the queue.

Thinking himself stylish – unaware of the dandruff that had escaped to his shoulders from his rather lank, unwashed long hair – his manner was cocky, straight out of the DI Smart school of charm, she quickly realised.

He had taken his time in filling out the requisition form, extracting details beyond the necessary minimum – but she knew he was playing a little power game; delaying her, even, and letting his gaze wander with barely concealed lascivious aspiration.

She could have tried a rational argument. However, that hers was a life-or-death matter of extreme urgency she would have struggled to justify with facts – and certainly could present no written order from on high. But he had pre-empted her by remarking upon them both working on a Saturday, and how he was unlikely to be finished until eight, such was the scheduled workload. How were single people like them expected to have a social life?

But she also divined that beneath the bravado was a lack of authority to which he did not want to admit. Quite likely there was no one present behind the scenes who could authorise her request for priority treatment. But in that she also saw an opportunity. While the cat is away.

Overtaking a supermarket truck rather more audaciously than she should, she cringes now as she recalls her winning tactic.

"Look – I'll buy you a drink – if you have them ready for me by lunchtime."

The young lab technician had frozen mid pen-stroke for a moment, as if not quite believing his success. Then he had affected to take the offer in his stride, and had signed off the form with a flourish – ripping off her copy, handing it over, and standing, watching smugly, as she apologised for her need for a swift exit.

A swift exit, before he could suggest the name of a pub.

Now she inhales and makes a face that a passing motorist might read as one of somewhere between revulsion and guilt; she'll take him a four-pack of Guinness when she returns to collect the prints.

She clears her mind; she must address the mission ahead.

She glances at the notepad on the passenger seat.

Skelgill had listed six visits that she may need to make. Starting from Penrith, and thence from each port of call, a minute spent interrogating her mobile maps app had produced the worrying data:

Penrith To Honister Pass – 28 miles, 44 minutes
Honister Pass to Wasdale Head – 37 miles, 1 hour 24 minutes
Wasdale Head to the Langdales – 38 miles, 1 hour 26 minutes
The Langdales to Grasmere – 11 miles, 23 minutes
Grasmere to Threlkeld – 11 miles, 17 minutes

Threlkeld to Keswick – 6 miles, 11 minutes

Even at a glance – a moment's mental arithmetic – she could see there is 4½ hours' driving to complete the circuit – never mind allowing for investigation at each stop.

But she needs to return to Penrith to collect the prints before she speaks to Skelgill at one o'clock.

She has considered instead taking in Threlkeld, Grasmere and Keswick, and thence up into Borrowdale to Honister. But from what limited fraction of his theory Skelgill has shared, she knows that sequence likely will not work. It would be like trying to do a treasure hunt in reverse, when finding each successive location has some dependency upon solving the clue at the former.

So she is driving to Honister, and she will just have to improvise from there.

She reaches the Keswick turn, the way into Borrowdale, and now wonders if she will cross paths with DS Leyton. Quite possibly he will be leaving about now, and the first stage of his assignment involves the same route – just as far as the little junction for Seathwaite. Or, if he has been really quick out of the blocks, she may see him coming the other way, perhaps leading a small convoy.

But neither eventuality comes to pass.

She concentrates on driving quickly and efficiently; it is still a little early for the tourist traffic that can make the winding Borrowdale road a nightmare for the emergency services. She counts down the landmarks that Skelgill habitually remarks upon. It strikes her that, so often a passenger, now she misses the leisurely views, and can only snatch glances. To her right, the blue expanse of Derwentwater shimmering between roadside oaks, with the distinctive green peak of Catbells beyond; the lake narrowing into its clear-running source, the River Derwent, broadening at the bridge at Grange where Skelgill sometimes stops to stare at fish; the Bowder Stone, the great post-glacial megalith which had its heyday as a Victorian visitor attraction; and the steepening wooded fellsides, their lower slopes pressing in, tree-clad and washed with a hazy sapphire tide of late bluebells.

Passing the track up to Seathwaite, she thinks about phoning DS Leyton. But she decides to leave it just now. Perhaps they each should get some progress under their belts before exchanging congratulations … or commiserations.

Leaving the hamlet of Seatoller the road begins to rise appreciably. It is narrow, winding and single-track in many parts; overhead dangle grey cascades of tree-hanging lichens, and lush green ferns spill from steep banks. But quite abruptly the habitat changes. Walls disappear and the open fellside sweeps skywards in a great V, by contrast bleak and barren; in the verges, bracken and hardy heathers replace the more delicate plants; running low, the exposed beck, Hause Gill, switches from one side to the other via subtle culverts.

Still there are passing places, and she must take care of oncoming vehicles – though straying sheep are now the more likely obstacle. She does not want to hit one – and she is reminded of the origin of their investigation.

And equally suddenly at the crux of the pass – Honister Hause – in the midst of so much wilderness she is confronted by an industrial blot on the landscape; there is no other way of putting it. The mine, England's last working example, produces Westmorland green slate, and offers cave-and-cliff adventure experiences to boot. No amount of trying – no thickness of rose-tinted lenses – can convince the disenchanted onlooker that it is anything but an eyesore, but perhaps the comparison to the surrounding landscape is a harsh one. Even its 17th century scars and spoil heaps have not yet been assimilated by nature, and stand qualitatively different to those many similar natural features carved out by the ice and sculpted by the elements.

But DS Jones has lowered her radar. The first building encountered from the east is the roadside youth hostel – a traditional stone edifice, at least – former quarry workers' accommodation, proudly advertising its 26 beds, licensed bar and no mobile coverage!

The turn into the makeshift parking area is just before the property, which is set down to the left of the road. Thus the hostel has its slate roof at road level, and its windows only bank-high – and it strikes her that any events on the road itself would be invisible from within. She notes, also, a little past the building on the opposite verge, the flattened roadside bracken where first paramedics stomped, and then her colleagues, in a peremptory search – just five days ago.

Despite their licensed bars and the ability to arrive by car, today's youth hostels retain some of their hair-shirt customs, one of these being that departing guests must clear out by 10 a.m. As DS Jones approaches on foot, she is guessing the staff will be here, beginning the daily clear-up and turning the rooms around. From the car park she mounts rough-hewn slate steps two at a time, startling a pair of hefty

Herdwick lambs that graze the short turf of the embankment between weathered pine picnic tables.

Inside, lingering smells of breakfast and body odour greet her nostrils. Squeezing past blue laundry hampers awaiting collection she finds herself at a narrow reception counter with an office behind. A stout middle-aged woman with prominent rosy cheeks and short brown hair is speaking on a landline telephone in a Scots accent. Between conversational snippets it seems she is placing the bar order. Though she offers pleasant eye contact and indeed raises her eyebrows in a gesture of frustration – as though it is the speaker on the other end that is the chatterbox – she makes no great effort to end the call. She must assume that DS Jones, sportily clad, is a passing outdoorswoman with some enquiry.

Beyond, through in the office, DS Jones catches glimpses of a younger woman, moving about with cleaning equipment. She is humming to the strains of a transistor radio; DS Jones recognises *Dreaming* by the American rock band, Blondie.

DS Jones casually places her warrant card on the counter top, as if getting it ready in order to introduce herself. But it does the trick; the loquacious manageress cannot resist a look, and she moves to terminate the call.

'That's the polis back tae see me.'

Abruptly, she hangs up and regards DS Jones with a good degree of relish.

'Whit can I dae for ye, hen?'

DS Jones has acquainted herself with all the interview notes and witness statements taken by her uniformed colleagues, in the rather late aftermath, on Monday morning. The manageress, in common with most present in the vicinity at the time of the incident, and traceable, had been in her quarters, and was unaware of the road accident until alerted by the authorities.

'Mrs Brodie, right?'

'Aye, that's me, hen.'

DS Jones introduces herself, and explains her purpose – that she is inquiring about a party of three guests that stayed on Sunday night, and who left promptly on Monday morning. She supplies their names.

The woman nods, but continues to look on with anticipation.

DS Jones, herself working on limited information, realises she is unsure exactly of how to couch the next question, or, indeed, precisely what is the right question.

206

'Did – er – anyone – among your other guests, perhaps – show interest in where these three walkers were going next? I know you can't be party to every conversation – but it might be something you picked up in passing.'

The woman looks momentarily baffled – but then a little idea occurs to her. She raises a salutary finger, and follows it around to a noticeboard at her back. She tears off a small sheet of paper and places it before DS Jones.

'They left this, hen. Lots of folks dae it. If ye dinnae turn up the nicht – the rescue ken where tae look.'

DS Jones pores over the form. It is a neatly typed itinerary, listing the stages of the route and the intended overnight stops, along with contact numbers of the various hostelries and personal details of the trio. She guesses it is the handiwork of route-finder Gerry. As a seasoned walker, he will be familiar with this simple safety protocol.

She looks up, and assesses the distance from where she stands to the noticeboard. At a push, the 12-point type would be legible – though it would be easy enough to lift the counter flap and gain closer access.

'So, anyone could have seen this?'

'Aye.'

DS Jones hesitates, thinking the matter through. While there is not yet a specific answer to her enquiry, this fits well enough with Skelgill's prediction.

'What about – anyone asking – in person? On Monday – after the incident on the road?'

The Scotswoman makes a disappointed face and shakes her head.

'Yes – I – I speak to –'

The manageress turns in surprise.

The voice comes from behind. It is the cleaner, standing now in the doorway. It seems she has overheard – and despite her obviously foreign accent she has understood enough to intervene.

'Katya?'

A young woman in her mid-twenties, DS Jones would guess – she has her blonde hair tied back; she is slender – almost too thin – such that her prominent cheekbones showcase deep-set very pale blue eyes, that are made mournful by dark crescents beneath. She steps forward – though she turns first apprehensively to her superior.

'*Vybachte.* It was when you speak with police.'

DS Jones's ears prick up. She knows the word, *sorry*.

She interposes before the elder woman can respond, and speaks directly to the girl.
'*Vy ukrayinka?*' Are you Ukrainian?
The girl nods.
'You speak?'
DS Jones makes a face of apology. '*Trishky.*' A little. But she can see she has put the girl at ease. 'Better if we stick with English, if you don't mind.'
She bows her head, to encourage the girl to be forthcoming. Katya looks first at the manageress, and then back at DS Jones.
'I clean here. At eleven o'clock.' She indicates to where DS Jones stands. 'Telephone ring and nobody can answer.' She glances again at the manageress. This was what she meant, that Mrs Brodie was being interviewed by one of the police officers. 'I pick up. A person ask for relative. If relative is safe.'
DS Jones is nodding evenly. Though her pulse is rising – she can almost hear a little thump in her head. Who would ring – especially when no news of the incident had been broadcast?
'What did you say?'
'I say, everybody here – they are safe.'
DS Jones stares at her. She feels like hares have been set running in several directions, and she strives to see which one she should pursue.
'Was it a man or a woman?'
But now the girl seems a little dismayed. It is immediately plain that she is unsure.
'It was bad line – crackle. I not sure. Maybe woman.' But she shakes her head as if she is not convinced. 'Some people local accent – some men – speak with creaky voice, like woman.'
DS Jones nods; she is actually right. She lines her sights on another hare.
'Who did they ask for?'
Now the girl frowns. Her clear eyes seem to cloud for a second. Then her focus returns.
'The lady. Lady – white hair – and green jacket. She take photos.'
DS Jones is staring.
'Not a name?'
Katya shakes her head.
DS Jones glances at the itinerary on the surface before her.
'What about her friends? Did the caller ask about them?'
Another shake of the head.

'Just old lady.'

DS Jones catches a glimpse of a third hare.

'Did the caller ask to speak to the lady?'

'I say they go already. It is rule. Everybody, they go.'

Now perhaps the girl experiences a pang of guilt. She glances at the manageress. But she continues before either of the others can comment.

'The person want to know – where can they talk to her?' She steps closer and DS Jones realises she wants to refer to the form. She turns it. Katya locates the entry marked "Honister Hause YHA" and then traces with a finger down to Monday night. She nods. 'Yes – I tell them *Wasdale*.'

*

DS Jones would like to have stayed longer to engage with the Ukrainian girl. But she sensed Mrs Brodie would intervene and keep her talking, given half the chance, and she had gleaned all that she could from Katya. She had made her apologies to the manageress, and to the girl had quietly mouthed *Slava Ukraini,* drawing a sad smile.

Standing at her car, DS Jones casts about. Some people are up on the ridge above the mine – she can tell they are taking a selfie, and the notion brings her mind back to the task in hand.

Literally in her hand, she has Gerry's itinerary, willingly yielded at her request.

She scrutinises the page.

Skelgill was right. Honister Hause first. Next, Wasdale Head.

She needs to go there.

But she needs to collect the prints – the prints (or one in particular) are not negotiable.

She has a little over two hours to spare.

To drive to Wasdale and thence return to Penrith will take her closer to four hours.

A *Catch 22*.

And jeopardy is rising. There was someone on the trail. And not a relative – they would have provided a name. The woman who takes photographs – someone was interested in her.

Skelgill's theory makes more sense by the minute.

She would ideally discuss this dilemma with him – but, of course, she has no signal, and quite likely neither does he.

She stares out across the fells.
If only she could go cross country.
Wait.

Skelgill's malicious glee in the vagaries of Lakeland topography reaches its acme when he talks about travelling from the Hopes' farmstead at Seathwaite to Wasdale Head. How many times has he told her? It is 40 miles (and 1½ hours) by road ... *and under five miles on foot?* Five miles is not even 10k.

She looks down at her trainers.

Her last 10k ... she clocked 38 minutes.

She can drive to Seathwaite in seven minutes.

*

'You look like you could demolish a pint, lass.' The stocky, middle-aged, ruddy-faced bar manager greets a perspiring DS Jones with a broad grin.

'A pint of water, perhaps – if you don't mind.'

'Are you training for the Bob Graham? It's not until next week, is it – the big event?'

DS Jones makes the man wait until she has downed half of the glass. In the meantime she slides her ID across the counter. She gasps with relief.

The man, who has no doubt seen all sorts coming and going, takes largely in his stride the arrival of the young police officer in running gear.

'Actually, you're not so far from the mark, sir. I'm making enquiries about some walkers who are following the route. They lodged here on Monday night. Retirement age. A tall gentleman, and two ladies – a redhead and the other with distinctive white hair. These are their names.'

She produces the walking itinerary that she has folded into the case of her mobile phone.

'Aye, I remember them. They had two rooms on t' ground floor.' Now he points to the form. 'They gave us a copy of this. It's on our guest noticeboard in t' passage. I thought, best keep it until their trip was finished – just in case, like? Touch wood.' He raps a knuckle against his temple.

DS Jones nods.

'May I see it?'

'Aye.'

He circles around from the end of the bar and leads the way through a door marked "Bedrooms – Residents Only". DS Jones notes that no key is required.

A little way along the corridor he stops and peruses a cork board hung between a pair of framed Ordnance Survey maps.

She sees immediately that he is frowning. He points to a clear space – although there are two drawing pins each with a small fragment of paper trapped beneath.

'That's funny – someone's took it off. Who would do that? I'm the only one that looks after this – I'm the designated contact for the mountain rescue.' He scratches his thick thatch of grizzled hair. 'Want me to ask the other staff? They're not all in, just yet.'

DS Jones is biting her lip pensively. She checks the time on her sports watch.

'I think you've already shown me exactly what I need to know.'

23. PERSUASION

From Seathwaite – noon Saturday 8 June

'FANCY MEETING YOU here, girl. I spotted your motor – couldn't work it out. Thought you were supposed to be off round the houses. Wasdale – Langdale – back of beyond. Tried your mobile – no signal. I was getting a bit worried, truth be told.'

DS Jones stands with hands on hips, recovering her breath. She tosses her head and puffs air upwards to deter the farmyard flies that find her glowing skin attractive. But the final stretch has been downhill and she is not too overwhelmed. DS Leyton has approached to intercept her at her car. She sees now that he has pulled away from a group of four hefty farmer types who are gathered at the back of a pick-up to which a silvered aluminium livestock trailer is attached. They seem to be sharing a hip flask – although they do not look the sort to need Dutch courage. Nearby, the Hopes' vintage Land Rover, engine chugging, has its door open. She catches Jud Hope's eye; he raises a hand to shade the sun, and he gives her a respectful nod-come-salute. She reciprocates the gesture – there is a lot she could explain, but she has urgent questions on her mind, not least for her colleague.

'I thought you'd be long gone?'

DS Leyton shakes his head.

'Turned out the Guvnor's pal Jud, there – he was down in Kendal at an auction. These other geezers –' He indicates towards the group with a small jerk of his head, 'it's Jack Thompson and his two lads – they were out and about. So it's taken a couple of hours to get the mob together. We were just about to split when I spotted you coming like flippin' Jessica Ennis-Hill.'

DS Jones looks somewhat diffident.

'Not exactly – but, look, I need to go – I need to collect the prints from the lab – for our conference call at one.'

DS Leyton looks her over in an avuncular kind of way.

'Emma, girl – you look like you could do with a break – and a couple of bottles of Lucozade. Why don't I drive you? And then we'll be together for the phone call.'

DS Jones frowns.

'But what about your brief?'

DS Leyton shrugs.

'It's waited a couple of hours – it'll keep another twenty minutes. That's all a detour will take us.' Plainly, he decides this is a good plan. 'Jump in my motor – I'll have a word with the lads and arrange where we'll hook up.'

*

'Guinness? I thought that was strictly for nursing mothers?'

DS Jones grins – she shows off that she also has bought a bottle of energy drink.

'It's not for me, don't worry.'

'Well, it's certainly not for the Guvnor, I know that. Him and his flamin' flat beer. You'd soon get short shrift.'

Unceremoniously he selects first gear and they shoot off from the little local Co-op; the clock is ticking. But he seems to notice a degree of quietude – perhaps reflection – in his partner that does not match the urgency of their mission.

'Something up, girl?'

She shifts forwards as though she wants to reply – but hesitates for a moment.

'Actually – would you mind going in – to collect the photographs?'

'Nah, course not – why?'

Now she makes a face of self-reproach.

'The creepy lab technician – I kind of told him a white lie – that I'd buy him a drink if I could jump the queue.'

DS Leyton cannot repress an amused chortle.

'Nice one – so that's what the beer's for! You didn't say he'd be drinking alone. *Ha-hah!*'

But still she harbours a degree of guilt.

'I thought it would save time if you went in. My only worry is if he cuts up a bit difficult.'

DS Leyton looks pleased with the prospect.

'Don't worry, Emma – I'll sort it.'

On arrival, DS Leyton reaches for the four-pack of cans in their famous black and gold livery.

'I know exactly what to do – I've taken the nippers to see *Aladdin* at the panto.'

And, sure enough, he reappears within barely two minutes, bereft of tins and bearing a large envelope in one hand; a broad grin creases his naturally ingenuous countenance. He sinks into the driver's seat, hands over the package, and starts the ignition.

'Two copies of each. I've got the negatives safe.' He pats his shirt pocket. 'Creep put in his place.'

He lets in the clutch and they begin to move away.

'I owe you.'

DS Jones's tone is grateful – but the temptation to examine the prints is too great. Carefully, she extracts one of two glassine sleeves containing a set of the photographic enlargements.

'Wow.'

'Got what you want?'

'Well – I don't know – it's just that these are superb photographs. She knows what she's doing.' DS Jones admires a panoramic shot of a hazy Buttermere, with Red Pike rising majestically above Sourmilk Gill.

Carefully, she begins to work through the prints. The one she seeks comes about halfway through.

Her silence, and her stillness, tells DS Leyton she has it.

He glances across.

'Well?'

She stares intently at the expertly framed landscape.

'I think it's exactly what we want.'

DS Leyton nods with satisfaction. He is keeping his eyes on the road – and not sparing the gas.

'So, the Guvnor was right?'

DS Jones nods pensively.

'It looks that way. And it corresponds to what I've learned this morning.'

She tilts the print up to the light.

'I think with a magnifier we'll even be able to read the plate on the vehicle. The image has such fine definition. She must have a good camera.'

DS Leyton drops a gear to take a bend, but maintains their velocity.

'Hold onto your hat. Next stop Matterdale – and the last piece of the jigsaw.'

*

'Looks like he's home.'

DS Leyton's car leading, the three vehicles rumble like an undertaker's cortege into the small untidy yard of Billy Higson's farmstead. The dogs are barking out back, as before. DS Leyton swings round in front of the cottage. The Thompsons' pick-up reverses its trailer to the barn door. Jud Hope turns his Land Rover and leaves it blocking its less-well-cared-for counterpart belonging to Higson.

DS Jones glimpses a movement at the right-hand window. Though it is grimy, there is no reflection, for the bright midday sun is close to its seasonal zenith. The yard is dry and pale ochre clay dust drifts from tyres. The dogs keep up their agitated howling.

DS Leyton looks at his wristwatch.

'I suggest you wait here – in case the Guvnor phones early.' He sees that DS Jones is about to mount a protest. But he reaches to place a hand on her arm. 'You've done more than your share – it's my turn now, girl. Here – hand me that print.'

Reluctantly, she acquiesces. But he is right on several fronts. And they must not miss Skelgill's call.

She sips from her bottle and slides down in her seat to wait.

She watches as the five grim-faced men split up, and the Thompson boys – twins by the look of it – slip one each side around to the back of the cottage. DS Leyton raps on the door and then tries the handle. It opens. She hears him call out, "Mr Higson, you don't mind if we come in?"

To pass the time she begins to leaf through the prints. The lady Rita has an extraordinary talent. DS Jones is particularly arrested by a shot of Skelgill at his bivouac. Though he would not admit it, it is actually a beautiful photograph, the low evening sun's rays highlighting extraordinary detail: primeval turquoise lichen encrusted on the stone wall; bright yellow stars of tormentil in the turf; the steam and smoke from his storm kettle; and Skelgill – his rugged countenance at once foreboding – and yet, knowing him – vulnerable.

Then a sound alerts her. They are coming out.

First is DS Leyton, and then Jud Hope, followed in a stained vest by the wiry form of a sheepish Billy Higson – though she reads flashes of suppressed anger and belligerence that vie for expression. The Thompsons follow, jaws set in familial congruence, and the glint of vindication in their dark eyes.

215

She cannot help thinking it looks like a prisoner being marched to face a firing squad.

They make for the barn – but a little to her surprise DS Leyton plainly bids farewell to the others; he peels away and joins her in the car.

'Cheeky little toad.'

These are not quite her colleague's words, but she mentally tones them down for the purposes of writing a report later.

'How did you get on?'

DS Leyton is irked, but also plainly amused and certainly mildly triumphant.

'Sly cove tried to claim he found them roaming. Reckons he was doing a recce of the Bob Graham crossover points with his brother – in his brother's van – and they just came across ten prize sheep, trotting loose along the lane. Reckons he's been keeping 'em safe until he could find the rightful owner.'

DS Jones further edits a "my backside" from her putative report.

All is very well – but missing is the essential fact she is yearning to hear.

'What about Honister Hause?'

DS Leyton pauses a moment – then she sees he has the photograph he took with him clamped between the pages of his pocket notebook. He clears his throat.

'At first – he didn't want to admit it.' DS Leyton now looks pleased with himself – there is to be the announcement of a small masterstroke. 'But when I said I'd be back – Wednesday next week – to take him into custody on a charge of theft – his memory drastically improved.'

DS Jones nods with approval. Next Wednesday is the day of the Bob Graham Round anniversary challenge.

Now DS Leyton displays the centre spread of his notebook.

She sees, in his neat script, a statement written out – but clearly signed in a different hand – that of *"W. Higson"*.

'I hinted we might overlook the sheep – safely returned – with a suitable compensation package for the owners' trouble – I left them to negotiate that.'

He jerks his head in the direction of the barn – where preparations are already being made to load the Texels into the Thompsons' trailer.

The print is too small for DS Jones to read at a glance – but DS Leyton now raises the photograph.

'The Higsons saw this. Not the accident. But they can witness the motor was there. And a description of the driver.'

216

24. FINAL HURDLE

Latrigg parking area – 4.50 p.m. Saturday 8 June

LATRIGG, AT A modest 1203 feet, languishes at 206 in the list of 214 'Wainwrights', fells trodden and described by the late great cantankerous biographer of Lakeland's mountains. But Latrigg is prized, despite its lowly rank, for its spectacular views over Keswick, Derwentwater and the fells that surround Borrowdale and the Newlands Valley. It is also appreciated for its easiness underfoot – 'Sunday best' is adequate garb, according to Wainwright – and its accessibility: the single-track lane from Applethwaite, at its terminus, widens into a makeshift parking area fewer than 300 feet below the summit.

To this very point, fell runners or walkers completing the Bob Graham Round in the anticlockwise direction descend from Skiddaw, (No. 1 peak, clockwise), and briefly follow the narrow lane before dipping down the thickly wooded fellside. The car park is thus a convenient meeting place for supporters, who join for the last mile to the finish line at Keswick Moot Hall. For those in no hurry, it is also a fitting spot for a celebratory photograph, while there is still some altitude to provide a worthy backdrop to the achievement.

A handful of cars shimmer beneath the late afternoon sun, arranged in a neat line, perpendicular to the boundary wall. No one is in sight on Latrigg. So these vehicles probably belong to more serious walkers, who have hiked up to Skiddaw and perhaps beyond.

The air is heavy.

Faint strains of lazy birdsong percolate from the woods below; a mild prelude to the dusk chorus.

Against the dry stone wall, a short distance before the first car, rises a small but venerable hawthorn tree, its tight wind-sculpted canopy inclined to the east. Beyond is a rough intake pasture gone to seed, looking more like a wild hay meadow. The tree shades a makeshift gate, more of a hurdle. These close simple features – the tree, the gate, the shade – offer not only a moment of respite, but also, with the great bulk of Skiddaw behind, a powerful metaphor for the photographer's eye. Journey's end.

And here, a trio of walkers.

Two females and a male.

A couple, it seems, are being posed for a photograph by the single woman.

The pair comprises a tall man and a shorter, red-haired woman, each of mature years. An actual couple, it would seem – for they act at ease, unembarrassed, joshing and shoving as they vie for space, leaning over the narrow rustic stile.

The photographer may be of an age with her companions – though it is hard to be entirely sure – there is a certain natural grace in her movements – and she is somewhat incognito, having the capacious hood of her lime-green cagoule raised, which she employs in the way of a photographer of yore, when large-format view-cameras were virtually entered by their operators, ducking beneath the dark focusing cloth, better to refine the shot.

Accordingly, she takes her time.

The camera, on its tripod, is set in the centre of the lane.

She seems relaxed.

But it is of course a dead end – so there is no passing traffic – an arriving motorist would naturally slow down and give plenty of notice, while anybody leaving would first get into their car, and so draw attention to themselves.

She checks back and forth.

She makes adjustments.

She tugs further at her hood and bows again to shade the viewfinder.

She is clearly a perfectionist.

Those behind the hurdle are becoming impatient.

Protesting voices carry on the still afternoon air.

'Come on, Rita – I'm getting a thirst on.'

She flaps a reprimanding hand; they must be patient; the maestro is at work.

Some way along the line of cars, an engine starts.

Perhaps someone has been seated at the wheel all the time.

'Hurry up, Rita – else you'll have to shift out of t' road – after all this trouble!'

But the woman in the green cagoule is unruffled; she merely raises a calming hand.

The car revs more urgently – the familiar precursor to moving off.
It is throaty; a large, powerful engine.
If the photographer is not expeditious, she will have to give way.
But still she waits – she crouches, poised on tiptoes, like a sprinter in her blocks.
And now, by proxy, the starting gun.
The car's note becomes a sudden roar.
Massive revs.
A burst of sound.
Tyres grind on the surface, spitting stones.
A blur of activity – almost too rapid to process.
A large dark shape bursts from the line – and accelerates.
In its path, the green-jacketed woman, and her camera on its tripod.
Only twenty-five feet of separation.
The driver cannot have seen her.
Perhaps the woman does not hear, impaired by her hood.
There must be a collision.
A warning cry from the gate.
'*Rita!*'
A strident crack.
The big car does not stop.
The camera and tripod lie crushed.
The big car surges onwards, trailing a dust cloud.
The couple gape helplessly after it.
And then – oncoming – headlights on full beam – filling the narrow lane – a small car.
Big car, small car.
A game of chicken.
But it is not the size of the dog in the fight.
It is the size of the fight in the dog.
The big car swerves – and crashes – lurches, stranded, into the roadside ditch.
From the driver's side of the small car leaps a stocky man, and from the passenger side another man, taller, rangy.
They dash to the big car.
They prise open its doors.
Handcuffs are produced.
From the back of the small car, a little gingerly, a white-haired elderly lady emerges.

At the hawthorn, from behind the wall – like a fell fox – springs the wearer of the lime-green cagoule.

She draws back its hood to shake out bronzed-blonde hair – and to reveal a young woman wearing a radio earpiece.

25. ADMISSION

Police HQ – 11.15 a.m. Monday 10 June

'MRS LAWSON, we believe we understand the motive for this crime – for the murder of Sebastian Sinclair – but in court the Prosecution does not need to prove a motive. While motive can be important to convince a jury, and in some cases pivotal, in this instance we believe we have more than enough circumstantial and witness evidence to gain a conviction.

'We are conducting this interview off the record, because we have reason to believe there is information that ought to remain confidential. The public being interested is not the same as the public interest. Specifically, it would be against the interests of certain entirely innocent parties, and others to whom only very limited culpability may be attached.'

Skelgill and DS Leyton look on; the latter, in particular, with not inconsiderable admiration at his female associate, and the sagacity of her opening words. An old head on young shoulders. Skelgill appears a little more ambivalent, but his expression goes unnoticed by Victoria Lawson, for he and DS Leyton sit in the shadows, while she and DS Jones face one another across a lamplit table in the centre of the interview room.

If the two and their table could be lifted out of context, they might just look like two young executives, stylishly dressed, and neatly groomed, circumspectly made-up, perhaps in a corporate environment, engaged in a meeting, discussing various papers and pictures arranged between them. They each have a small bottle of mineral water and a glass. Indeed, such a scenario must have played out many times at Sinclair Design, with Victoria Lawson being briefed or consulted by one of her underlings.

But here the roles are plainly reversed. It is the younger woman who radiates the aura of seniority. DS Jones is calling the shots. But she does so with delicacy and respect. And perhaps this is what causes the conflict for her own superior – she is undoubtedly much better at this kind of thing than he has ever been, or ever will be. DS Leyton harbours no such qualms, and grins affably from the sidelines.

Victoria Lawson, however, despite her immaculate appearance, and trained confidence in formal meetings, plainly has no muscle memory for such a situation. To DS Jones's mind the woman appears to suffer a more enhanced state of the ongoing anguish that she has witnessed during their encounters hitherto. On no occasion has Victoria Lawson seemed genuinely at ease; a fretfulness the young officer has constantly sensed, and has communicated such to her colleagues.

Now – and despite DS Jones's opening words of reassurance – Victoria Lawson looks ever more like the proverbial rabbit in the headlights. At the phrase "the murder of Sebastian Sinclair" she had visibly cringed. Her palms, nails perfectly manicured and subtly coloured sky blue to match her outfit, are pressed flat on the table surface, as though she needs these extra points of contact with reality. Her taut expression seems to be barely containing an inner dread, that threatens to escape via the white sclerae of her widened eyes.

At last, she seems to nod, understanding.

DS Jones gives a small exhalation of relief. She is not without emotion herself. She inhales and quickly resumes her oratory, speaking calmly and evenly.

'Given the series of traumas you have suffered – we feel you do not need another piled on top of it. And this is such a personal matter, with wide-ranging ramifications for several parties. There is arguably your privacy that can be invoked. And the revealing of that information – if at all – should be done in a considered and meticulous way, with expert advice and support.'

It is perhaps a challenge, even for the articulate DS Jones, to paint such an abstract and indeed obtuse word-picture – but Victoria Lawson, despite her distress is nonetheless listening intently. She leans forwards a little.

The tension in the room is palpable.

DS Jones now offers a prompt.

'I think you know what I am talking about? You don't have to say it aloud.'

Victoria Lawson nods.

Amongst the materials laid out on the table are several photographs. Included are the small, slightly curling prints borrowed from the Lawsons' refrigerator.

Now Victoria Lawson slowly extends a hand.

The others watch on in frozen silence.

Her index finger with its pale blue nail hovers over the snapshot of her late father and the two small boys. Specifically, it comes to rest upon the younger boy, William. The brown-eyed boy.

Her own blue eyes make deep contact with the hazel of the young detective.

DS Jones nods; her lips part a little, perhaps to release an inaudible sigh.

Skelgill and DS Leyton, also bent forwards in their seats, in tandem lean back and fold their arms, their brows knitted. But their actions do not penetrate the little bubble of concentration in the centre of the room.

It is DS Jones that breaks the spell.

She sits upright. She rests her elbows on the table and intertwines her fingers. Now she resumes in an entirely more informal manner. She prefaces her words with a smile of apology.

'Mrs Lawson, we believe there is a DNA paternity test. We do not need to see it. If necessary we could apply for a warrant to present to the private medical practice in Carlisle.'

Victoria Lawson does not gainsay the statement; clearly, she anticipates there to be an actual question.

And she is right.

'Is it possible that your mother, Isobel Beslow, gained the knowledge of such a report?'

After a long delay, Victoria Lawson, biting her lip, nods.

'And that would have been without your intention or consent, correct?'

A small pause.

'Correct.'

For the first word she has spoken, her voice is surprisingly clear and free of tremor.

'And in your judgement, that information would have been considerably troubling to her, correct?'

'Correct.'

This time there is no delay, and it is DS Jones who requires a moment to find the right words.

'There is a question that we shall need to put to you on the record. It is a formal matter that can be dealt with in due course. But we will take on trust your answer today.'

Victoria Lawson – as if she knows the crux is coming – without taking her eyes off DS Jones reaches for her drink; indeed she holds the rim of the glass to her lips, as though it might sanitise any answer she should give.

DS Jones, for the first time, glances briefly across to her colleagues; DS Leyton is agog; Skelgill, implacable, gives the faintest nod of encouragement. She fixes her gaze upon Victoria Lawson; in the woman's eyes she is sure she reads a plea for the coup de grâce.

'Mrs Lawson, did you have any idea that your mother had killed Sebastian Sinclair?'

26. WHAT GOES AROUND

The Highwayman, Keswick – 5.45 p.m. Monday 10 June

'RECKON SHE WAS telling the truth, Guv – that she didn't suspect her old Ma?'

DS Leyton's question is spoken quietly, although at the moment he has only his two colleagues for company, and others in the bar are well spaced and engaged in their own conversations.

Skelgill is momentarily distracted, tilting his glass against the light from the leaded window. He scowls, but it may be dissatisfaction with the clarity of the pint; it is not his regular brand of bitter, but a sulphurous guest ale from Burton-upon-Trent. He presents a deflecting palm.

'That's one for you pair. You did all the legwork.' He takes a draught of beer, keeping his hand raised, to show he intends to add a rider. 'But I can see why she wouldn't.'

There are nods all round. In the loose (and undocumented) conversation that had followed DS Jones's question to the effect, Victoria Lawson had poured out sundry rather irregular thoughts and feelings, not always consistent or even comprehensible.

Indeed, her first response might on the face of it have seemed somewhat hyperbolic.

"I've been confused – since you made it plain quite early that you didn't believe it was an accident – I'm sorry to say, I've been thinking that – well – it's ridiculous – but that Morag Sinclair must have organised a hit-man. And then you were asking about that unpleasant runner – the 'Goat' character – I thought, of course, that made some kind of sense."

Hyperbolic, perhaps, but there is no refuting that Billy 'The Goat' Higson had been firmly in their sights (latterly of his own making). And to say that none of them had considered the little paradigm of motive, means and opportunity in relation to Morag Sinclair would be further to deny what was understandable speculation – moreover, not to have considered the victim's spouse as a suspect would be both remiss of investigating officers, and flying in the face of long-standing statistics.

DS Jones, however, does have an answer to her colleague's question.

'I think she was too overwhelmed by the situation to properly analyse what was going on around her – or to judge what actually might have happened.' She takes a considered sip of her own half pint, but does not exhibit any of the fussiness of Skelgill. 'When you think about it – she and Sebastian Sinclair, they'd made a momentous decision – in her mind she'd crossed the Rubicon ... then she found herself stranded midstream.'

Skelgill remains phlegmatic, but DS Leyton seems more enamoured of the metaphor; perhaps it is he that is best placed to empathise with the predicament in which Victoria Lawson had become embroiled.

'I don't envy her. It was never going to be easy, before the Sinclair geezer died – and it ain't any easier now. Is she going to tell Frank Lawson that she was about to up-and-leave him – on flippin' Father's Day, an' all – because one of their nippers ain't his? Is she going to tell the kid who his real father was? And what's she going to say to Morag Sinclair?'

Skelgill shifts a little in his seat.

'That's where it's going to be tricky to keep a lid on it. Morag Sinclair and her bairns have a right to know why their husband and father was murdered.'

They stare at their drinks, as though wisdom swirls within, like the fortune teller's crystal ball.

DS Jones is first to speak, her gaze still lowered.

'Victoria Lawson will need counselling. She's on autopilot, like a zombie. It must be overwhelming. She's been carrying the death of her father – the consequential burden of her widowed mother – a needy husband. She's been carrying the stress of the child's paternity for what – two, nearly three years? And then all this. She's got the survival of the company to worry about – responsibility for all the staff. And now, she's lost her lover and soulmate.'

She looks up to see that Skelgill is staring at her.

She forces a smile – and he snaps out of his momentary reverie. He nods slowly.

'Aye, it's nervous breakdown territory, alreet.'

DS Jones regards him intently, as though she would wish to read his deeper thoughts.

'How could she ever forgive her mother? Think of what she has done – to the small boy, William. Murdered his father – out of selfishness for her own circumstances.'

DS Leyton, mid-drink, makes an inarticulate growl.

He swallows, and finds some words.

'Wicked old crow. Or do I mean crone?' He looks for accord among his colleagues. 'Can I say that?'

DS Jones smiles.

'Maybe not in the report. Leave it to the sentencing judge.'

But DS Leyton is shaking his head.

'You know, I had a bad feeling about her from the start – prowling about the house and spying on us. I mean – the nanny, Ellie, was defensive, at first – but she came round. But the old Ma – she was protective – and more than that. Course, now we know she was earwigging when I caught her in the little library room.'

'Leyton, now we know she specialised in it.'

DS Leyton concurs with Skelgill's remark. DS Jones had asked Victoria Lawson to be more specific about how her mother could have found out. Her explanation is fresh in their minds.

"Frank was away on business. Sebastian was working late – but he'd just picked up the DNA report from the private clinic and called in on his way home. Ellie had gone and my mother was getting the boys' supper and watching TV with them. We had a glass of wine in the conservatory. We agreed – this was it – we had to do it – that we couldn't leave it any longer. William was already calling Frank *"Daddy"* – it was killing Sebastian. He said we had to grasp the nettle – tell our partners by Father's Day. His own parents are getting old – he said they ought to know their grandchild. I said, okay."

They had changed the subject, drunk another glass of wine – out of sheer relief. And that is when they had discussed other things, such as the Bob Graham Round – and how, anyway, they had to wait until after that event – while Sebastian was so entwined with Frank. The magazine, *Fell Running*, lay on the coffee table in its sleeve – Sebastian Sinclair pointed out his 'other' rival, in the form of Billy Higson.

And that is when Victoria Lawson's mother Isobel, listening-in from the adjacent rooms, began to hatch her plan.

And it nearly worked.

'Should we have some sympathy for her?'

DS Jones's words might seem out of kilter with the tenor of their discussion, but her tone tells her colleagues that she is unequivocal as far as her opinion goes. Yet it behoves them to consider the alternative perspective, for this will be presented when Defence meets Prosecution.

'Sympathy for what she felt – aye, maybe.' Skelgill perhaps surprises the others – but he quickly adds a caveat. 'After that –' He takes a swig of his beer, and his expression leaves them in no doubt as to what he thinks.

DS Leyton is shaking his head, still it seems a little in disbelief.

'Okay, she'd lost her husband – the grandkids and the Lawsons were all she'd got. But just to protect her personal situation, her version of the family – she was willing to commit murder. Double murder. *Struth.*'

Skelgill nods pensively.

Thus far, Victoria Lawson's mother Isobel Beslow has not responded to questioning. Their assessment of her motive, therefore, is necessarily based on a degree of conjecture. But the pattern of observed behaviour, they agree, smacks of panicked self-preservation. She acted rashly to stop Sebastian Sinclair in his tracks. And she acted rashly to cover up his killing. Only in the idea of the red herring – the threat placed in *Fell Running* that cast suspicion on Billy Higson and others – did she show some premeditation – and even that, ironically, placed her precious son-in-law Frank Lawson in the frame.

But in her ruthless and relentless pursuit of Rita – human proxy for the incriminating photograph which Isobel Beslow realised had been taken from such a distance that she was powerless to prevent it – in her successive attempts at theft and destruction she demonstrated a degree of cunning and absence of remorse that borders upon the psychopathic.

If these are Skelgill's sentiments, he baulks at the fleeting hint of admiration for the criminal psyche that crosses his own thoughts. But, thankfully, they do not need to trouble themselves too far in this regard. As DS Jones succinctly pointed out, the Prosecution does not need to prove a motive. The police do not need to enter the twisted mind of the murderer. It is sufficient to demonstrate that the act took place, and who was the perpetrator. And now they have a watertight case.

They have a photograph of Victoria Lawson's late father's dark Mercedes at Honister Hause at the time of the incident. (The car otherwise kept garaged at the grandparents' property.) In the photograph, the figure of a woman apparently delving into the roadside bracken. Impounded, they have the car, with the damage to its bonnet and grille. They have a DNA sample from the point of impact that is a match for Sebastian Sinclair. They have the statement of Billy Higson (and his brother, indeed), who saw the stationary car and, standing beside the road, its female driver, whom he was able adequately to describe. And they have more still. From a nearby business in Portland Square, they have CCTV of the same woman delivering a large envelope out of hours to the letterbox of Sinclair Design. They have CCTV from the very hostelry where they now sit – The Highwayman, Keswick – again, the woman, entering and leaving at times that correspond to the break-in.

There is also the evidence of the pursuit.

And in this regard DS Leyton is hungry to know more. Since his impromptu mobilisation on Saturday morning there has been limited opportunity to learn of the build-up to Skelgill's eureka moment.

'When exactly did you realise, Guv?'

Skelgill understands that DS Leyton refers to Victoria Sinclair's mother.

Skelgill shakes his head, almost dejectedly.

'I can't say there was an *exactly*, Leyton. When we pulled her out of Victoria Lawson's Dad's old Merc? Search me.'

DS Jones does not buy the evasion.

'But you did know – you knew to get the photograph developed – you knew she was stalking Rita.'

Skelgill retains an expression of discontent.

'I reckoned *someone* was stalking Rita. Remember, I was out in the wilds.'

'But you were gathering information, all the same.'

He cannot help a grin at her rather formal description.

'Me – I was getting the Chinese water torture. Drip, drip, drip.'

The mention of drips seems to prompt him to drink. Though he checks himself and scrutinises his glass, as if he realises he ought to conserve some of his present ration. He begins to recite, reflectively, indeed his gaze fixes on an old dark oil painting of Blencathra on the far wall, and his eyes seem to glaze over.

'I can't believe I didn't twig straight away that Rita had taken an early-morning photo at Honister Hause. Gerry even said summat about it – the smell of breakfast enticed her back from her snapping.

'Little did she know she'd captured the aftermath of the crash. Just a tiny fragment of evidence in a great landscape.

'And Isobel Beslow saw her – and knew she'd been photographed.'

'But I didn't.'

'I spotted the trio in the fells – a good couple of hours after Sinclair and Lawson had run past, going the other way. I didn't link the two. I didn't think much at all about Rita and her friends.

'The first I really knew of Rita – she's wanting to photograph me with the Kelly kettle at Wasdale.

'Then, later – next day – I hear their rooms have been rifled.

'I didn't think too much of that – I mean, even they thought it was the cleaners tidying up. That's what I dismissed it as.

'At that point none of us knew she'd tracked them from Honister. She'd been at Wasdale all right. Searched the rooms – but Rita keeps her camera glued to her. But she stole their itinerary – she knew where to follow them.'

Skelgill glances briefly at DS Jones, to acknowledge this to be her discovery – her legwork, literally.

'Then I didn't think owt about the woman in the bar above Grasmere. Your crossworder.' (Another glance at DS Jones.) 'She eavesdropped. Made herself scarce when she twigged I was a cop. Saw us pair chatting near the bar. She even checked up on us afterwards – you and I. I glimpsed her. She's a widow – she's not a carer or a regular childminder – she's free to come and go as she pleases. She was using her own car when she was doing a recce – perhaps going back to the Lawsons' in the evenings. And the Merc when she meant business. Like next morning. She'd heard enough to know Rita would be taking photos at the gingerbread shop – and later up at Dunmail Raise.'

Skelgill lets out a sigh.

'Rita had a narrow squeak. Her camera had a narrow squeak. Perhaps Isobel Beslow thought all she had to do was destroy the camera.'

He looks now at each of his colleagues in turn.

'Meanwhile, you pair were putting the heat on, back at the Lawson's place.

'She senses you're getting warm – that you've found out about the threat.'

DS Jones lifts a hand; she wants to interject. Skelgill gives way. She looks first to DS Leyton, in anticipation of his corroboration.

'Remember, in the kitchen – when the little boy, William, came running in? She swooped out of nowhere to snatch him away – and she called him by his full name – she emphasised the Lawson.' (DS Leyton is nodding.) 'I think she was worried – that we'd recognise him – his paternity, I mean.'

Skelgill's brow is furrowed.

'She was getting more desperate, that's for sure, lass. She sees you in the Traveller's Rest – next thing you turn up again at the house.

'She didn't try owt after Dunmail Raise – not at Threlkeld. But she went to Keswick and broke into what should have been Rita's room the next night.

'That was maybe when the penny eventually started to drop. *Duh!*'

Skelgill hits the heel of his left hand off his forehead.

'Rita was injured, so they never made it to Keswick.

'By then I was thinking, someone *is* stalking them – but I didn't consciously make the link to Sinclair – why would I? I'm with three retired folk who have nothing to do with the district. No enemies. Not even any friends.'

He turns to look more intently at DS Jones.

'Then you showed me those photos – the family snaps.

'I knew I'd seen her – the mother.

'I didn't know where – but I knew it was recently.

'A little voice was yelling at us – there's a connection between my crew of pensioners and your investigation.

'Then when you told me Frank Lawson's prints were on the outside but not the inside – that the magazine with the threat had come from the Lawsons' property. Well – someone did it – and they left no prints. If it wasn't him, there's only his wife and his mother-in-law. And I had nobody fitting his wife's description on my radar – which narrowed it down.'

He sighs and finishes the last of his drink, as though it is a thirsty business, and now earned.

'Only a few minutes before – I'd had this – call it a *premonition*.'

He raises a hand and points across to the landscape painting. Sharp Edge is just discernible at the top right of the mountain. He jabs a finger to add emphasis.

'And there's Rita on the precipice – on Sharp Edge – and someone closing in. My sixth sense kicked in – I scrambled up to her.

'Sure enough, the person made themselves scarce. The blue cagoule.'

He turns to DS Leyton.

'Next seen when we pulled her out of the Mercedes.'

After a moment's silence, of the satisfied and relieved sort, DS Jones raises the ante once again.

'Do you think she would have pushed Rita off Sharp Edge?'

231

Skelgill grimaces, staring hard at the little line of highlight and shadow on the distant representation of the mountain.

'I reckon she knew she had to destroy the films – but, failing that? If Rita's not around – her photos would probably be ignored – perhaps never developed.'

They all nod in agreement.

Skelgill sinks down in his seat and gazes a little forlornly at his empty glass.

'Then you know the rest. She reverted to type. The MO that had worked on Sebastian Sinclair at Honister, and nearly worked on Rita at Dunmail. So, she tried it again.' He grins at DS Jones. 'She just didn't bank on Spring-heeled Jack!'

DS Jones flashes him a quick, darting glance – but then her gaze is drawn to a group of figures hovering at the entrance.

'Well, perhaps I should spring to the bar – it looks like your gang has arrived.'

Skelgill turns to see the distinctive shapes, sizes and colours of Gerry, Rosheen and Rita – they are politely waiting until they are noticed, and then invited, not wishing to interrupt what might be an official meeting among the three detectives.

Reintroductions of a more informal nature are now completed, and DS Jones delivers a drinks order and resumes her seat. A smattering of small talk is exchanged, until Skelgill shifts the subject back to the underlying nature of their gathering.

He grins wryly at Rita.

'Room not burgled, today?'

She chuckles.

'I still take the same precautions.'

She demonstrates the camera bag, slung over her shoulder.

Then she turns to DS Leyton, her expression showing concern.

'Sergeant, I do hope your employer will reimburse you for the camera you sacrificed. I feel guilty it was not mine that was put on the line.'

DS Leyton flaps a hand.

'Never fear, madam – it was gathering dust in the attic – my old uncle gave it to me, and I could never get the hang of it. Shutter speed, aperture, focusing – all that malarkey. By the time I got it right, whoever I was trying to photograph had got fed up and hopped it. *Nah* – I'm better off with me mobile – that's about as foolproof as it gets, thanks all the same.'

'She certainly made mincemeat of it.'

It is Gerry's observation.

'And to think – that could have been you, Rita.' Rosheen's exhortation is more caring of the flesh. 'And that she tried it at Dunmail Raise, when you weren't even on your guard.'

Rita is a little shaken, still – and DS Jones reads this.

'How did your witness statements go? It means you can put it behind you.'

'Until the trial.' Again, Gerry is quick to interject. 'Unless she pleads guilty.'

He looks questioningly at Skelgill, and then at each of the inspector's subordinates in turn, perhaps seeking an inkling of their expectations in this regard. But there is something of a collective shrug – and he continues.

'Cards on the table.' He pats the table top illustratively with a large gnarled hand. 'You'll read it soon enough in my statement – naturally, I told your young DC who interviewed me – I'm a retired copper myself. North Yorkshire Police, man and boy. I've been keeping a keen interest in your investigation. I haven't liked to poke my nose in. I have to say – hats off, to you all. Now I know something of the full story, I doubt there's many detectives that could have joined the dots like you three have. You've got her bang to rights, that's for sure.'

Skelgill regards Gerry with undisguised intrigue – and renewed respect. He wonders, had their roles been reversed, could he have restrained himself with such diplomacy – or would he have been unable to resist sticking in his two penn'orth? He clears his throat a little self-consciously, for the latter seems more likely.

But when he does not speak, it is Rita that detects he is momentarily tongue-tied, for she now picks up the subject that Gerry has raised.

'Will *I* need to come – for the trial?'

Although Gerry is already nodding sagely, it is DS Jones who furnishes a reply.

'You could probably provide evidence on camera.'

Gerry gives her a friendly nudge.

'*Hah* – that'd be apt, for you, Rita!'

But Rita demurs.

'I would willingly travel.' She glances at Skelgill, a twinkle in her eye. 'Now that we have set our record time for the Bob Graham Round, isn't it the done thing to beat it?'

The proposal generates a round of amicable conjecture – and the suggestion of trying the route clockwise, as was their original intention. Gerry addresses Skelgill.

'Course – you'll be doing your round of the tarns, long before all that. Have you got a proper name for it yet, lad?'

Skelgill sticks out his jaw. This question has dogged him since his very first discussion with Professor Jim Hartley. The last he heard from his old mentor, the DAA committee had come up with the suggestion, 'Fisheround' – but were still open to persuasion.

He is about to mention this, when he is reminded of the possible delicacy of former relationships – that Rosheen and the professor were erstwhile colleagues – when Rosheen pre-empts him, and raises a finger as if to test the wind.

'It's a pity your name's not Rod.'

'What?'

Skelgill's retort is so quick, and its inflexion so revealing that he has both his colleagues staring at him. They recognise this statement has struck a nerve; while the others are oblivious.

But Gerry is already chiming in; he pats his partner on the forearm.

'Hah – that's a beauty! *The Rod Graham!* It'd be perfect, wouldn't it?' He sprays grins about, canvassing nods, and then – although no explanation is needed, he gives one – perhaps for his own satisfaction. '*Rod* – for fishing. *Graham* – to show where the round is, the route, the tradition. There's no flies on Rosheen!' He raises his glass to her. 'You should have been in advertising, not archaeology.'

Polite murmurs circulate – but there is no doubt that Skelgill's prominent cheekbones are flushed, and DS Jones, in particular, regards him with inquisitive intent. However, now it is she that senses he is discomfited, and she moves the matter on, questioning him on behalf of the group.

'Will you report live online?'

'Hah – you'll have to have it online!' Gerry again, beaming. He turns to Rosheen, seeking acclaim. 'You get it? On line. Fishing line. Ha-hah!'

She taps his arm, in friendly reproach.

'Gerry – you've not even had one pint.'

'I've got to find some way of keeping up with your wit, love.'

Now Rita has something to add.

'If you did post live as you went round – it would mean I could follow your progress from the States.'

She regards Skelgill hopefully.

Skelgill contrives a look that seeks not to disappoint, when that is plainly what is coming.

'I'd like to try – but at most of the tarns, they're set so deep in their coombs – I'd have no signal. I'd need to lug a satellite phone.' There are nods of collective disappointment. 'Happen I could carry a GPS tracker – you'd be able to see where I was up to.'

Rita pats her camera case.

'Well – that's a good compromise – I can cross-reference with my photographs. I shall not even need to picture you in my mind.'

She winks at Skelgill – perhaps in case he might let slip about the surprise calendar for her friends.

Reference to the photographs prompts DS Jones. She hauls her shoulder bag off the back of the chair. She extracts a large envelope and a smaller padded packet.

'Here are your negatives. And all the spare prints. We've made copies of everything we need.'

Rita appears enthralled.

'How wonderful – it is quite a bonus that you have given me all these enlargements.'

She delves into the envelope – and pulls out the image of Skelgill at his bivvy at Wasdale.

She regards it reflectively.

'Our first meeting. I never thought for a minute I'd become embroiled in a homicide investigation! That I'd captured a tiny vital detail – I was watching the early morning light changing on the fells.'

She gazes longer at the photograph of Skelgill – and then suddenly offers it – but not to Skelgill himself, instead she hands it directly to DS Jones.

'Would you like this one? Please – keep it. Here, look – there's a spare sleeve.'

Skelgill inhales, as if to protest – but their round of drinks arrives, and the waitress produces a pad to take their order for bar meals – and he obeys his own meeting room motto, "never talk over the tea lady".

DS Jones slips the print into her bag.

*

Farewells completed and DS Leyton having left on foot in the opposite direction, Skelgill and DS Jones wend their way down the market place. Despite their pub meal, Skelgill's step falters as they are touched by invisible tentacles of frying fat and salt and vinegar as they pass a chippy.

It is a balmy evening; a party of swifts makes screaming passes, a sporadic crescendo, grating by comparison to the lazy background melody of a chimney pot blackbird. Pedestrians, mainly visitors, window-shop outdoor gear, or peruse pubs on tiptoe, trying to see what beer is on offer, and whether food is still being served. Skelgill, out of superstition, it seems, causes the slightest of diversions as he stretches his free arm to brush fingertips against the stone of the Moot Hall, like a fellwalker passing a cairn. The implicit reference to the Bob Graham Round provides the invitation that DS Jones has been waiting for.

'Okay, so – are you going to spill the beans?'

'What beans?'

'Come off it – Rosheen's idea – the Rod Graham.'

Skelgill scowls defiantly. But he realises she has sussed him. He tries one more weak line of defence.

'It's nowt.'

'I don't think so. Besides – there are things I'm entitled to know.'

Skelgill silently hems and haws. He casts about in vain for distractions.

Eventually, however, there is nothing else for it, but to come clean.

'Rodney.'

'Yes?'

'It's my middle name.'

'*What!*'

He rounds on her.

'See – exactly – that's it exactly. You're taking the rise.'

But DS Jones is merely baffled.

'How can it be your middle name? This has never come up. I've filled in forms for you. I've seen your warrant card – your driver's licence.'

Skelgill makes a face of long-suffering resignation.

'I was Christened it – after some relative or other – but it was never put on my birth certificate. Luckily, the arl fella had been in the Queen's Arms before he went to the registrar.'

'But – well – how come you've never mentioned it?'

Now he looks at her askance.

'Would *you* mention it? Imagine if Smart found out I was called Rodney ... Rodders ... Rod.'

236

DS Jones hesitates for a moment.

'Well – there's nothing wrong with *Rod*. Look at Rod Stewart.'

Skelgill scoffs.

'Aye – and what have I got in common with him?'

He inadvertently raises a hand to pinch his nose. He realises she is staring at him, her grin widening.

He retrenches.

'Besides – I've banned it – since I were a bairn. Never used it. Never mentioned it.'

'But, why?'

'Why? When you've got three big brothers, evil like mine were – and *Only Fools and Horses* on the telly – what do you think they called me, all the damned time?'

'A plonker?'

Skelgill chokes.

'Thanks a million.'

DS Jones is now suppressing an insistent giggle.

But she waves a dismissive hand.

'Siblings can be cruel. They don't mean to be. You probably wouldn't be so tough.'

Her back-handed compliment seems to confound him for a moment, and they begin to drift on.

She is first to speak again, her manner now more analytical.

'You should consider it. I think the Rod Graham's a really good name. Gerry is right. It would give you a kind of ownership of the concept of the angling round – just like happened for Bob Graham – except it wouldn't be so brash. It would just be a small mention in your Wikipedia entry.'

'That'll be the day!'

'Oh, and your mother's a Graham.'

Skelgill does not answer.

DS Jones decides to let her words sink in; she senses she is winning the argument. They have reached the supermarket where her car is parked; she is driving, having partaken of only a half pint of bitter.

She jangles her keys.

'What do you want to do?'

Skelgill rounds to the passenger side, and regards her across the roof of the car.

She recognises in his expression a familiar incorrigibility.

'How do you fancy a bivvy breakfast on Blencathra?'

'What?'

But even in the single word, her tone already admits a weakening. He presses home his advantage.

'All the gear's still up there. I didn't want to lug it with that crowd, in case of some kind of rumble. I've not had chance to recover it. Besides, I've still blanked at Scales Tarn – and there's not long left until the – the *Fisheround.*'

She regards him censoriously – and points her remote at him. The vehicle bleeps as its locks disengage. As she ducks down she looses off a parting shot.

'Actually, I think Rod is a really cool name for a boy. Especially in an angling family.'

***

EPILOGUE

SELECTED EXCERPTS FROM
THE WESTMORLAND GAZETTE

Reporter, Kendall Minto

SHOCK AT BOB GRAHAM EVENT

Friday 14th June

DRAMA BEFELL this year's Bob Graham Round anniversary challenge when odds-on favourite and record-holder Billy 'The Goat' Higson trailed home in 5th place, not even in the medals. It seems misfortune struck on the fells above Stonethwaite, where he was chased, butted and knocked unconscious by a rogue Texel tup. Mr Higson was found wandering by a fellow runner, and was gradually coaxed back into the race – but to no avail as far as his winning streak was concerned.

The bookies were on cloud nine. Moreover, the race was won by an outsider, first-time entrant Frank Lawson, a businessman residing at Wetheral. Mr Lawson was training partner to the recently tragically killed Sebastian Sinclair (see *Gazette*, 7th June). Indeed, in his victory speech from Cumberland Infirmary where he was admitted with dehydration, Mr Lawson dedicated his win to Mr Sinclair, stating that, "he was a better man than I".

NEW ROUND FOR LAKELAND

Friday 28th June

'RUN-AND-FISH' are the watchwords for an exciting new challenge that will have enthusiasts flocking to the Lakes. Born out of the legendary Bob Graham Round, it incorporates the added test of catching a fish in each of 12 mountain tarns en route.

Under the aegis of the Derwentdale Anglers' Association, the round was officially launched by its pioneer, DAA member and well-known local police officer and amateur fisherman and fell-runner, Dan Skelgill, a Buttermere man. Mr Skelgill completed the inaugural round over the night of the summer solstice, 20th-21st June, and – get this – not only did he succeed in catching his twelve fish ("six brownies, three perch, two eels and a schelly"), but he completed the round *inside 24 hours* – indeed, with 21 minutes to spare ... and where have we heard that statistic before?

Modest to the last, when asked if he expected the round to be named after him, Mr Skelgill merely stated, somewhat cryptically, "Well, it's got to be the Rod Graham, aye?"

GAZETTE EXCLUSIVE!

BOMBSHELL IN HONISTER DEATH CASE

Friday 5th July

REGULAR READERS will recall that Mrs Isobel Beslow is due to stand trial in August at Carlisle Crown Court, when the prosecution will allege that on 3rd June at Honister Hause she wilfully murdered Mr Sebastian Sinclair by intentionally knocking him down with her car, and that she concealed his unconscious form in roadside vegetation such that he died from his injuries.

Last evening, Cumbria Police made the dramatic announcement that a SECOND PERSON has been charged in connection with the death of Mr Sinclair.

Detective Sergeant Emma Jones spoke exclusively to the *Gazette*: "Following the arrest of Mrs Isobel Beslow on 8th June, analysis of her mobile phone records revealed suspicious activity in connection with her son-in-law, Mr Frank Lawson. Subsequent investigation has led to Mr Lawson being questioned, and today he was arrested on suspicion of murder. Mr Lawson will remain in custody while our inquiries continue."

Eagle-eyed readers might notice that Mr Lawson was the former running partner of Mr Sinclair (*Gazette* 14th June), to whom he dedicated his victory in the Bob Graham Round anniversary event.

HONISTER MURDER TRIAL OPENS WITH GUILTY PLEA

Friday 9th August

IN A SURPRISE development, the Honister Hause murder trial opened today at Carlisle Crown Court with a statement from the Prosecution that one of the two accused, Mr Frank Lawson, has at the eleventh hour changed his plea.

Leading counsel Jane Sigmund-Smith KC outlined to a hushed courtroom that the Crown has accepted from Mr Lawson a guilty plea to the lesser charge of accessory to murder. He will tell the court of his shock of witnessing from afar the incident that killed Mr Sebastian Sinclair – however, he will confess to subsequent collusion in an attempt to cover up the crime. He will aver that he noticed a photographer in the vicinity of Honister Hause, and that he communicated this to his fellow accused, Mrs Isobel Beslow. He will further admit to advising Mrs Beslow in her attempts to recover or destroy incriminating photographic evidence, acts for which she faces a series of additional charges, including burglary, dangerous driving and attempted murder.

Following the Crown's statement, the hearing was adjourned for further deliberations between Prosecuting and Defending counsel. It is anticipated that Mr Lawson's turning King's evidence will lead to a guilty plea on behalf of the remaining accused, Mrs Beslow.

Speaking afterwards on the courtroom steps, DS Emma Jones stated, "While we are not entirely in agreement with Frank Lawson's denial that he was an accessory before the fact, such may be difficult to prove beyond reasonable doubt. However, should Isobel Beslow now plead guilty to murder, as is expected, it will preclude the need for a trial that would expose personal information that would be damaging to innocent third parties. Instead, the affected families will be afforded privacy to deal with reconciliation, and to receive professional counselling. With this outcome, we are comfortable."

The Rod Graham Round

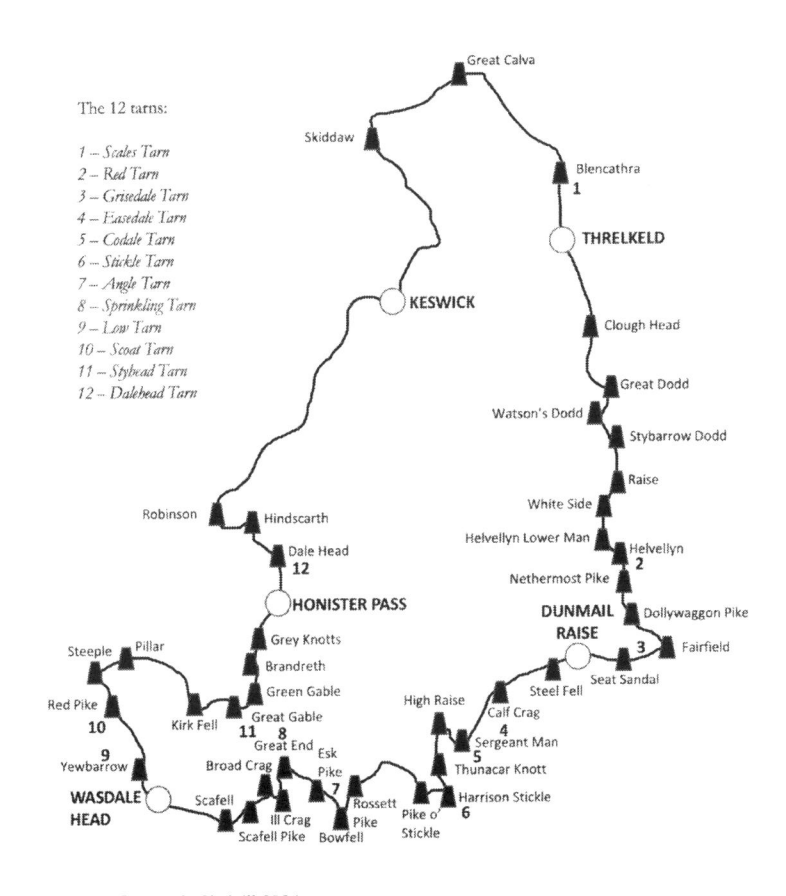

The 12 tarns:

1 – Scales Tarn
2 – Red Tarn
3 – Grisedale Tarn
4 – Easedale Tarn
5 – Codale Tarn
6 – Stickle Tarn
7 – Angle Tarn
8 – Sprinkling Tarn
9 – Low Tarn
10 – Scoat Tarn
11 – Styhead Tarn
12 – Dalehead Tarn

© D.R.G. Skelgill 2024

NEXT IN THE SERIES

LADY OF THE LAKE ...

IT IS ALMOST three decades since the body of a young housewife was pulled from Wastwater, England's deepest lake. The corpse had been weighted and sunk twenty years earlier – wrapped and concealed in a carpet, a submerged landmark that was actually known to leisure divers. Such a grisly fact only added to the horror that haunts the neighbouring dales; how long before another picturesque Lakeland water gives up its dark secret?

'Murder Mere Murder' by Bruce Beckham will be released in January 2025.

FREE BOOKS, NEW RELEASES, THE BEAUTIFUL LAKES ... AND MOUNTAINS OF CAKES

Sign up for Bruce Beckham's author newsletter

Thank you for getting this far!

If you have enjoyed your encounter with DI Skelgill there's a growing series of whodunits set in England's rugged and beautiful Lake District to get your teeth into.

My newsletter often features one of the back catalogue to download for free, along with details of new releases and special offers.

No Skelgill mystery would be complete without a café stop or two, and each month there's a traditional Cumbrian recipe – tried and tested by yours truly (aka *Bruce Bake 'em*).

To sign up, this is the link:
https://mailchi.mp/acd032704a3f/newsletter-sign-up

Your email address will be safely stored in the USA by Mailchimp, and will be used for no other purpose. You can unsubscribe at any time simply by clicking the link at the foot of the newsletter.

Thank you, again – best wishes and happy reading!

Bruce Beckham

Printed in Great Britain
by Amazon

9f47b8b5-d1de-4817-9537-adf0e98c6150R01